Green Monkey Dreams

Also by Isobelle Carmody

The Obernewtyn Chronicles:
Obernewtyn
The Farseekers
Ashling

Scatterlings
The Gathering

Green Monkey Dreams

Stories by

Isobelle Carmody

VIKING

Viking
Penguin Books Australia Ltd
487 Maroondah Highway, PO Box 257
Ringwood, Victoria 3134, Australia
Penguin Books Ltd
Harmondsworth, Middlesex, England
Viking Penguin, A Division of Penguin Books USA Inc.
375 Hudson Street, New York, New York 10014, USA
Penguin Books Canada Limited
10 Alcorn Avenue, Toronto, Ontario, Canada M4V 3B2
Penguin Books (N.Z.) Ltd
182–190 Wairau Road, Auckland 10, New Zealand

First published by Penguin Books Australia, 1996
1 3 5 7 9 10 8 6 4 2

Typeset in 12/14 Adobe Garamond by Midland Typesetters, Maryborough.
Made and printed in Australia by Australian Print Group.

National Library of Australia
Cataloguing-in-Publication data:

Carmody, Isobelle
Green monkey dreams

ISBN 0 670 86750 0.

I. Title.
A823.3

Some of the stories in this collection were first published in a slightly different form:
'Roaches' in *Into the Future*, edited by Toss Gascoigne, Jo Goodman and Margot Tyrrell, Viking,
1992; 'The Monster Game' in *Family*, edited by Agnes Nieuwenhuizen, Mammoth, 1994; 'Corfu' in
Crazy Hearts, edited by Frank Willmott and Robyn Jackson, Hodja Educational Resources
Cooperative Limited, 1985; 'The Witch Seed' in *Bittersweet*, edited by Toss Gascoigne, Puffin Books,
1992; 'Seek No More' in *Goodbye and Hello*, edited by Clodagh Corcoran and Margot Tyrrell,
Viking, 1992; 'Long Live the Giant' in *The Lottery; Nine science fiction stories*, compiled by Lucy
Sussex, Omnibus, 1994; 'The Pumpkin Eater' in *She's Fantastical*, Sybylla Feminist Press, 1995.

for Stephen, to whom all of my stories truly aspire

ACKNOWLEDGEMENTS

My thanks to those editors whose requests prompted me to pen a number of the stories in this collection. The rest were written for this book, and I would like to thank the Australia Council Literature Unit for the grant and grace which gave me time and space to write them. Thanks also to my publisher, who agreed that it would be good to have all of my stories under my name; and especially and always to Erica Irving, who edited and nurtured the voice of these stories – my truest voice.

In particular, as well as friends and family, I would like to thank Rachelle Moore, of Indian Valley High School in Ohio, who told me about the green monkey dreams, and Kerry Greenwood for rummaging through her vast store of arcane knowledge to source and find the exact wording of the Chuangtse quote for me.

CONTENTS

'Chuangtse dreamed of being a butterfly, and while he was in the dream, he felt he could flutter his wings and everything was real, but on waking up, he realised that he was Chuangtse and Chuangtse was real. Then he thought and wondered which was really real, whether he was really Chuangtse dreaming of being a butterfly, or really a butterfly dreaming of being Chuangtse.'

Lin Yutang, *The Importance of Living*

PART 1

THE
HigH PatH

*'There are many sorrows in heaven
waiting to be sent to us as Angels ...'*

THE GLORY DAYS

They ask me to write down all I remember of the Glory days. A hard thing, because there is so much of Sorrow in the telling. My mind shies away from it, looping backwards and forwards in time.

Last night, I thought of a girl I grew up with in the sister-house who told me that minebirds sing a song just before the deadly gases kill them, to lift their souls to heaven.

Wakened this morning by the bells that toll the beginning of the solar day in Freedom, I tried to remember her name, and found I could not even recall her face.

Hearing the bells ring now, for dusk, I realise an entire day has passed like the blink of an eye, and it comes to me that if death is a kind of song that lifts the soul out of the body, sorrow, too, can steal a soul and carry it away.

Perhaps that is what is wrong with me.

Yet the story must be told, and there is no other but me to tell it. I must make them understand that there are many Sorrows in heaven, waiting to be sent to us as Angels of death. I have told them, of course, but they nod soothingly and their eyes glide away. They think I am hallucinating or perhaps that I am mad because of all that happened. They think of me as a child, telling themselves I was too young, blaming themselves.

But if I learned one thing in Glory, it is that flesh is the greatest lie.

My youth was the main objection when I was proposed as an agent, but my sponsor was Erasemus, Tribune of the body that administers Freedom. He had been a very young man when he became Tribune of Freedom, first of all cities. He was one of the initiators of the plan to establish autonomous self-regulating cities which would have the same rights as a country once had over its citizens, and it is rumoured that it was his decision that bells be rung at dawn and dusk in gratitude that we wake and sleep in freedom.

Erasemus is also my father – an archaic word. Very few children of Freedom know or care who their progenitor is. Before the nation and country wars that changed the world forever, a woman bearing a child would remain together in one dwelling with that child and any others spawned by her, and the man who impregnated her. The woman was owned by the man, and the children born to them were owned by both. There was even a contract of slavery in which she would vow to love and obey him, before witnesses, as if loving was something that could be commanded. It was all part of the vast greedy possessiveness of those times that people bound themselves together in little nations called families.

Despite the fact that such conditions were inevitably destructive, and more often than not produced psychologically flawed adults, this custom of families continued right up to the wars. Fortunately the anarchy that followed, while dreadful, broke down the old corrupt and meaningless systems. Now, it is not forbidden to know who one's mother or father is, just not important.

We are all now sons and daughters of Freedom, sisters and brothers to one another. A computer tells us when blood is wrong between a male and female, for safe mating, but otherwise there are no divisions. In my mind, Erasemus was an older brother, and I was faintly shocked that he named me daughter. I put it to his being of the generation that straddles the changes. Though he was one of the initiators of the modern age, he was a son of the old world and it had left its mark on him.

He saw my discomfort and said, 'I tell you of the close blood between us because I would ask you to do a thing which is more than I have the right to ask.' I remember that I thought his eyes very sad and beautiful in his ugly boulder of a face. I had not been so close to him before, having only ever seen him during public addresses, and the contrast struck me. There was an expression in his eyes I did not understand. I know now it was guilt at the knowledge that his truest daughter was Freedom, and that one daughter may be sacrificed to save another.

'What do you want of me?' I asked, without the slightest sensible twinge of unease. I had grown up in Freedom and knew that I might say no if I wished to whatever he proposed, though he was the most powerful man in the city. It meant nothing to me that he was my father. I was about to learn that one could be compelled by honour and pride far more easily than by force.

'You know that Freedom sends emissaries to the other cities – to Serenity and Winter?'

I nodded, I think. 'Because of trade and to stop inbreeding?'

He nodded too, but a little impatiently, as if I was behaving like a clever student when something more was wanted of me. 'Among other things, for trade, yes. Other sorts of emissaries are sent to the frontier cities like Fury.'

'Agents,' I said, remembering some gossip I had overheard.

He blinked and, though his expression did not alter, I sensed his appraisal deepen. 'Do you know why we sent agents rather than diplomatic and official emissaries?'

I didn't. I had only overheard the word and assumed it was another name for emissary.

'Have you heard of Glory?' he asked.

Another piece of gossip surfaced in my mind. 'It is a frontier city.'

He smiled then. 'It is not common knowledge that we have located another city on the very edge of the wastes, but it does not surprise me that you have heard of it, my dear. I have kept an eye on your mentor reports over the years and it has been observed more than once, and not always as a compliment, that you are in the habit of noticing rather more than people generally do.'

'You monitored my progress? Why?' Embarrassment made me brusque.

'Curiosity. Your mother . . .' I flinched and he frowned at me, but changed the subject abruptly.

'We needed a child who could . . .' His voice trailed off, and I remember being startled. One did not think of the articulate brilliant Tribune being lost for words. That did make me feel a quiver of apprehension, but before I could fasten on it, he was going on, telling me that Glory had been visited by Freedom's emissaries, and as with many of the frontier cities, they were refused entry. Only people wanting to join the city were allowed inside.

'Agents are sent in when emissaries are refused entry,' Erasemus said.

I was shocked because this flouted everything that Freedom and the cities represented. Officially a city might close its borders if it chose. Cities were small and could not increase beyond their walls, preventing the need for physical expansion. All cities were the same ground size. Numbers could increase, but only in so far as there was capacity for them. Cities like Winter were built up to house their population. When the population overgrew, another city would be built, and its builders would then design their own inner city matrix and modes of governance in accordance with whatever rules or ideals they had. No city could amalgamate with another, though people might shift between them. No city could interfere with another.

'We need to know what is happening in the new cities that are formed,' Erasemus said. 'We send agents in when emissaries are not permitted merely to examine the social matrix to ensure Interference is not part of its mindset. None of the agents sent to Glory returned but we received enough information from them to indicate that Glory has begun stockpiling ancient weaponry.'

'How many agents were sent in?' I interrupted.

After a pause, he said: 'Twenty, but that information is strictly confidential.'

My mouth fell open. 'When you say they did not return . . .'

'I mean they were never seen again. It is likely ... most certainly likely that they died. Were killed to prevent them speaking of what they witnessed. We must know why and what is going on in Glory.'

I knew then.

We need a child, he had said. I had been consistently high in lessons with whichever mentor I chose, as he had observed, and I had already taken on the position of mentor to three younger sisters and a brother. One mentor told me I had a mind that leaped ahead of logic and reason which made my work patchy and inconsistent, but occasionally inspired. I had been voted to lead the youth tribunal, but had preferred to sit as an independent and speak when the mood took me. In truth, I had feared boredom.

Hearing of my refusal, my favourite mentor brother told me that there were three kinds of people: followers, leaders and scouts. Scouts were capable of leadership, but they could not tolerate the responsibility of it. Disinclined to take orders either, they invariably flouted authority and fomented strife. This was why scouts, he said wryly, were the first to be sent into danger. It was half hoped they would be killed.

'I fear you are destined to trouble us as a scout, little sister,' he said.

'All of the agents lost were adults,' Erasemus was saying. 'We now feel that the deepest heart of Glory is ... too rigid for an adult outsider to infiltrate ...'

I was nodding, and so he stopped. He was too clever to overstate. 'You must think it over,' he said, but he knew and I knew, that there was no choice. Twenty dead because they had entered one of the closed frontier cities. Dead, why? What had they seen? That was what I was to find out. To seek knowledge was not Interference.

'Have you any information about the city?' I asked. 'About its culture and traditions. Its laws?'

'Little enough, I am afraid,' Erasemus said. 'Closed and focused around a central religion called the High Path, its people worship a figure known as the Angel.'

It was to his credit that he did not baulk at the word.

'The Angel?' I asked. 'Is their religion another version of ancient Christianity? Do they worship an Angel as a god, or is it an idol?'

'The Angel is a real person with the power of life and death over his followers. As you know, we do not interfere in internal politics or religions so long as citizens are free to leave a city if they choose it. But in this case, agents were prevented from leaving and there is the real possibility that Glory will use its arsenal against other cities. We want to know if they plan to make war on nearby cities or on one city in particular. If possible, we need to know where their arsenal is stored.'

'Information, then?' I asked crisply, thinking that was not too great a thing to ask; forgetting that what Erasemus wanted and what Glory would demand of me might be two different things.

The healer, Laurai, visits me, interrupting my memories. I cannot say I regret it.

'You must get up. Go outside. It will do you good to walk about and exercise your limbs, lest they begin to atrophy,' she says somewhat sternly, as if my inactivity is wilful and stubborn.

I have a sudden muddied memory of being dragged from rubble, my bones grinding together, my face streaming with blood and tears.

I had not known, when I first woke, why I wept. The memories of the last day had been crushed out of me by the stone teeth of Glory, lethal even as it fell. A blessed, if fleeting forgetting.

When I woke the second time from a nightmare of drowning, I was in Freedom and Laurai was leaning over me. I had never met her before and thought I was in Glory still. Then she spoke and I knew I was home. There were no healers in Glory.

When she realised I could not speak, she pressed a pencil and paper into my fingers. I lay there cradling them, without the strength even to write and ask what had befallen me. The last thing I could remember clearly was running along the main street in Glory. It was Erasemus who told me, when he visited later that day, that Glory was gone, destroyed along with all of its inhabitants.

'What happened?' he asked. 'Jack Rose saw the city explode.'

It took all of my will to write. He looked at me searchingly after reading my scrawl. 'You don't remember?'

I had not strength enough then to shake my head, but he read the answer in my face. He asked the healer if the lost contents of the rooms in my mind would ever be restored.

'They are not empty,' Laurai said, her cool eyes blue and watchful. 'It is only that her mind has suffered a sort of blindness.' She had looked at me then. 'You must teach it to see again.'

She touched the pencil with the tip of her finger. 'That is the key to the memories locked inside you. Write what you remember and the rest will follow. Go gently, for if you force the memories, they might vanish altogether. Go back to things that you remember well, then move carefully forward in time. You must stalk the thread of memory like a cat stalks a bird.'

And of course, I did remember.

Like all frontier cities, Glory was walled, but getting into it was more unpleasant at first than dangerous. Indeed, I thought I might as easily have walked in openly, for the guards on the gate seemed relaxed and inattentive once the entrants swore fealty.

'Do not let them fool you,' whispered Jack Rose grimly. 'That is a Venus flytrap. Easy to enter, hard to leave.'

He had been my mentor and trainer in the art of spying, and he had brought me to Glory. I had thought Rose rather a soft name for a spymaster, but Jack had thorns aplenty, and he did his best to help me develop my own on that long journey. There had been no time for proper training at the little-known agents' academy, and I was not sure I could have borne it, had there been time. I felt trained agents were a symbol of Interference, and Jack Rose and I argued our way to the frontier.

'We must be safe,' he said once. 'We must guard Freedom.'

'Freedom is more than our city. It is an ideal and you are

breaking it. You and Erasemus and the academy. You deny to the other cities the very freedom you guard in ours. One city is no better than another. No larger, no stronger . . .'

'If Freedom is threatened by another city, it must protect itself.'

'But you don't know if it is a threat when you send in agents.'

We could not agree, and yet we became close on that journey. Despite our differences, it was he who would drag me from the ruins though I was a scout and dispensable.

'We are fairly certain that everyone new who enters the gate is followed,' he told me, when we were finally crouched in the dank and odorous sewer drain of Glory. Peering out through the grille, we were waiting for the street to be empty long enough for me to get out unnoticed.

'The other agents went too casually,' Jack Rose said. 'The one advantage of entering this way is that, because it is so apparently easy to get into the city, no one would bother watching the drains. Remember . . .'

'Be invisible,' I finished, quoting his creed and grinning despite the jitter of my heart against my chestbones.

He squeezed my arm, ever unsmiling. 'Stay only long enough to find out what goes on, Rian. In and out.'

I nodded, believing it would be that easy; truly imagining I was well prepared for what lay ahead. Secreted weaponry, stun pills and gases, a rudimentary training in the amalgamated martial art of Taiche.

'One last thing,' Jack Rose said. He took my hand and pushed a ring onto my finger. 'If you need help, activate the first setting on the red seeker ring. I will find you if I can. But only do it if you are desperate.'

I stared at him, because agents always went in without anything that would prove they were agents. Always. He had told me that himself. I stared into his fierce wild eyes, trying to frame a question, but he prodded me unceremoniously and said the way was clear, so I climbed out into the empty street throwing off the grey coverall that had kept the drain muck from my pale tunic. He pulled the grating back in place and hissed at me to get away from the duct before vanishing into the fetid darkness of the caverns. I walked away without looking back.

Of course, what lay at the heart of Glory was Sorrow, and I was defenceless as a babe against that.

Glory was not much different to Serenity in its layout: utilitarian, and constructed along a squared grid. A mentor had taken me there once to show me that anything could be taken to excess, even the desire for peace. But what was bare and grim in mind-numb Serenity was in Glory gentle simplicity. Glory was clean and pale as the mountain city of Winter which had been the first city growing out of us, and shared many of Freedom's laws and customs. As in Winter, most constructions in Glory were of white softstone, though they were not the tall pale towers of our sister city, but low flat-roofed dwellings for the most part, all unadorned. The clean, bare, bonelike whiteness of Glory gave off a radiance in the solar rays that hurt my eyes, and I was glad the day was near to ending.

We knew the ceremonies conducted by the Angel occurred at sunset, hence my entry to the city at that time. We had agreed that any mistakes would be less likely to be noticed if people had their minds elsewhere, and besides, I could attend the ceremony and observe what went on there.

In and out, I promised myself.

A stooped man stepped from a doorway ahead, and I followed. He led me into the broad avenue I later learned was the main street, and suddenly we were only two in a whole stream of people. I was startled to see how many of them looked ill and frail in their spotless white tunics. Many bore savage burn scars, though they looked content enough. I was uncomfortably aware that I was too healthy looking, but no one paid the slightest attention to me.

Ahead, I could see the thickening crowd stream up a set of broad steps and go under a stone arch. This must be the Chantry Jack had told me about.

'We know there is a place called the Chantry where the populace meets to hear the Angel speak each day. That will be as good a place to start as any. All the children live in communal carehouses dotted about so you can follow some of them back to a carehouse. None of them have names and I doubt you will be noticed for they do not seem much for lists and order in Glory.'

Passing from the pink-stained dusty street and into the shadowy interior of the Chantry, I could hear the susurrus of hundreds of voices.

After a moment, my eyes adjusted with relief to the dimness. People were pressed in close and stood staring up at a raised dais. A plain wooden seat was set atop the dais and sitting on it was the Angel. Dressed in a white shift, and barefoot, his feet not quite touching the floor, fingers clasped loosely together in his lap, he looked like a child at its lessons. Though he did not wear a crown, his hair was yellow and rose up in fine down to float about his head, catching the sunlight in a nimbus.

Behind him, in shocking contrast, the outermost wall of the city lay open and showed the black ruinous lands. The wall surrounding Glory literally ran along the edge of the frontier beyond which no one could walk and live for long.

Jack had told me the Angel was young, but the light behind made it impossible to see his age. I felt uneasy at this face of shadows crowned by light, surrounded by darkness. I told myself the effect was deliberate, aimed at binding awe and mystery.

Then the Angel shifted and light fell onto his features.

I gasped but fortunately it was lost in the cries of the people pressed around me. I felt as if someone had kicked the breath out of me; the Angel was beautiful.

Even as I write that word I am seeking another, but I am defeated, for there is no word made on this earth that can describe the solemn glory of the Angel's features. No wonder he called himself Angel. To look into a mirror at that incredible luminous perfection, and think himself anything less would be a blasphemy.

I was stunned, for surely the other agents who had managed to get some information out of the city to Jack Rose would have mentioned this. And if so, why hadn't he told me? Then a second later I realised that the appearance of the Angel would not be thought important to adult agents searching for power and corruption. They would not see that such incandescent beauty was power, for anyone seeing truly must know that no corruption had ever touched that face. Here was goodness personified. Here was an Angel.

And I knew then that Erasemus had been right to send me. An adult would see a child in the Angel's face, and search for a manipulator. Indeed Jack had spoken often of the boy's controller. But I saw a beauty so pure it must inflame those who looked on it with a kind of madness of adoration that might be shaped or honed to any purpose; and, in its midst, eyes with the sad wisdom of the ancients.

I missed quite a lot of what he was saying that night in my shock at his appearance, but I visited the Chantry every day from then on with the rest of the populace, and heard him say these words again and again. Before long, I knew them well enough to chant with him, as the rest did.

'There was a sickening of the spirit of heaven.'

He always began without preamble, his voice sweet and low pitched, shaped to the story, so that his words became a sort of wind that breathed itself into you.

'Therefore, heaven separated this sickening spirit, lest it infect the rest, imprisoning it in a cage of flesh. Sent forth upon the earth, that flesh which called itself humankind, multiplied, as is its nature. Far from transcending the flesh, purified by its ordeal, as heaven had hoped, the spirit became further corrupted, wholly absorbed by its physical prison.'

Here his beauty became a sort of reproach, and his voice shaded into an implacable subtone. 'In grace and infinite mercy, heaven sought to undo this binding of flesh to spirit. But heaven erred, misjudging the virulence of flesh, for some survived the wars. Thus did heaven bind pure and uncorrupted spirit into flesh. I am that spirit and that flesh sent to bring about Geddon – the end of all flesh and of the spirit that clings to it and worships it.

'I tell you now that these are the Geddon days; the days of Glory during which you may prepare for the end of flesh. That spirit in you which does not rise above the flesh will perish with it. This is the judgement of heaven. I am the Angel, descended by heaven's grace, to offer, to those who will seek it, the two-fold High Path – the Harrowing of the flesh and the Anguishing of the spirit – that will loosen your spirit from the flesh which binds it to the earth, so that when Geddon comes it may fly free.'

Then He asked who aspired to the High Path and a lot of people lifted their arms and streamed through doors to the left and right of the dais at the front of the Chantry. After a few visits I realised most of the sick and ailing and scarred went to the right, while the others went to the left.

I watched them go curiously, thinking to myself that this High Path and the whole story of being an Angel was pretty much a mish-mash of the old religions – mostly standard Christianity straight out of the Bible.

Jack Rose had predicted as much.

'All religions run along pretty much the same lines. God or heaven made humans, didn't like how they came out, and wanted to be rid of them,' he had said one day as we travelled. 'This Angel is using tried and true dogma, but that hardly explains how he has amassed so much power by it. Nor does it explain the weapons he has his followers collect. If it were only weapons we might disarm them stealthily and let them keep their toys, but there is more to it than that, and this Angel is at the centre of it. To find out anything, we have to get to him, and to whoever controls him. That is where you come in, because it seems the Angel needs playmates.'

He meant this literally. The Angel spent some of each day in a garden playing with the children of Glory. I learned how easy it would be to get to him the first day I woke in a carehouse, when the attendants asked over a simple breakfast who would like to visit the Angel. There was a great clamour of delight, and ten were chosen. This happened every day, and I saw it would not be too difficult to get myself chosen, but first I was determined to learn a little more about this two-fold path advocated by the Angel.

I learned that the Harrowing of the flesh was literally that: people letting themselves be physically tortured. I learned it by lifting my hand and following those people ushered to the left door in the Chantry. I had discovered that the two doors literally represented the two-fold path. I went with the awareness that I would be forced to undergo some sort of physical torture, certain I would be equal to it. I had seen several of the people who went through the doors afterwards. Those who went in healthy came out battered and thin and pale, but they were alive.

I have spoken of those days of pain in detail, and I will not revisit them again now save to say that when I began to remember, those days of Harrowing came to me first in nightmares; and I was again swimming and swimming desperately in a vat of water, pushed by poles from the edges until, utterly exhausted, I could swim no more. I would sink screaming for Jack Rose and Erasemus, cursing them, and I would breathe in the oily water. There would be agony, then unconsciousness. Then I would be revived to undergo the same thing. The pain of drowning was dreadful, and drove me to the edge of madness. Only the mental disciplines of the Taiche training enabled me to endure.

Some died on this first brutal step on the High Path, and the Angel gave praise that heaven had accepted their spirit before Geddon. Many more went mad, but all who survived were eligible to go on to the final step – the Anguishing – which was supposed to enable their spirit to rise to heaven spontaneously when Geddon came. I had not managed to find out much about the Anguishing of the Spirit. I was on the verge of offering myself for the second door, thinking it could not be worse than the Harrowing of the flesh, when I was selected to visit the Angel.

Unable to refuse, I went with trepidation and a little excited flock of children, expecting rituals and brainwashing, or maybe some sort of sexual interference disguised as play, but all the Angel did was to play with them. The children loved it. They squealed and giggled and begged for more. He tickled them and crawled after them, growling and pretending to gobble them up. He laughed and told them stories of heaven and he sang to them. I hovered on the fringes, wondering how one who so obviously adored children could allow them to be tortured, and preach of death. I was not the only child who had undergone the Harrowing.

As if he felt the intensity of my scrutiny, the Angel looked over the children's heads at me.

In that moment, I learned that there truly is love at first glance: a mingling of souls that surpasses all sense, all words, all flesh, all life. That first single look we exchanged wakened in me a voracious longing. But the most shattering thing of all was my awareness that the Angel experienced the same jolt of recognition and shudder of longing.

I saw his lips part to half shape some word, perhaps a curse or prayer, then he beckoned. If he had called me to him at the heart of an inferno, I would have gone. The doomed children of Glory parted to let me pass and I came to him as smoothly and inevitably as a blade sliding into its sheath.

'Welcome, my dearest love,' he whispered, taking my hands. 'I have been wondering when you would come to me.'

I was completely bewildered. I opened my mouth but somehow I found the lies I had created would not shape themselves into words. *Dearest love*, my heart sang.

'I am Rian,' I said at last.

He smiled and it seemed to me there was something new in his face. 'Yes.' He released one of my hands and reached out to stroke a finger along my cheek. 'I am Sorrow and as an Angel, I am beyond Harrowing. Even Anguishing is near beyond me, yet how else shall my spirit transcend flesh at the end, except by its grace? Therefore heaven swore that I would find Anguish ere Geddon came, in the face and flesh of a girl called Rian. My name was given me as a seal for that promise – Sorrow – for it was said I would know its truest meaning only when I saw you die, and with that pain would come the release of my soul.'

I swallowed a dry hard lump of terror, trying to still the panicky madness that skittered around the edges of my mind, gibbering of love and Angels and death.

'I . . . I don't understand. You are saying you knew I would come here today?'

'I knew you would come from beyond this city to stand before me. I have left you to wander freely throughout Glory where other agents sent before you were taken at once.'

Now I felt cold to the bone. 'I . . . other agents?'

He sighed. 'You are sent by the denizens of the city of Freedom who fear Glory will attack and attempt to convert the other cities to Angel worshipping. You came through the drainage caverns led by a man who, even now, waits for you outside Glory, his fear of losing you gnawing at him with the teeth of a rabid rat.'

I blinked at that, remembered the look on Jack's face as he pushed the ring onto my finger.

'You have undergone the Harrowing of your own choosing,' the Angel went on. 'This I foresaw. You have seen all of the city in your wanderings. You have asked questions and have been given true answers. You know my face and my name, and you have spoken to me. In this last, you have surpassed those who came before you. But only because heaven bid me give you the freedom of this city. I know that you have yet to be touched by the Highest path – but we shall find that path in one another, for only by love can the soul find its highest Anguishing.'

I gave up all pretence of confusion. I had been trained to accept and prepare for death when it was inevitable. I, who understood that I had been sleeping until the Angel's Janus face of death and love wakened me to womanhood, let the fear of death his words generated mingle with the terrifying madness that was love. Then I let my emotions fuse into a shield for the inner stillness that was the core of Taiche, and waited.

'An opportunity will always come to turn the tide, even in the darkest moments. There will inevitably be one split second when you might act and alter the course of events. Miss it, and you die,' Jack Rose had told me, and showed me how to be still at my core, and watchful.

'What are you going to do with me?' I asked the Angel.

'First, I will show you what you have not been allowed to find,' Sorrow said, and he led me out of the enclosed garden. The children followed in a subdued train as he brought me through the city to the silos where the weapons were kept. Ancient missiles which, when activated, would rain acid chemicals to poison the earth and sear the flesh.

'How did you find them?' I asked, aghast. Surely this was enough to destroy twenty cities.

I froze, seeing what I had not seen before. Not twenty cities – but all cities – Geddon.

'Heaven guided me,' Sorrow said, his fingers caressing my arm.

'Why?' I breathed. But I knew. Had I not shaped the words a dozen times with my own lips? As if reading my mind, he said them for me.

'These are the Geddon days – the end days – in which the spirit that is not prepared to abandon the flesh will perish with it. This is the judgement of heaven.' He touched one of the missiles as gently as if it were an animal that might startle. 'In a sense, my Rian, I am an agent as you are, sent to infiltrate. Expendable but with one chance for redemption. Just as your Jack Rose gave you a ring to summon aid, so I have you.'

He smiled and led me back to the garden. Strange though it seems, we sat and he held me and stroked my hair and whispered words of love into my ears. He went for a while to deliver his usual sermon, but he returned. I did not try to run, nor he to bind me, because he was an Angel with all the omniscience of heaven, and knew I was snared by love.

'You have seen the people here, Rian,' he told me when he returned. 'They know that Geddon casts its shadow over them but they are not afraid. They know what will come once the flesh has gone, and they will welcome its loss.'

'Will you kill me so easily?' I whispered.

And then he wept and I wept too. He reached out and pulled me into his arms. I was surprised at the strength of him under his soft, white flesh. His hands trembled as they rested on my bare arms, and he leaned towards me and put his lips on mine. I pulled away; I froze. I meant to, but my lips were not mine any more. They flowed forward and seemed to fuse with his. I did not know where I ended and he began.

'Flesh keeps our spirits from heaven,' he said, without taking his mouth away from me. 'When Geddon comes, we will never be parted. Not in all eternity.'

'But we will not be ourselves in your heaven.' I shivered with a desire for him to kiss me again so powerful it was like a knife in me.

'Sorrow,' he murmured bleakly, and I saw the shadow of longing, the pain of parting, mirrored in his eyes. 'You see,' he said. And he kissed me again.

We sat all night, and he told me of his coming to Glory and the years of his rising to power. He told me of the death of the agents – not murder but chosen deaths met on the High Path. They had been converted, he said. I knew he was seeking to convert me, and that in convincing me to accept death, he fought his love. In my turn, I sought to win him from his oaths to heaven. Every minute that we were together, love seemed brighter and more dangerously alluring. We walked the High Path together, exalted and despairing.

The next day, or perhaps many days later, for time had ceased to matter, he showed me the maps that indicated the stockpiles set under all the other cities, confirming what I had guessed. To destroy Glory was not enough. Heaven wanted all humanity wiped from the face of the earth. In Freedom, ironically, the cache, now isolated and harmless, is right beneath this healing centre where I now sit and write. It was installed even as the foundations for a new wing were laid. The Angel had told me of his own agents, moving like shadows through all of the cities to lay the foundations of Geddon. I wondered that no one in Freedom had noticed what had been done.

'It is the essence of Freedom that its citizens will not interfere with one another,' the Angel told me. Then he showed me the room on the perimeter of Glory, where the explosions and weapons would simultaneously be set off.

'This time, it must all be destroyed. Heaven cannot raise flesh easily and it will be aeons before it can happen again.'

'You'd kill all of those thousands of people after they survived the madness of the worldwars?' I asked, as we stood in that small machine-dominated room.

'I would free those souls left behind,' he said gently. 'I will free them from fear and death and pain and sorrow.'

'And from love and beauty of the sort that only flesh can know?'

Again there was a flash of pain in his eyes, and he stroked my cheek, then pointed to my ring. 'Why not summon him then? He will come here though it is forbidden. He could kill me and save you.'

I thought there was a flare of hope in his eyes.

'You would not let him,' I said, knowing that this was true but not all the truth. I could not bear the thought of Sorrow dying.

'You believed he was an Angel?' Jack Rose asks. I have let him read the words written down. His eyes are filled with pain and he makes no effort to hide it. He does not care if I know how he feels.

'He was,' I say. 'He came to bring Geddon. He fell in love and he trusted me. But I am not an Angel.'

'You loved him?' He turns away to stare out the window, bracing himself.

'Yes,' I rasp, and wonder how many shapes Sorrow can take.

'You killed him,' Jack says flatly. 'You had to. He would have killed himself and me and you and all of us. All the children left – not just the ones in Glory. He would have killed humanity out of love. You killed him so that we would survive.'

I feel the pain and memory of Sorrow well up and spill out of me. Again I see his face, suffused with radiance, for he walked the Highest Path of all in the moment of dying, knowing that he failed because of loving me, knowing that I remained behind, and was lost to heaven. Again I feel the whoosh of the explosions, and the flaring heat of the flames as they coiled around me. The sound of Glory dying was the sound of my anguish.

'Tell me again what happened at the end,' Erasemus said. 'I know you have written it, but . . .'

He stopped, not wanting to say what I saw so clearly in his face. That if I thought Sorrow had truly been sent by heaven, then perhaps I was mad. If that was so, perhaps I had been mistaken in reporting that the control centre had been annihilated, and was incapable of detonating the explosives hidden in the other cities, in Freedom.

'He showed me the control room, and when I had the chance, I went back to destroy it. I rewired it so that it would be blown up. I didn't realise the city would go up with it. I thought it would just be the room.'

'He might have lied when he said the control room was the only control centre. Maybe the weapons could be triggered some other way.'

I looked at the wall, and after a moment he went out. Unless he believed Sorrow had been an Angel, he must doubt. He could not understand that an Angel is truth. Erasemus believed Sorrow had been mad, and I could not tell him any different. People see what they want to see. Sorrow told me that. People can look into the face of the sun, and see only the eternal night.

'It was foreseen that it would come to this moment of balance,' Sorrow had said, standing in the doorway of the control room. His eyes were on the weapon I held. Jack Rose had made it himself – a little sheathed knife that, triggered, ejected its blade. My hand trembled.

'You love me,' the Angel said.

I nodded, weeping. 'I do, but I have to stop you. I can't let you destroy everything.'

'Only flesh, my love. Only the material world. I would never harm you.' He was smiling because he was an Angel and Angels are love and only know love. He loved me, but he did not understand the nature of flesh, the need of it to survive. The drive to go on which is stronger than fear or hate or even love.

'Heaven calls – can't you feel it?' he said, his face exalted. 'It is time. It is not too late, even with all you have done. We will end it together.'

He reached for the lever which would bring Geddon to the world before the control room could explode and sever Glory from the other cities.

I triggered Jack's knife and a red flower bloomed over the Angel's heart. He fell like a snowflake, as the city around us juddered. His head was in my lap. He smiled and tried to lift his fingers to my face.

'Too late,' he whispered, his hand falling back. 'I failed heaven. I failed you, my dear love. We must part.'

'No,' I whispered, but he was gone, flesh and spirit.

I do not know what it means that I have survived. I meant to follow him, for we had begun the High Path together. Yet I live and suffer. Perhaps the path is longer for me, because of my betrayal. But in one thing, I did not betray. He went to heaven, I saw the pain in his eyes as his spirit left the flesh – his name was a foretelling – for his Anguish at the last was terrible.

'What will you do now?' Jack Rose asks.

'I will survive,' I say. 'That is what we humans do. You taught me that. It's what flesh does best, you said. Nothing is more important than that. To survive, we will do anything – starve, hunger, claw. Kill an Angel.'

'We are what we are now, Rian,' he says softly. 'If we once were just spirit, we're not that any more. We're flesh and maybe we have a different path to tread than heaven intended. Maybe heaven will leave us alone now.'

'Maybe,' I murmur, and my heart twists, but I do not let my pain show. 'I heard you are leaving.'

He nods. 'I've had enough of being a watcher. The authorities have heard of lands beyond the wastes where there are a few isolated settlements. There might be no truth in it, but we need the gene pool so I am taking a boat out. It's likely to be a one-way trip. All I have to do is let them know there are others.

They'll come when they can and if they want.' Jack Rose hesitates. 'You could come with me, Rian.'

Survive and go on, I think, for accepting, too, is part of surviving.

'I could . . .' I say.

ROACHES

The day was bright and cold, casting sharp-edged shadows over the crumbling city. Framed in a sagging doorway, the boy stood motionless and pale, wary eyes skimming along slabbed grey surfaces, alert for movement.

But that alone was not enough to be sure.

He listened with ears so attuned to the noises of the dead city that he did not register the gritty hiss of the wind, or the rustle it caused at the fringe of great sodden banks of debris on the cracked footpath.

His eyes rested on a spiral dance of leaves, a voice inside his thoughts warning of the danger that lay in moving around in the daylight: Gordy's voice speaking to him out of the past, stiff with warning.

'Day is dangerous because you might be seen, and night is dangerous because you can't see who might be watching.'

But the scrapers fell when they willed. The boy sniffed at the air, ripe with the rain smell, knowing anything exposed would be destroyed. But he noticed the way the sun shone fair on the ruins. You could be seen for miles out in the open like that.

He chewed his knuckle, trying to decide.

The Carnies living in that part of the city had passed by that morning as he watched unseen from his high window. Usually they stayed away all day. But you had to act as if they might be back at any moment.

'Don't expect the Carnies to be like us,' the Gordy voice said. 'Their brains are scrambled. They are not like us. Don't try to out-think them. If you let them see you or guess you are there, they will hunt until they find you, and they will eat you.'

As they had eaten Gordy.

'Be careful . . .' the boy whispered to himself in Gordy's voice.

He swallowed a sudden dryness at the back of his tongue. Gordy would call it too much of a risk, but if there were books . . .

He took a deep breath and stepped out. The sun felt delicious and dangerous on his skin. His bare feet made no sound and he walked as Gordy had shown him: very slowly, ready to freeze at any moment, always staying close to the edges of buildings and shadows. The fall of the scraper had covered the road in a fine white dust, and the boy flapped a cloth automatically behind him, erasing foot marks as he picked his way through the rubble.

Excitement clawed at his gut as he spied the edge of a book. A quick glance around, then he knelt and reached into the narrow gap between two slabs. He groped and felt the book move fractionally, sliding just out of reach.

Sweat beaded his chest and face as he struggled to make his arm longer, his fingers more certain. The cracked stone gnawed at his armpit.

'Book . . .' he muttered, the word as fierce as an oath.

Again the book shifted tantalisingly. But this time he managed to get the edge of it between thumb and forefinger. 'Be careful, be slow, be patient. To be too quick is to die quickly.' Gordy's words were a litany as he inched the book out.

Gordy had told him about books.

'That's all there is left of the old world,' he had said. 'The days of books are gone for good.'

He had explained how the black scratchings that filled the pages hid words. Only those who knew the secret of the scratchings could know what the words said.

Gordy had told him the messages of many pages, and had begun to teach him the magic of understanding the scratchings. He still remembered how to make his own name.

The wind breathed its cold breath and the dust stirred unnoticed as the boy made the mark of his name in the dirt as Gordy had done.

'What does it say?' he had asked, for he did not know what his name was and was filled with curiosity.

'It says Roach,' Gordy had told him. Then he had made another mark. 'That says my name. Gordy. See?'

'Roach . . .' The word had sounded mysterious and powerful. Then the older man had told him the story of the roaches.

'Before the Carnies and the red dust came, there were lots of different things in the world. There were dogs and cats and snakes and horses and birds and fish. But the red dust came and made them all mad, and so they ate each other in the Dying Times. And all that was left were the human Carnies, because there were more of them than any other kind of creature, and us. But there was one other kind of thing that didn't go mad and that was those little bugs you call scritchins. In the Olden Times they were called roaches. The red dust didn't make them mad. They were tough. The world's best survivors and that's what you are too. You and those scritchin bugs are the same thing, and so you share the same name.'

For a while the boy made the marks that told his name everywhere they went in their twilight excursions. Then Gordy told him the Carnies might notice the markings and wonder who made them. It seemed the Carnies might know the secret language too.

'Who knows how much they might remember?' Gordy had mused.

The boy did not believe the dirty wild Carnies were capable of such knowledge, but he kept his doubts inside his mouth and did not let the words show his thoughts

Before Gordy came, the boy had been alone. For as far back as he could remember, he had hidden from the Carnies. There had been more of them once, but he supposed they just kept eating one another and so there were fewer and fewer.

Each night he hid the wardrobe in his high scraper room, and when the sun disappeared he would hunt scritchins until the moon came.

The night Gordy came, he had heard the Carnies' hunting calls from the street below, and noises that told him someone had entered his scraper.

He heard the sounds of footsteps and his sweat was cold as he imagined the Carnies grinning their horrible mad grins as they squatted, waiting in a circle.

Stiff with terror, he had lain unmoving in the wardrobe for long hours. He had peed himself, and he bit his tongue rather than cry out when the cramps twisted his muscles. In the end, he came out because he was exhausted with the dreadful waiting and imagining. Better to be eaten.

But when he came out, there was only Gordy asleep across the doorway. While the boy was trying to make up his mind what to do, Gordy had opened his eyes and spoken.

Roach recognised the word 'eat' and thought Gordy was announcing his intention.

'You might as well eat me and get it over with,' he had said. Roach remembered those words and now he understood what they meant.

Somehow they had sorted it out. Roach could hardly recall how, though he remembered vividly the terror of the hiding and the waiting.

Gordy had escaped from a Carnie camp and his eyes had been filled with hurting as he told his story. The Carnies had hunted him, but he had given them the slip, and ended up in Roach's wardrobe room.

'Makes you wonder, doesn't it?' Gordy had said.

Once they understood each other, Gordy had wanted to know everything Roach could remember until his head hurt with all the thinking and remembering.

'Why do you hide in the wardrobe?' Gordy asked.

His questions were like picking a scab you thought was healed. Sometimes there was more there than you thought, and it hurt. Sometimes he would remember a new thing.

One night Roach dreamed of a woman. Not a Carnie woman with breasts that sagged like old waterbags and filthy matted hair, but a woman whose hands were as smooth and

27

warm as the insides of his legs. He dreamed she was much bigger than he, and had pressed her lips on his mouth and face and put him into the cupboard. 'Be very quiet, my sweet,' she had whispered. 'When I come back we'll go to the country where we'll be safe.'

The next morning he had told the words of the dream to Gordy.

'It might have happened that way,' Gordy decided. 'It might be that this woman was your mother. Maybe she was one of them who didn't give in to the dust so quick. Maybe she tried to lead the Carnies away from you.'

'She'll come back for me,' Roach announced.

'Maybe,' Gordy responded.

Roach could tell from the way Gordy's eyes slid away that he did not believe the Mother would return, but he had not seen the look in the dream-woman's eyes as she made her whispered promise. Roach had been unable to find the words to show the look to Gordy, but he knew the woman called Mother would come back and take him to Country where there would be no Carnies or crumbling scrapers, and where there might be other roaches who had resisted the madness of the red dust.

After Gordy was taken, Roach discovered loneliness was a thing that ate into your belly like hunger, and which no food would ease. He began to long for the time when the Mother would return. He dreamed of Country, and it became a fantastical place where green grass covered the ground like in the park where the Carnie gangs fought their battles.

Gordy had explained the Carnies belonged to gangs. They hunted one another and the few mad loners for food, and also fought wars which were bloody savage gang battles where the losers were thrown shrieking into the cooking-fires as part of the victory feast. He said the wars were part of an older madness.

Roach had dreadful silent nightmares for a long time over what he saw in the park the day Gordy had taken him there. And he never forgot Gordy's warning.

'Be careful. Never let the Carnies see you or guess you exist, or they will hunt you until they find you. And they will eat you.'

Gordy had tried to convince him to sleep outside the wardrobe, but Roach had refused. In the end this saved him, for the Carnies came one night while they slept.

'Stay! Stay!' Gordy had screamed, and the Carnies had laughed, thinking he pleaded to be left. But trembling in the wardrobe dark, Roach had understood that last desperate message.

Days passed before hunger drove him from the fetid urine reek of the closet, his mind filled with pictures of the man he had seen thrown screaming onto the fire in the park. Only this time, the man had Gordy's face.

He had never seen Gordy again.

Not long after, the mother dream began to recur.

Sometimes the dreams turned into nightmares at the last minute when the Mother smiled, revealing sharpened Carnie teeth. Roach began to think of going out to look for the Mother-woman, or for Country. But he did not know where to begin.

And then he remembered a thing Gordy had told him about books. 'You can find the answers to any question in books, if you know how to read. Some books can even teach you that.'

And so he had begun the search for the book that would give him the magic knowledge of the black markings. The wardrobe room was filled with books which were yet to reveal their secrets.

He had asked Gordy once to scratch the 'Mother' word, and he especially kept books where he could find that marking. Each night he dreamed of the Mother, and each night it seemed to him she was more real, and closer, and that she would come very soon to bring him to Country.

Perhaps this book was the one. His heart juddered in his chest as he heard a faint sound behind him.

'Be careful ...' His mouth shaped the Gordy warning.

Anna stared down from her vantage point at the lone boy crouched over the ruins of a fallen building.

She guessed it was the skyscraper she had heard fall in the night, and her stomach rumbled at the thought that the boy had found food packets. She was bone-weary of the bitter taste of cockroaches and wondered what kept her from leaving the woman and the dead city. In her heart she believed there was no end to the city, but sometimes she dreamed of a place where there were endless trees and great expanses of grass, and even a great pool of water called Sea. Sometimes she thought of searching for the dream place.

It was cold outside the cellar.

The woman called this cold Wintertime. The boy below was clad in ragged shorts and did not seem to notice the chill in the air. She had seen him before since she had begun to roam more widely in search of food packets.

She had told the woman about him, but the woman said he was a Carnie or some sort of trap to catch them.

'You want them to come here and eat me,' she had accused.

Anna had not answered, but she did not think the boy was a Carnie. For one thing, he was too skinny. The Carnies were well-fleshed, though she sometimes wondered what they would do when they ran out of people to eat. The boy was even thinner than she was. The sun showed the knobs along his spine where the scant flesh stretched tight. And he was always on his own. The Carnies travelled in packs.

But most of all, Anna knew he was no Carnie because of the silence. That was one thing about the Carnies – they were always gibbering and screaming at one another. You could hear them long before they appeared. They were stupid and loud and clumsy.

She could see the boy was straining to reach into a crevice and again the thought of food stirred in her.

The woman hated being alone and had not wanted her to come out. She was deaf – easy game for the Carnies. If Anna had not stumbled onto the cellar where the woman hid, she would probably be dead. Even though there were fewer Carnies than there used to be, the woman would not leave the cellar, and each time Anna went to search for food, the woman seemed more reluctant to open the bars to let her back in.

The woman had not always been so. In the beginning she had taught Anna a way of making words with her fingers, and they had spoken for many hours in the darkness of the cellar.

But now the woman lamented her own survival endlessly, talking of the past with longing and despair until Anna was tempted to hit her on the head with a brick. What was the sense in talking about 'before'? Now was now, and that was all there was to it.

Anna checked the knife in her holster. She had killed three Carnies with that knife and two with the one before. She always hid the bodies and left them for the cockroaches to finish off, though she doubted the Carnies even noticed the disappearance of their companions.

Hiding the bodies, she had sometimes wondered if it would be such a terrible thing to eat manflesh. Before she had found the woman and the cellar, she had begun seriously to consider it. The only thing that stopped her was a fear that the madness in the Carnie flesh would somehow get into her.

The woman had been captured by the Carnies and had managed to escape, but her daughter and man had been eaten, so Anna had never brought up the idea of eating manflesh. The woman's daughter had been called Anna and this was the name the woman called her, pressing wet lips on her face.

Anna rubbed her cheek unconsciously at the memory. Somehow the name had stuck though she could not see the use of names with only the two of them left in the world.

'And we won't be here much longer if I don't find some food,' Anna murmured to herself. Food had been difficult until the woman had told her which packets were all right. She was grateful for that knowledge. But now the packets were getting scarce. There were always plenty of cockroaches, but you got sick if they were all you ate.

If only the woman would agree to come out of the cellar, they might find a better place. For the hundredth time, Anna wondered why she did not leave. Twice the woman had almost got them killed blasting away at shadows with her gun-weapon.

Absently, Anna ate two dried cockroaches and let her hand rest on the ridged hilt of her knife. She decided to go down, telling herself food *was* worth the risk. She could kill the boy and take the food packets if she had to.

She moved through the disintegrating building to street level, relieved and disdainful to find the boy had not moved. How stupid to sit out in the open like that for so long! Surveying the street with narrowed eyes, Anna left the shelter of the building and felt the sun on her bare head like a warning finger.

She resisted the temptation to look behind her. There was a kind of madness in too much looking behind.

She was little more than three steps from the boy when he swung round without warning. The shock in his eyes told her he had not heard her. She saw that the thing he had in his hands was not a packet of food, but a book.

The immediate fright faded from the boy's narrow face, and Anna saw that he read in her the same qualities that distinguished him from the Carnies. Close up she could see he was not as young as she had thought.

'Are you going to kill me?' he asked, his voice unexpectedly deep and rusty, as if it were not often used. That voice told her he was a loner. That was how her voice had sounded once.

She was startled to realise her knife had leapt into her hand. She let the point drop but did not put it away. 'Why do you gather books?' she asked, her own voice pitched low.

'You're not a Carnie,' the boy said.

'I'm called Anna,' she said, deciding there might be some point in having a name after all.

'Where do you come from? Do you come from Country?' His eyes were fever-bright, though he did not have the hectic red cheeks that went with that sickness. Anna noticed the way his ribs defined themselves through his skin and the bones of his knee joints stuck out. When she did not answer, he began to sidle away.

Anna felt baffled. 'Why do you collect books?' she demanded.

The boy flinched at her tone and his eyes scanned the street around them, reminding her of the risk they took standing in the open. He carried nothing to defend himself. She wondered how he had survived even this long.

'I know where there are lots of books, if you want me to show you,' she said, sensing the boy would run any second without some bait to keep him. She could not say why she wanted to bind him to her. Perhaps it was that he was another survivor, who knew what that might mean. And it was true that she knew of a building where a giant room was filled with books.

'Books?' His voice was intense. 'Show me,' he whispered.

Anna looked around and shook her head firmly. 'I will come back another day and show you. It's going to rain.'

The boy stepped closer to her. 'Take me to the books.'

Anna lifted her knife warningly. 'No. I told you I'll come back.'

The boy seemed not to hear her, and the sky was heavy with rain clouds. Any minute it would pour. Anna backed away. 'You'd better get in before the Carnies come.'

This seemed to penetrate the boy's trance and he looked around him convulsively. Anna took this moment of inattention to slip into a doorway and disappear.

She made her way straight back to the cellar, knowing the woman would not let her in if it began to rain. She could not distinguish between the rain vibration and the vibration Anna made hammering on the cellar door.

Picking her way over the partly crumbled building that rose above the cellar, Anna passed the lettering which told the building's name: IBRARY. Entering the section of the building which was still intact, Anna gagged slightly at the rotting musty smell of the shelves filled with books. Once, she had hidden between the shelves because the woman had locked her out when the Carnies came hunting. The smell of the books made her feel sick and she wondered again why the boy collected them.

Belatedly, Anna realised she had not found anything to eat. She hammered a long time before the woman responded.

The cellar bar slid open with a wooden rasping sound, and she waited a moment before descending the metal steps. As usual, the woman had retreated into the darkest corner of the cellar in case it was not Anna who knocked.

'Food?' the woman asked in a guttural half-grunt.

Anna shook her head and tilted her face so the light showed her lips. 'I'll find some. Tomorrow. I saw that boy again.'

'Carnie,' the woman snarled, coming slightly forward.

'No. I spoke to him . . .' Anna began, then lifted her fingers to make the finger-talk. She told the woman about the boy and the picture in her mind of bringing the boy to live with them, of talking in low voices and hunting together. He was small and skinny but she would teach him the way of killing silently to protect himself. And maybe they would try to find a way out of the city.

'Carnie,' the woman repeated.

Anna opened her mouth, but before she could utter a word she heard the sound of a footfall, and whirled to see a bare foot touch the first step.

The woman made a long keening sound that made Anna's hair stand on end, and time seemed to slow as the boy jumped into the cellar. In the grey light falling from above he seemed bigger, his face an inhuman plane of angles and hollows.

The girl heard a distinct clicking sound that told her the woman had her terrible gun-weapon. She waited for the sneezing cough that meant it had spat out death at the boy.

The boy's head tilted and then was still as he spotted the woman in the shadows. His lips moved.

The woman stepped hesitantly into the light, her bone-white face strangely still. She lifted one hand and the fingers flicked out a question.

Anna pressed her fingers into the woman's palm. 'He says, "Are you Mother?" '

Though her legs were numb the woman did not move for fear of waking the children whose heads lay in her lap.

The girl had often slept that way when she had first come to the cellar, but in recent times she had seemed to withdraw into herself.

No, the woman thought with wry honesty. She drew away because I pushed her away.

She shook her head, wondering that her mind was so clear.

Very gently, she laid her hand on the girl's head, and spoke the name of her dead daughter. The one who wore her name now was tough and violent, yet still a child for all that.

She looked at the boy and shook her head. He looked about eight or nine, but he might be older. He was nothing but skin and bone and that made it hard to tell.

The woman remembered her own childhood, long before the red dust came, in the lost world of yesterday. She had been frightened to sleep with the cupboard door open for fear of what might come out of that dark space. Queer that she could recall so easily the terror of lying rigid on her back, waiting for morning to come and drive away the night terrors. She stroked the boy's matted hair and wondered that he slept so trustingly. His trust made a calmness in her, so that the long terrible years since the dust came seemed like shadow years.

It occurred to her that she had made the cellar into a kind of wardrobe all these dark years of hiding – both a place of refuge and of writhing terror.

I climbed into the wardrobe with my nightmares, she thought.

The cellar door was unbarred and moonlight shone obliquely through the opening. The air was cold on her arms where the blanket had slid from her shoulders, but still she did not move.

She looked at the boy again. He had spoken of Gordy. How queer that their paths had knitted together again. She had thought him eaten, but he must have escaped at the same time she did, and found the boy as she had found her cellar and the girl.

Her fingers closed around the boy's wrist easily. He must have been little more than a baby when his mother hid him in the wardrobe.

He called himself Roach and she had almost laughed aloud at that, knowing who had given the name. Trust his ironic sense of humour. Roach. Survivor.

She breathed in deeply, swallowing great mouthfuls of the clean cold air.

'I am Mother,' she whispered to the night. 'Tomorrow we will go to the Country.'

THE BEAST

As he emerges from the black taxi with its tinted windows and sleek carcass, I can see at once that he is one of those grave, serious children whom one would not notice in a crowd. He stands quietly waiting as if he has done it often, clad in spotless black shorts and a jacket that has obviously been tailored for him. These are clothes of a politician's son or some high official, perhaps a blackmarketeer's boy.

Centuries ago in another land, I wore similar garments to be confirmed. I cannot imagine why a boy dressed in such clothing has come here. This is an Industrial Zone, to begin with, not Residential, though there is little enough industry going on in it. The rows of factories are silent, inhabited by the mysterious, rusting machinery of another age, cogs still joined intimately in some unknowable rite from the Dark Age of Technology. Some furtive use of machinery still takes place in corners of these enormous places, but for the most part they are poor chop houses with almost everything being done by hand.

Glancing into them at night when they brought me home after my last Renewal, I caught sight of the fitful orange glow of forge fires being stoked in the cavernous darkness, and the gleam of a sweaty muscled arm. I felt I was looking into the Age of Stone said by many to be the first age of humankind.

It is not all factories, of course. Here and there are vacant lots studded with the inimical glint of dusty broken glass. Once this was prime land but no one builds factories any more so land has no value. In fact, no one builds anything any more because there is no need. There are far more dwellings than people to fill them, and even the wealthiest live like those crabs that once existed, scuttling from shell to shell.

It is almost funny now to think how people feared that the Renewal Vaccine would end up destroying the earth by over-population. Instead, people just stopped having children almost overnight. There was no need for them to inherit or provide a dynastic immortality when you could just stay around yourself. Then, instead of everyone choosing to go on and on forever as experts predicted, they still died at pretty much the same rate after a hiatus of a century or so. During that time the population growth was virtually at a standstill, but various wars and pogroms killed off thousands either immediately with bombs and bullets and poisonous gases, or eventually because of the destruction of food supplies and the onset of disease.

A lot more died when they stopped taking the Renewal Vaccine. People could go on and on, but what would be the point with the world the way it was? Better to see if there was any afterlife after all.

Of course, just because it is zoned Industrial does not mean people did not live here. Nor were they poor scrabbling workers. There were a few streets with grand houses on the edge of this sector. You can see the places where trees grew in their yards and even – the extravagance of it – in the streets as well, to shade and perfume the paths perhaps. These dwellings would have been inhabited by the factory bosses who ruled the world for a time. The trees have long been lopped down and even their stumps have been hacked from the ground by the Anti-Green lobby which was established after the dismantling of any industry deemed to harm the environment. When the Rainbow Ban was announced, people wept for joy in the streets in just the same way as they had once wept when the wall keeping the old Germany in two halves came down. It was a great moment. It was a Happily Ever After. But nobody ever wonders what happens After That.

No one thought about all the people who lost their jobs, because the poor have always been powerless. They didn't reckon on the fact that for people with no life tomorrow was irrelevant; they need not trouble themselves about the consequences of their fury. The first great uprising was of the poor and nobody guessed how many of them there were until they rose in a great crashing churning tidal wave.

I remember the feeling of power that surged through me like molten gold as I marched with the rest, holes in my boots and my lice-ridden clothes in tatters. The sun shone that day because I felt we were doing something. A girl with red hair kissed me with a mouth that tasted of honey. Back then, in the beginning, I was capable of all kinds of love. I could be surprised and shocked.

The grand old houses used by the factory bosses in their days of glory were destroyed by the Anti-Green's because of their gardens and the trees, of all things. Or they might have been razed during one of the uprisings of the poor. Sometimes it's hard to remember who killed what and why. Or perhaps the police troops burned them under the command of the Elite who resented the union power of the labour bosses. Or maybe they were destroyed in the Neighbourhood Wars that followed the breakdown of countries and other such territorial boundaries. All of this happened before anarchy settled the world comfortably into a sort of general apathetic peace, so it could be left to meander to its demise.

There is no way of knowing what happened except by personal remembering since the scribes mark time no more. Most historians were killed in the Riots against Elitist Intellectuals half a century ago. Myself, I think of that as being the end of my world, and the Neanderthals now toiling away at their rough forges are the inheritors of the future. Time is circling back, devouring its own tail. Soon we will be slime and dust and then a whimper.

Of course things still exist. We humans are good at blindness. How else could we have failed to know the beast in our midst, except by wilfully not seeing it? There are schools run by the few Intellectuals who escaped the Riots, and who are trying to preserve and collect the lost knowledge of all the ages. And there are the New Intellectuals who teach whatever crystal and ley-line gibberish occurs to them, and who dream of the new world which they will ruin as fast as the old. There are the barter markets where you can exchange anything with the help of the Facilitators. There are men who call themselves Politicians who rule districts with brute squads, and blackmarketeers who sell their services and mercenary squads for hire to any Politician wanting to move in on another, or to Facilitators needing to deal with reluctant suppliers. There is even the odd car that escaped the Carbon Monoxide Ban that was set in force once the connection between automobile gases and mentally defective children was finally published.

People still marry if they can find someone to perform the ceremony, though love died long ago. Married or not, a few even have children.

But the thing is that nothing is connected to anything else.

Once when I was a small boy, a teacher dissected a frog. In those days there was a law that said you had to go to school; and a frog is a small amphibious creature that lived in waterways when they could sustain life. I was not worried until the teacher inserted a pin into the creature's brain and ran a mild electric current along the pin. The frog's legs began to kick ferociously and I screamed at the teacher to stop. The teacher assured me that the frog was dead, but its leg nerves were simply stimulated by the current. The nerves did not know the frog was dead because it thought that the electrical stimulus was a message from the brain to jump. He reminded me that chickens could run even after their heads were chopped off. In those days, chickens did not hatch and die in cages. They had legs and beaks and eyes and they could run about.

This world is like the frog or the chicken that runs even though it has no head. It is dead but it does not know it yet.

That this apartment building survived suggests that no one thought it worth destroying. Its walls are blackened with ancient machine filth, and the rooms are small and squalid. Rats inhabit the basement in droves making the odd expedition upwards. Yet despite all of these things, it is always fully occupied. It collects human detritus as a grate collects fermented leaves. A certain sort of people come to live here. Those of us who are closest to the bitter end of everything. Refugees from politics, still twitching in its death throes, or people hiding from blackmarketeers paid to kill them, people who have cheated their Facilitators. All seem borne on the muddy tides of chance: refugees, drunks, slatterns and lesser vermin in search of a hole to hide in.

In a decaying world, this is a graveyard.

Yet at the same time, this street is a small but powerful eddy in the great tides of the world. Things seem to be drawn here by invisible undercurrents which have their own hidden purposes. Events of significance occur here, things happen, which reflect and even change the wider world. From my window, I am watching the end of the world. Nothing will stop it now. It has gone too deep.

Just the same, it seems to me that this boy's arrival presages an Event. I squint to see him better and what I do not see my inner eye conjures.

The pupils of his too-big eyes are charcoal-hued, but there is the faintest hint of grey at the centre; a flaw as subtle as a wisp of cloud on a dark night. His face is finely textured and smooth, but sickly in its very purity: pale, as if he has lived his life under the moon like some midnight-blooming flower.

It came to me all at once that this pallid moony boy has been brought here by his mother to die. He is thin as a stick insect, his great nodding head too heavy for the thin stalk of his neck and body. His legs are frail and spindly, poking out like sticks from the wide bottoms of his shorts. A few strands of hair float up from the dark damped-down mass on top of his head.

He looks across the street, his eyes coming directly to my window.

The breath snags in my throat, for though he cannot possibly see me, I feel his awareness of me like the touch of a wet hand on my belly. His gaze conjures up my granny who said in a hot fierce whisper that death bestows strange powers on those drawing near to it. She told me that in the old land an age ago, sitting up in her bed. I was then a boy, slurping tea and dreams from my mother's saucer. I know that sweet green land was amongst the first to go, destroyed utterly when it was used as a killing ground between two greater powers. It had been ravished too hard and for too long. Yet I dream that green things still grow there: where in my youth they called children with that fey look 'changelings', and everyone recognised them and treated them carefully.

Once my granny gripped my chin and told me I was the hope of the future. 'Hope you are,' she hissed. 'The hope of us who are dying.'

I sense this boy staring up at my window has not been treated carefully but there is an air of power crackling about him. Can he be hope now? Surely hope died with the red-haired girl and her honey mouth. But if not hope, then what is he that comes amongst us?

His gaze shifts at last, running slowly along the walls of my apart-ment house, as if he can see through the grimy facades and their layer of angry graffiti to the squalid little worlds behind them. So must the angel visiting the Evil City have looked about him, intent and fearless. Then I remember another man with such a look.

It was in the old country. A young priest, new to our troubled district, visited. The call took us all by surprise, my older brothers fighting and screeching like a pack of mongrel dogs trying to decide who was top dog, my sister in her oldest gown with her hair half up and half down and me locked between my mother's thighs as she wielded scissors and a comb. I had not seen the priest before and his black flapping cloak frightened me. I began to bawl in terror, and my da came in from the porch carrying his paper. He stared first at me, then at the priest, before patting at me and saying, 'Whisht lad.'

The priest had stared at our home, curious and fascinated, for he had come from a rich city family. He did not quail at the grubby, noisy disorder any more than the boy below flinches from the ugliness of this street where his mother has brought them. The likes of the boy and that young priest, who must surely have perished in the Anti-Religion wars, do not expect to find a place that fits them. They are fearless in their solitary strangeness.

The boy's mother climbs out of the taxi at last. She is a complete contrast to him, all guile and sharp angles with a shrewd, foxy little face and a way of holding herself that makes her stomach protrude grotesquely. There is nothing of her in the boy's face and one would not think of her as his mother at all, except that her hand hovers longingly over his shoulder for a moment.

Only as they turn from the taxi towards the building across the street does it occur to me that they are the new tenants, and I who have lost the capacity for surprise, am surprised. The building opposite is in terrible condition – much worse than this one. There are only four habitable apartments in the half-derelict complex. Three have been occupied continually since soon after I came. These days, a young woman lives in the left, lower-storey flat. In appearance she reminds me of my sister, dead these long years. Mary was one of the first to refuse Renewal. She was called a fanatic in a time where people had enough energy for zealotry.

'It is going to get worse,' she told me before she died. 'No one will stand against it. No one will see and say what they see. Even I do not dare so much. I close my eyes and pray, but prayers are not enough. One must have the courage to speak out. There is no courage left in the world and I hate sad endings.'

The young woman in the building over the road has the same frightened eyes as my sister, and I know that she sees as well.

That is partly because she is little more than a child herself, despite the paint she uses to disguise it. She lives alone and has no callers, no Facilitator protector. I have long watched her from this window and it seems to me there is a mystery about her that is unresolved. I have seen her coming home at dusk, hands folded across her breasts and her face saturated with pain. I cannot guess where she has been or what has been happening to give her such a look. She never goes out at night and I have speculated that her pain is caused by some sort of treatment. The hospital opens in day hours. Or, more likely, I am pre-occupied with death and try to glue all the ragged bits I see together with that dark unguent.

The other ground-floor apartment has only recently been vacated. Its last occupant wore an overall and answered the factory siren's call each morning. My neighbour thinks there was a mishap where he worked. The rate of accidents in factories where they use the old machinery is such that a person wanting to commit suicide would be more certain of success by taking a factory job than in jumping off a bridge. Nothing is replaced and everything is old and failing. The machinery they use is lethal with rust and mishandling.

The only occupied flat upstairs has had the same tenant for many years. He arrived soon after I did. I have never seen his face, for he only comes out in the darkest hours. The door opens, and at first it seems the wind has blown it ajar. Then he slips out, a big misshapen shadow laboriously forging a path. Though I cannot see his features, I see by the way he walks that he is old. He puts his feet down carefully as if his bones are brittle and mend uneasily, like inferior solders. He does not like the daylight. His blinds are always closed and I imagine the dimness behind them must be as thick and brown as old syrup with him wading through it slowly.

The other upper flat has been vacant since a woman and two children were killed there, axed by an unknown assailant. I was in hospital when they found the bodies. One of the aides, seeing the address on my papers, told me of it. I remember she spoke of my home and the street in the past tense, as if I would not be going back there. Ironically, I was discovered to be suffering from the lung blight they once called cancer. The Renewal Vaccine could not deter its ravenous progress.

'The beast killed the babies,' I told her, half lost in febrile memories after they operated to remove the corrupted lung.

The aide shook her head pityingly, for she thought my mind had wandered from itself. 'It was a man who killed them. They think it was a neighbour but there is not enough proof for a conviction. Everyone claims they saw nothing. It must have been some sort of maniac.'

I nodded, but she did not understand the beast is a creature born out of and within ordinary men and women. It makes them stalk the night as murderers and torturers and hides behind their ordinary faces.

I have known the beast was in the world since I overheard my mother tell my sister that her grandfather had a beast in him. He was a thin, stooped man with slitted eyes and dreadful long hands with all the fingers the same length. I had never liked him but he was still just a man. My mother's words made me realise I shrank from him because the beast was inside his skin, hidden behind his human-seeming face.

I was never afraid of the dark after that, because I understood the beast did not have to hide in cupboards or dark cellars. There were better places to lurk.

At my first confession in a lather of terror, I told the young priest I meant to kill the beast which had taken possession of my grandfather. I would fling a canister of stolen holy water on it. I did not want to admit my plans, but eternal damnation for murder seemed less fearsome than bursting into flame for making a bad confession. But the priest had only shaken his head.

'An admirable if fierce aim, my boy. But that beast will not be so easy to kill without killing your grandfather as well,' he said gently and rather cryptically.

I have often wondered if the long-term inhabitant of the upstairs apartment in the opposite building was disturbed by memories of the old violence across the hall from him. After all, they took him and questioned him for hours, thinking he was the culprit. Had he seen the person who did it? A yellow glint in his eye, the hint of a claw in his words? And what of that night of blood? The walls in all of the buildings are as thin as paper, so the man upstairs must have heard the screams and shrieking of the babies. Why had he not intervened?

In my mind's eye, I saw him cowed in terror hearing it all. He could not fight the beast. He closed his eyes and pretended he was deaf and blind.

Lying in the hospital in an amniotic fugue of morphine just after the murder, I thought of my vow that I would kill the beast when I grew up. I had not realised that as an adult I would no longer see him. He came into me as sweetly as honey melts into toast.

I did not even know he had been there, until those occasions when he abandoned me, having sated himself on my depravity. It was then I realised he was trapped in me, and henceforth I relished my decay. If the beast had me, I would rush to my end but it is long in coming. Much longer and sadder than I imagined. In the beginning, I prayed that one would come who would name the beast in me. I felt if someone saw him in me, then I could fight him, and drive him from me and the world.

But no one saw.

The second-storey flat has been empty for a long time because of the murder. The aide told me there was blood from one end of the apartment to the other, and that the wallpaper was soaked in it. The murderer had chased the woman from room to room. There were handmarks all over the place. The blood had been cleaned away but that kind of thing makes it virtually impossible to rent a place. Of course the agents tried to hide the history under a coat of paint, but the old violence had left indelible prints in the air that could not be painted over. To begin with the To Let sign was changed regularly to stop prospective tenants realising the apartment had lain fallow for so long, and asking why. Ask me no questions and I'll tell you no lies – that is the way of salesmen and agents and men, my granny told me.

Watching the boy and his mother mount the steps to enter the building opposite, I imagine them stopping to examine the foyer with its mouldy red carpet winding up half-rotted stairs. Then they turn into the ex-factory-worker's room. Perhaps they find a few grease-stained rags and some empty State Beer cans. Maybe even a letter or two chewed to lace by rat embroiderers. Any minute the mother will hurry the boy out to the waiting taxi with disgusted grimaces. There has been a mistake, she will say.

But they do not come out and after a moment, the taxi glides away. The removal van arrives. Men bring furniture in. They are sullen and careless. They do not understand why anyone would bother bringing furniture here. They heave and grunt as they unload the van, and then they rest before shifting everything inside. The furniture is finely made and expensive. From the crude identity tattoos, I see the removalists were once police troopers. They shake their heads as if they recognise the incongruity of this pair coming here. At one point, the mother appears to be having an argument with the van driver. I imagine him trying to tell her she should go somewhere else. *This is no place for the child or you. This is a bad area.*

Where is there a place for us that is not bad? she must respond, if she would speak the truth. She points insistently to the apartment, and the rest of the furniture is brought in.

After a week, the newcomers have settled into a routine which suits me very well. If the day is fine, the boy is let outside late in the morning. He plays there quietly on the step until his mother whisks him inside when the factory sirens announce the disgorgement of their staff. The mother never leaves the house except to go to the barter market. On those occasions, she locks the boy inside.

The beast cannot help but stir at the thought of him in there alone.

I let the sickness come into me for a while then to weaken the beast, for even now it is capable of striking out. How long I am ill, I cannot tell, except that when I return to my senses, there are several pails of milk gone rancid on the step. The landlord bangs on the door and asks am I alive and do I need an ambulance. He is annoyed because he thinks I should get Renewed or go to one of the Gentle Death vans and get my dying over and done with. *I am well*, I croak, but that is a lie. I am better but I toss in my bed, longing for release. Tenacious, I drift in and out of memories of the old green country. The boy gazes at me from the eye of a fox I once exchanged stares with, when I was a boy.

In the last dream before the fever broke, I was crouching in front of the fire, feeding wood into its maw and watching my father talk to the young priest with drunken, melancholy dignity. I was fingering an old piece of candle and wondering how a voodoo doll could be made, and whether that sort of magic would kill the beast that has shifted from my grandfather on his death to my father. My mother stirs a pot, her hair falling to curtain her battered face.

When I can rise again, the bed is crumpled and evil smelling as the lair of a wild animal. I make myself a cup of tea using a new teabag. I can barely hold the cup. I decide to have it black because there is no milk until tomorrow. It is not really tea, of course.

I cross to the window and look out eagerly. The boy is there and I am pleased because I feared I had imagined him, or worse. I feared the beast had sought him out, despite its weakness. He has his back to me and he is looking up. I cannot tell which apartment holds him so rigidly attentive but I guess that he has learned somehow of that old murder and, boylike, ponders it.

The young woman comes out and smiles at him easily. This tells me that they have met and spoken while I lay ill. I am disappointed to be denied the visual revelations of that meeting.

She leans forward as he speaks, and I imagine his voice softly accented. She points away down the street and as he turns to look, I see the peach-suede curve of his cheek. Perhaps he has asked where she goes and she is making some vague reply.

He says something else and points up, tilting his head expectantly at her. I sense that he has asked a question about the murder.

It alarms her, for she steps back. She looks upstairs and shakes her head and says something. I have seen her glance up at the apartment above hers when she comes home at dusk. I had always supposed it was part of a general nervousness of men, given her lone state. But she might have got the murder story confused and think the man up there is the murderer of babies and wives. He was a suspect for a time and he has never been the same since that night. He murdered truth rather than name the beast he saw. It occurs to me he might even fear the beast will come for him eventually.

The boy is watching the young woman. He is drinking in her fear, absorbing it. What is the pale stone of her fear doing to that clear mind? I wonder, as she hurries away.

The boy gazes after her for a time, then turns his eyes fleetingly to my window.

For a while, like an Indian Summer, I am well in the midst of my dying. I come to the window each morning and the boy is there clutching a bit of protein toast, or drawing in the dust. Sometimes he reads. That tells me he is educated. I wonder what he is reading as a breeze riffles the pages. Occasionally he looks up at my window.

He knows I am here. Often, he looks up at the apartments where the man upstairs lives. His attention seems divided between his upstairs neighbour and me. Two people he has never seen. Once the man in the room above him bumped the old blind as we watched from our two vantage points, that boy and I. Or perhaps it was only a breeze. The boy nodded to himself. *What does he see?*

A picture comes into my mind of the boy and his mother listening to the man upstairs shambling back and forwards through the yellow murk, stopping occasionally to scratch at the floor. A despair fills me at the thought of them fearing the man and fearing the beast. All this fear creates a stink that will rouse the beast and draw it to them.

That night I crossed myself, then gave the warding-off sign which my granny had taught me. A gypsy showed her. The priest had told me God could help drive off the beast if it ever came to me, but I felt my granny was a more serious contender. I wish now she had told me more about how to deal with the beast. But all she did was warn me that I could not run from what ailed me, or the world.

'It's all linked, lad. You are the world and it is you. You can't flee from one bit of the world by going to another. You can't run away from your mouth or your feet.'

I had laughed and kissed her and swung her round till she squealed and whacked me across the ear. The red-haired girl laughed.

'Ow!' I laughed too. 'What makes you think I'm running away and not running to something?'

She had only smiled, showing blunt, naked gums. 'You can't run from what you are.'

I had gone over the great seas, saved and worked and done a few shady things before I got a librarian's certificate. I thought I would educate myself the rest of the way. With the world in such a state, I wanted to get away from the beast on the rampage. I lost myself in books. I loved them, but in the end the oldest books began to smell to me like the cottage I was born in. The papers reeked of my mother's dank tears and my father's desperate rages; the words smelled of despair taken from the heart of trees of sorrow. I sensed the beast all about me as if he had come there and urinated over everything, marking his territory.

I smelled of the beast.

Only then did I understand what my granny had meant when she said I could not escape. She had not meant the beast would follow me, but that he was already everywhere. I had a wife and a child and friends when the beast slipped into me, and before he was done, I had lost them all. I did not care until he withdrew from me, leaving me limp and flaccid. Utterly spent.

For some days rain blurs the window like tears, and I do not bother to rise, knowing the boy will be kept in. But when the sun comes up again, I shuffle to the window and peer out in hope and dread. The boy is on the step, shining like a star, and there is an ominous thudding at my temples.

The young woman comes creeping along the street now, and she is almost on top of the boy before she seems to see him. Maybe she is on drugs. The boy asks something and her lips move. Perhaps she is saying: 'What are you doing out so early?' or 'Why do you shine?'

She points to the apartment above hers. 'That is where the beast lives,' she is saying.

I can almost hear her words.

'That is where the slayer of children and babies dwells. That is the blackener of women's eyes, the lip-splitter and wielder of lit cigarette butts. That is the dealer in broken arms and jaws and necks. That is the king of the bullies and brutes. That is where the lover of pain and bullets hides.'

The boy shakes his head, and he turns to face my window.

He points to me. His eyes are like searchlights, fearless and innocent. 'There is the beast. Up there,' he says. 'He is watching us now.'

The Beast

I start back from his terrible brightness, shivering with terror and hope, for perhaps at the uttermost end of all things, there is hope. If one can come who will see the beast and name it, perhaps it may be defied and driven back.

THE LEMMING FACTOR

The music trilled and fluted, at once wooing and commanding, imperious and intoxicating. The notes were faint, but Sim strained his ears to catch the edge of each one. The tune reminded him of the smell of hot buttercups, of greengrass and the milky mothersmell of his blinddays. It reminded him of the first time he had held his baby brother against his chest. It reminded him of dusk when the light was so beautiful; it ached his throat.

He let the music possess him and fill him up with memories and dreams, because it stopped him thinking.

'I am so tired,' Rill said softly.

Sim gave the youngling a startled look for Rill might as well have stolen the words out of his own head. Neither Rill nor his older sisterblood noticed Sim watching them.

'I am tired, too, Rill,' Kora responded softly. 'But we must keep going, for see how far behind we have fallen. What will happen if the song fades before we reach the end of the road?'

What indeed? Sim thought, but he could not make himself believe it would come to that. It had been promised that the second piping would gather up those who had been left behind in the first great exodus.

To be slow was not to doubt the Piper. It was not lack of faith.

Of course, Sim had not always believed in the Piper, though it shamed him to admit it. There was no proof he existed. Nothing tangible. Just rambling memories and half stories passed on through generations of the first time the Piper had summoned their people to the road. Then, it was said, he had walked before them, tall in a coat of many colours, a long silver pipe held between his fingers and set to his lips. He had led them, piping all the while, working his ancient magic to bring together road and land and Great Blue above, so that they might cross to Evermore.

'But how do we know it is true?' Sim had asked when he had grown old enough to understand the gaps in the old stories. 'I mean, if all of our people went with the Piper to Evermore, why are some of us here still?'

Not all had gone, he had been told sadly. The sick and the halt and some mams fearing for their younglings had stopped their ears with wads of grass and stayed behind. Some had stayed out of doubt and others out of fear of discovering nothing, for it was said those who set their paws upon the road were bound to it forever. Without the Piper's magic to bring together earth and the Great Blue, the road ran on endlessly.

Someone else told him everyone had taken to the road when the Piper piped, for his music had been irresistible, not just a command but a wooing. But many had fallen by the way, for the road was a test – long and hard, requiring endurance and faith. No one had been allowed time to rest and there had been no water and very little food along the way. Some had given up and turned back. It was said by all that the magic required to bring the road to the Great Blue, so they could cross, drained the land and the Piper himself so that the road could only be held together for a certain time. Hence the fear of falling behind, that they would miss the way to Evermore and be bound to the road for eternity.

There was another story that said the earth was not bound to the Great Blue, but that the Piper had spun a bridge of sunlight and water between one and the other. The bridge had been all but transparent. When the moment came, some could not bring themselves to step onto it. Others missed out when they arrived too late, for the bridge lasted only as long as the last note held.

'When you see the bridge of colour and light in the sky, it is the Piper's sign that he will return for those of us who failed the first time. It is his promise, written in the Great Blue.'

Sim had heard all the stories.

'How do you know he will come again?' he had asked his mam before she died.

She had smiled a weary smile. 'He left one behind – the Prophet – who travelled among the ones who had not gone and told us what the Piper had told him: that he would not ever come again, but that he would send his song to bring us to the place where the land will meet with the Great Blue. And a way will open to Evermore where there is no hunger or sickness or fear or pain, and where there will be a celebration to end all celebrations, as our people are reunited with the Ones Who Went Before.'

His mam had died that night, and he had wept and hoped she had found her way to Evermore, for he had then believed that death was the only real way to go beyond the Great Blue. He had believed that, right up to the moment the Song swelled into the air, filling his veins and his sinews with sweet fire.

That had been many days ago. Days beyond counting. Days and nights of running and stumbling and of the song woven into the air, calling and pulling at his soul. At all of their souls. Even poor Sorah with his crippled paw. And Kora whose face Sim's eyes had been resting on at that very moment, and who seemed to change before his eyes. The hard aggression and the ambition had dissolved into a kind of light that reminded him of the milky dusks where everything was uncertain and half formed, fraught with possibilities.

Sim stole another look at her, knowing that whatever she said to comfort Rill, she was not tired. The pace was nothing to Kora the Bold, who could have been running alongside the other front-runners. Would have been, except that her mam had died of the bloat only two days before the song swelled on the winds, summoning them all to the road. That had left Kora responsible for her four little brothers: Rill, Mif, Lekkie and silent, solemn little Floret, just out of his blinddays.

It was hard to know who to pity more – the mam for missing the pilgrimage to the Great Blue, or Kora, saddled with the younglings. She could have left them to fend for themselves. The old Kora would have. She was big and strong and athletic, and she had run further and faster than most. When the Piper called, it was clear to anyone with half a brain that she would be one of the first to reach the Great Blue – maybe even the Firstcomer, who it was said would sit at the right hand of the Piper at the celebration in Evermore.

Her decision to pace her brothers was received with incredulity, for it meant sacrificing her chance to be the first. A lot of the others thought Kora a fool, and had said so loudly, as if personally affronted by her decision. She might have made someone else stay back with her little brothers, they said. No one would have blamed her. After all, everyone was supposed to run their own race.

But Kora had run along with the little ones, chivvying them and encouraging them, falling further and further behind.

Sim wondered if she regretted her decision now.

It was different for him. Even if he had not been pacing Sorah, he would never have been near the front. In the ritual runs which he now understood were training for the greatest run of all, he had never managed to be anywhere near the front. His mind would begin to drift and before he knew it, he would be running with the stragglers. The elders called him a lazy dreamer who ought to have run harder.

'He does not put his heart into the run; the Piper knows,' his da had once sighed to his mam in Sim's hearing.

Even now, it was all the same to him if he was last or nearly last. Surely all that really mattered was getting there, and he would not leave Sorah to limp last and all alone.

Any more than Kora would leave Floret.

Sim had always been more than a little awed by Kora before this. She had never so much as looked at him, of course, and that had been as it should be. *Each according to their place in the race, each to run the best they can.*

But in choosing not to run the best race she could, Kora had made herself into something different. He was not the only one who thought it. The day the exodus began, a fight had nearly broken out when one of Kora's rivals said loudly that she ought not to be allowed to come. That had ended when Kora hunched her shoulders, and snarled the traditional prelude to a challenge. The other had started back in alarm and lifted her head in submission.

Kora had turned her back insultingly, as if her rival's life was nothing.

She was still formidable, though now streaked with sweat and road dust, but something had changed. Ordinarily as things went, Sim would not even have dared think of Kora for fear the Piper might strike him dead on the spot for his insolence. But her deliberate slowish lope, and her gentleness with her brothers separated her from the haughty frontrunners who had only days before been her comrades.

He wondered how she felt about the Piper finally sending the song of summoning so soon after her mam died and before her little brothers were old enough to fend for themselves. A month more would have done it, yet she had never railed at her fate and even now, when the stragglers were falling further and further behind, her face gave nothing of her thoughts away.

'If the music stops,' Lekkie was saying now to Floret, 'we will have to run and run forever until we fall on the road and die and maggots come to gnaw at our innards and big birds with knife-beaks come to peck our eyes out ...'

'That is enough,' Kora said sharply. 'There is no need to frighten him.'

'But if he is afraid he will run faster ...'

'No,' Kora said sternly, and Lekkie fell silent.

Sorah stumbled, and, reaching to steady him, Sim noted with a pang that the limp had grown worse. 'We ought to stop so that you can rest that for a bit.'

Sorah shook his head, not saying what they both knew. No one rested until the road reached up and touched the Great Blue. The stragglers had fallen behind in a little clump, and there was a widening gap between them and the tail end of the main group. The road was completely covered by the swarm of pilgrims. So many millions of them – a stream of life running ahead as far as the eye could see, all grown out of those few left behind.

'*May the Piper pipe forever,*' Sim whispered reverently.

By the time night fell, Sorah's limp had grown much worse, and two others had fallen back with them. Liff, and his mate, fat jolly Wirun who had lived in a burrow near Sim's mam and da for as long as he could recall. In his youth, Liff had been one of the elite frontrunners. But now the endless running and the steep hills were taking their toll.

'Is the Great Blue the sky?' inquisitive Mif asked Kora, again calling Sim's eyes to her.

'It is, but when the road brings us to it, it will be more than that too,' she said. 'The Great Blue is where this world dissolves and becomes something new. It is where all dreams come from, and beyond the dreams is Evermore.'

'Mila told me that there was no such thing as Evermore,' Mif said.

'Mila said there was no Piper either, a little while ago. And now she runs as eagerly as any other.'

So do I, Sim thought wryly.

Sorah stumbled and righted himself again before Sim could help. He felt guilty because he ought to have been watching instead of dreaming.

'We must go faster,' Liff wheezed. 'The song grows fainter.'

In the moonlight, Sim saw Kora exchange a look with Wirun.

'As the Piper wills, so plays the song,' Wirun said at last. 'The run is a test and maybe getting to the end first is not the main thing.'

Liff gave her a disgusted look.

'Did the Piper make the road?' Rill asked her, his eyes as dark and shiny as wet black stones.

'I do not know,' Kora said shortly.

'The Piper made everything,' Liff said sternly. 'He is all powerful.'

'Then why didn't he take everyone the first time? Why didn't he just wait?' Lekkie asked, shifting his pace so that he could trot along beside Liff and Wirun.

'The Piper plays as long as he can and it is up to us to hear and run the best we can,' Wirun said. 'If you run your best, no matter how slow, the song will not end until the road does. But the Piper knows what is in your heart. If you do not give your best the road will never end, though the song will.'

'Why can't we just rest a little?' Mif whined.

'We must run when the Piper calls,' Kora said in a tone of voice that wanted an end to the conversation if nothing else.

Sim's lips twitched but his amusement evaporated when Kora have him a hard stare, almost as if she had felt his thoughts.

'How much longer?' Rill asked as the long night wore on. Now the land either side of the road fell into deep misty hollows, rocky and steepsided. The air felt clear and thin, and it seemed they were climbing steadily.

Liff hissed in disapproval and increased his pace.

'You must not ask that,' said Kora.

'Now the Piper will punish all of us!' Mif wailed, sounding on the edge of hysteria. 'The music will stop.'

'At least we would be able to stop if the music did,' Lekkie said with some asperity.

'Kora!' Mif shrieked. 'Make them stop.'

'Shh,' Kora said. 'Shh. Crying out like that is sure to make the Piper stop if nothing else does.'

Mif gulped down a sob.

'The Piper hates us,' Rill said.

There was an astounded silence, and Sim felt Liff's fury radiate back towards them. He had drawn some way ahead now, driven by outrage and fear of being tainted by the heresy of little ones. Wirun laboured along behind him, heaving.

'He loves us and that is why he sent his song,' Kora said, but absently as if her mind was elsewhere.

'Then why does he make us run and run? Mam would never make us run so.'

'Hush,' Kora said. 'Mam will be waiting in Evermore for us.'

Dawn flushed the sky with rose and violet streaks, and Sorah stumbled twice. There was a small sobbing sound in his throat as Sim came up beside him. In the night, the main body of the exodus had drawn out of sight and even Liff and Wirun had gone over the crest of a high hill rising up before them. Beyond this hill lay one even higher, and they could see the road, gleaming and empty. Sim felt a stab of fear at the realisation they had fallen so far behind.

How long has it been? he wondered, his arm burning from the weight of dragging the stumbling Sorah along behind him. Sorah's eyes were glazed and his tongue was hanging from his mouth. If not for Sim pulling him along, he would have fallen to his knees.

How many days since we began to run?

'Better not to think of that,' Lekkie said in a conspiratorial whisper, having attached himself to them in the night after getting a clip over the ear from his sisterblood for teasing Mif. Sim shook his head realising he had spoken his thought aloud. It would not do for him to lose his concentration.

'Lekkie,' Kora said warningly.

'He is all right,' Sim said. 'I mean. We do not mind him coming along with us.'

Kora regarded him for a moment, then turned her face forward. Sim was unable to decide if she approved or not.

By afternoon they had slowed to a trotting walk. They came to Wirun, lying panting brokenly by the side of the road. It was such a shock to find her alone that Sim stopped.

'Get up!' he urged. 'You must not stop.'

'I must,' Wirun said despairingly. 'My body will not obey me and so I will die by the road. Better that than to run on and on forever.'

'I will help you,' Sim said, seeing the bleeding pads.

'No. One must run one's own race, and mine is done. But you have the strength to be kind, Sim, and that is rare.' She glanced over at Kora, who had stopped as well, and he had the feeling that something passed between the pair.

Sim turned his attention to Sorah who stood swaying beside him, a milky cast to his eyes.

'You might as well leave him too,' Lekkie said, with cheerful ruthlessness. 'He's not going to make it much further and they can keep one another company.

'No,' Sim said, taking Sorah's paw firmly in his own. 'We will go to the end together.'

'So be it,' Wirun sighed. 'Run then, for the song fades.'

'We must rest a bit,' Kora said calmly. 'A few moments will not make so much difference. We will stay with you for a while and perhaps . . . '

'No,' Wirun said. 'I will not be the cause of delaying you. Go. I do not want you here.'

And so they went on.

It was nearing dawn, and they had almost reached the top of the highest hill. They were all walking, for none of them had strength left even to trot, not even Kora. Sorah was leaning heavily on Sim when Mif gave a wail of despair.

'The song! It has stopped! The Piper has abandoned us.'

They all stopped, aghast, for it was true. None of them could remember the moment it had ended, and yet, for the first time in days, Sim could hear the wind in the sparse grass alongside the road.

'But I can hear something,' Rill said, tilting his head.

'Something,' said Floret, speaking for the first time.

Kora looked at Sim, her eyes gleaming yellow in the predawn blue. 'It is the wind,' she said, but there was hope in her voice.

'Not the wind,' Sim said certainly. 'Maybe it is not too late.'

'Too late,' Floret murmured and fell silent again.

'Come,' Kora said, and they crept the last bit of road to the top of the hill.

And then they were gazing down to where the road stopped and the land ended as if someone had sliced it. A dark shimmering shadow lay beyond, undulating and uttering a rasping whispering growl.

'The road ends, but what is that beyond it?' Mif whispered fearfully. 'Has the night leaked down over the land? Are we to be drowned in the darkness?'

'Where are the others? Where is the pack?' Lekkie asked in a voice that shook.

'It is the Great Blue,' Sorah croaked.

Sim stared down at his friend, thinking him delirious, but his eyes were clear.

'What else can it be?' Sorah pleaded, as if it was up to Sim whether it was or not.

'It is black,' Rill said. 'Like the sky at night. In the day it is blue and at night it is black.'

Sim did not know what to say. The side of the land, bitten off into a jagged cliff rearing out over the inky blackness full of drowned stars and the moon like a white hole, filled him with dread. The road had ended, but was this liquid darkness the Great Blue? And if it was, where were the others?

'Let us go down,' Kora said, and walked forward as if in a dream.

The sun had risen in a molten ball by the time they reached the edge of the world.

'I feel no desire to run on and on forever,' Sorah said as they sat by the road. He sounded puzzled and relieved.

'I don't even want to walk,' Mif said earnestly. 'Besides the road does not go on forever.'

'Do you suppose the Piper was here waiting for them when they came?' Lekkie wondered wistfully. 'Imagine how the bridge would have looked going up with them all swarming over it. They will be celebrating now in Evermore. All the ones who went and the Ones Who Went Before. They will have honey and nuts.'

'Perhaps,' Kora said. She was standing on the very edge of the jutting cliff, staring moodily down at the stones rising above the churning waves at the base of the cliff.

She looked up into Sim's eyes, and in hers, for a moment, he seemed to see the others, thousands of them, leaping off the cliff into nothing, falling down and down onto the black teeth below, drawn by the Piper, drawn by the song and their longing for Evermore.

Sim's heart beat fast and painfully as he wondered if it could be that all of the pilgrims had come here only to be swallowed by the voracious whispering dreams of the Great Blue? Had they not been warned by the darkness of it? Could it be that there was no Evermore? Had the Piper brought them to be devoured by the crashing water below?

Or perhaps after all, death was the only way to Evermore, and so the Piper had brought them there the only way he could.

'What will we do now? The Piper will never come again,' Sorah asked forlornly. 'Must we go back along the road as penance? We cannot go forward.'

'Maybe we could gather up everyone who is left and maybe the Piper will send another song some day . . . ' Lekkie said.

Kora looked at Sim, and her eyes were full of the bright sun and the arching sky. The dusk of uncertainty became a sharpening dawn of promise. 'We will go back to where Wirun was, and rest awhile. Then . . . '

'Then?' Sim asked softly, warmed by the radiance in her eyes.

'Then, we will leave the road and see what there is in the wide world. The Piper no longer plays for us. Either he has failed us, or we him, but it is over. We are no more bound to him now than the Great Blue is bound to the earth.'

'Leave the road?' Sorah said, sounding shaken. Even when their people had not dared tread the road, they had lived beside it for as long as anyone could remember. Waiting faithfully.

'Why not?' Kora asked, but she was looking at Sim.

He took a deep breath, sucking in the salty smell of the dreams crashing against the land, growing more blue by the moment, shimmering with sequins of light; he sucked them into his thrilling soul.

'O why not indeed?' he whispered.

PART 2

THE WAY OF
THE BEAST

*'Sometimes it seemed the giant's hand must be
shaped into a plea for mercy ...'*

The Monster Game

Well then, the Monster Game.

This would be a good name for childhood, but the Monster Game I'm talking about is not childhood itself, though it began there for me.

Children's lives are mostly monstrous games in which they strive to understand the forces that regulate their existence. Some never do learn that there are no rules, no regulations and no rhymes large enough and complex enough to give living any real purpose.

Childhood was no place to be in the Depression. I can't remember the first time I heard that word. Maybe it created itself. The hunger and the poverty seemed to come from nowhere too, like a mushroom born out of nothing on a green lawn. And once born, it went on forever. The only thing about it that affected me directly was the hunger. There never seemed to be enough to eat. Always bread and dripping to fill up on.

Dripping then wasn't the same as it is today.

There was nothing unique or poetic about my hunger. Almost everyone was skinny in the Depression. Except Mr Bracegirdle.

But I don't want to think about him. Not yet, anyway.

I remember little of all the people who traipsed and dragged their feet through our lives and our living room during those years. Everything runs together – hazy, ill-connected incidents and scraggy bits of this and that.

I remember my mother feeding the boarders.

We had been comfortable before the Depression. My mother had come from a good family who owned their own home. My father had not been of her class, but he had offered prospects. How we fell into trouble and debt, I don't know. Maybe it was all part of living through that time. People lost fortunes overnight, prosperous businesses faded into shuttered obscurity with no one knowing why. There was simply no money and no work. My father dying of something to do with his lungs might have been part of it. There was less and less money after that. Then one evening, my mother announced that we would take in guests. Her lips trembled when she said these words, and she held her head very high.

Poppy was ashen but the rest of us goggled, wondering what sort of guests could produce such a reaction in her. Only in time did we come to realise that by guests, my mother meant paying boarders. But she never spoke of them as such. 'Our guests' she always called them, uttering this euphemism to the last.

I was moved in with Annabel and Poppy.

'You can't put him in with the other boys. They'll bully him,' my mother explained.

She was attractive, of course; delicately built with soft skin and none of Poppy's boldness. But she had a stubborn streak and a fierce desire to redeem herself from marrying my father, from being poor, from having so many children. She had a determination not to sink into the mire beneath these disadvantages, and that meant keeping clean.

She was the cleanest woman I've ever known. She didn't even smell of sweat.

I remember she used to say to us: 'No one will say my house is dirty because I've got so many children.' She would examine every face anxiously for condemnation. She feared people would brand her ill-bred or slovenly for having so many kids and scrub, scrub, scrub all through the years, all the while sighing as though God and the whole world had made her get down on her hands and knees and rubadubdub.

Why she had so many kids when she seemed perpetually

embarrassed by her fecundity, I do not understand. Yet she loved us. I think we were a compensation of some sort, a protection from whatever monsters menace grown-ups.

I was never close to her. Sons are supposed, I know, to have this bond with their mothers. Ben and Tommy certainly did, and even Dave in his devil-may-care way. The girls were devoted to her too, except Poppy who was too wild to be devoted to anyone.

When I was young, I loved her in the same quiet, desperate way I have always loved. The dramatics in my family were doled out liberally to Dave and Poppy, and even in some measure to Annabel and Gertie. But not to me.

Maybe because of being the youngest, I was a sort of after-thought in most people's minds. I suffered from a crippling shyness – as if I was forever coming into a room filled with disapproving strangers. I must have seemed a pathetic creature beside the others.

The guests came and went.

They could eat, for a small consideration, the meals my mother made for the family. Depending on how many took advantage of this offer, we kids either ate with them in splendid elegance at my mother's precious cedar table, or in the kitchen. On the whole we preferred the kitchen because it was cosier and you could eat with your fingers and clean up the boarders' plates on the rare occasion any scraps were left.

Of the parade of smiling or scowling guests that passed through our doors in those years, I remember only two clearly.

Mrs Barstow had flaming red hair, blue eyes and faintly green-ish skin. She may have been a martian. Certainly she was not quite human. She rented our smallest room, a tiny annexe that had once been a sewing room. Unlike many of the others, she paid her rent promptly and in advance. Yet like some slinking criminal mastermind, she would creep into the house, leaping comically into the air if anyone spoke to her.

We discovered that she would come home early sometimes

and sit for hours in our old cubby before coming inside at her usual time.

'Mrs Barstow's in the cubby again,' Evan would whisper.

Evan and I were thrown together by virtue of our ages, but we were wary siblings for the most part, conscious of our essential differences. Evan spent hours up the peppercorn tree in the front yard on hot days and you never knew what he'd have up there with him, whether he'd let you come up or bombard you with cow dung.

Once he had a bottle of cooking sherry he had pinched from the kitchen, another time it was a dirty book he had got from one of the boarders' rooms.

Another time it was an insect farm.

He had seen an advertisement in the back of an American comic and had decided to start his own business marketing ant farms. He thought it was just a matter of domesticating the ants. When I climbed up, he had advanced from the ploughshare to the sword and was staging battles between various insects. The tiny creatures were proving uncooperative, preferring to examine the gauze lid for an escape route to being gladiators.

They would only fight, Evan explained, if he shook the bottle, and that was what he did. He waited for them to scale the edges, then just as they reached the gauze he would shake and the ant or spider would fall back. Infuriated, it would become aggressive and attack anything that moved.

Evan said he was priming his fighters for battle, but I think he liked the futility of their minuscule struggle for freedom against his omniscient and malicious power.

It is no surprise to me that now he is a prosecuting barrister, presiding coldly over this or that life, goading people to give away more than they mean to.

Perhaps the reason why Mrs Barstow so fascinated Evan lay in his own essential oddness. Evan wanted to know what she did in the cubby house. He wanted us to spy on her and find out. I was too scared. Evan would not go alone and I refused to go at all.

Nevertheless, the cubby was a magical place because of the

mystery surrounding it. Maybe Mrs Barstow put the magic in there with the drips of candlewax and cigarette butts. No one ever discovered what she did. She probably just smoked and thought her weird thoughts, but it seemed to us she was a witch who cast spells there and did unspeakable things to frogs.

My mother told us to mind our business. She didn't care what the boarders did as long as they did it quietly and brought no one up to their rooms. For the most part, she preferred to behave as if they did not exist.

So why did she choose Mr Bracegirdle as her special pet?

Not for his appearance, surely. He was a plump, untidy little man with hair that was too long and lank, and soft grapelike eyes. His mouth, sandwiched between a narrow moustache and a bulbous chin, was red and small like the mouth of a cat, and curiously feminine.

Within hours of paying in advance for the largest room in the house, he had a workman change the lock on the door, as though we were a lot of thieves. The first night he came he shouted at Gertie for playing too loudly, and he called my mother 'my good woman', which ought to have put anyone off.

I think it was his plumpness that caught her, for in those lean days it suggested plenty. He must have understood this for he wore his fat with the same pride as he wore a gold fob watch with the chain strung ostentatiously across his middle. Why this should make him an object of admiration in my mother's eyes when all around us people were starving, I don't know.

Mr Bracegirdle nurtured and took advantage of my mother's softness over him. He would discuss politics with her in a pompous voice and defer to her opinion as she doled out a second helping to him. He lent her books in foreign languages which she could not read, and exchanged sly and pointed looks with her over the dining table. He fluttered his eyelashes at her until my mother was beside herself.

When he reproved Poppy for going without stockings in the house, my mother sighed and shook her head. Poppy loathed him and would mimic the waddling movement of his fat behind. She dubbed him the Meat Man, and the nickname stuck though we only used it behind his back.

We started playing the Monster Game before Mr Bracegirdle came and after my father died. It started as a hide and chase game, but Poppy, who could not let anything go without embellishment, thought it would be far more thrilling not just to be hunted in the dark, but to be hunted by a monster.

'Let's play the Monster Game,' Evan would say, and when she was in a good mood Poppy would grin a crooked grin with her crooked mouth and nod. Then everyone, even Dave, would hide in the darkened two-storey house. After a minute and a warning, Poppy the monster would come after us.

We would hear her clearly from our hiding places, growling and slavering, horrifically realistic. Almost suffocated with terror and excitement, I would lie still in the wardrobe or behind a curtain, listening to her coming closer.

Sometimes she would artistically drag one foot and breathe raggedly. I always felt a bit sorry for that monster who seemed to be on his last legs. Sometimes there was a drooling maniac who would cackle and make quick, sudden dashes. I didn't like that one, but the scariest creature in Poppy's repertoire was the breather.

That monster would move stealthily, stalking its prey in utter silence. You would not hear it until suddenly, heart-stoppingly close, there would be heavy, hungry breathing. You never knew if it was just someone looking for a better hiding place, or the monster. If you made the mistake of calling out softly, a savage howl of laughter would slice the silence and you knew you were doomed.

Those monsters were remarkably clumsy when it came to catching their victims though. Years later, it occurs to me that they were a special breed of monster: a hybrid that lived on fear rather than flesh. There is a lot of that sort in the real world.

Cornered, you would always sacrifice someone else if it would save you. There were no heroes in the Monster Game. Heroes got eaten.

'Evan's under the bed!' Annabel would shout when she heard the monster approach her own hiding place.

Then we were all on the run, rampaging up and down the stairs, Poppy lumbering after us, and it was chasey, locked doors, giggles and thumping hearts. And when we were tired, or more to the point when Poppy was tired, we would go to the kitchen, thirsty, hot and overexcited, to dissect the game and laugh at near-fatal accidents.

Like the time Tommy climbed the tree to escape the monster and was left behind when the rest of us fled into the house. Poppy knew somebody was still hidden, and she growled experimentally. Tommy was so frightened at hearing the monster below that he forgot to hold on and plummeted to the ground screeching and crashing through the lower branches.

Oh boy. Those were the best times. Days of milk and honey.

Poppy asked us once why we got so scared.

'You know it's only me,' she would say.

'But you might turn into something else. A real monster,' Annabel told her.

'Or a murderer might get in and kill you and then come after us and we wouldn't know,' said Gertie, wild-eyed.

Those were reasons to run, but maybe the real reason the game had such power was because Poppy believed. Not that she would undergo a monstrous metamorphosis, but that she would bring some nightmarish thing to life with the potency of her imagining. She once told me that when everyone else was running from Poppy the Monster, she would run even faster so that she would not be left alone.

As a family we were believers. Not just in God, but in fairies and magic, vampires, werewolves and the power of the full moon. When times became harder and boarders often ran out without paying their arrears, when the house grew cold and our stomachs were empty, it was Poppy who would make us forget with her games and her stories.

'I am a storyteller and I have magical powers,' she once announced, just as she might announce she was a monster or a leper. And we would believe her for she did have power.

Stories gushed out of her and we all wallowed in them.

Truth was never a constant for Poppy. It was a thing that was to be transformed by her storytelling into something wondrous and larger than life. She would recount an adventure and the wilder it got, the more believable she made it. She was the kind of person who could make you believe in anything.

The real-life dramas occurring all around us – the evictions, the breadline queues, the sackings and the suicides – were irrelevant to the world Poppy wove around us. She used the real world but whatever her words touched, altered. Even my father, who died too soon and too quickly, became another of her malleable characters, so that in the end you forgot what he was really like and remembered only Poppy's creation.

Thus did she subtly change our history.

'What did Our Father do?' Gertie would ask. She remembered him least.

And it was always Our Father. Not dad or da. Our Father who art in heaven. Hallowed be thy name.

I have only a single true memory of my father. He was taking me somewhere on a bus. He pointed to a round tower in the field next to the cemetery where he was later buried, and told me that this was where they buried a giant. Rigor mortis had set in before the giant's body had been laid out, leaving one arm stuck out in front of him. Rather than dig a much deeper hole to incorporate the extended arm, it was decided to bury the body and then to entomb the arm in a tower of grey cement.

Whenever I pass that cemetery, I think not of my father, but of that dead giant's final rebellion against the rigid conformity of death. 'Long live the giant,' I whisper to myself.

In later years, I have seen little of my family. Things were never the same after Poppy left us. I don't sleep as soundly as I used to. I am an insomniac now, a legacy contracted, no doubt, from the toilet seat.

'Don't sit on the toilet seat,' my mother's ghost warns.

When Poppy was a girl before the truces of womanhood, she and my mother fought endlessly. Terrible screaming arguments when words flew through the air like knives, wounding anyone who got in the way. These arguments sent my mother white, but I think Poppy relished the drama of them. She had an unfailing sense for atmosphere. Her life was a canvas of purple passions, chaos and colour threaded with dark skeins of fear and pain, and not the sad, pathetic scramble I have found my own life to be.

Maybe it was the essential innocence in Poppy that gave her words magic. She was undefiled by reality. It did not bind or restrain her. Only her audience mattered and she had a gift for knowing them.

'Children are not subtle creatures,' I once heard her say. 'They are like new rocks, all jag-edged and half-formed. Time alone renders them smooth and lets you see the grain beneath the surface.'

'Stories for children,' Poppy said. 'Must be as rough and ready as their audience.'

Poppy was the best part of those years in which people starved and wept and despaired. With her we inhabited a fantasy world where anything could happen. Nothing in the real world could touch us. As kids, we had few friends because it was difficult for anyone else to enter the complex imaginary world she built about us. And in adapting, we were alienated from those about us.

We all adored her, even Dave, though her favourite was clumsy, sweet-faced Tommy. I felt I bored her, but with Poppy that was no distinction. She was easily bored. She was an impatient dreamer, rarely finishing anything and never meeting anyone who measured up to the beings that peopled her imagination.

Poppy did not get along well with adults, though they were often attracted to her. Once in a shop she ate a five pound note rather than pay a price she found exorbitant for a pie. She said that gesture had been maliciously misunderstood by the newspapers who reported her as hysterically unbalanced. She claimed that ours was not a good world for gestures.

Mrs Barstow crept into the house not long after that, clutching an oddly shaped parcel.

Dave and Ben were in the kitchen playing cards as they did day after day. At the beginning of the Depression they had queued up for jobs, confident in their youth and their strength, but that had worn off. Evan and I were in the hallway when Mrs Barstow came in. Evan was tormenting Gertie by pretending to torture a toy cat someone had made for her from a moth-eaten fur tippet.

'Come on, Nicky,' he said, pointing up the stairs when she had disappeared into her room. 'Let's climb up the pear tree and see what she's got.'

'I'm not,' I said. 'Mum'll kill us.'

'She won't find out, stupid,' Evan said contemptuously. 'How can you stand not knowing what she has. It could be the head of a body.'

'No!' I gasped, delighted.

'It could be a swag of money,' Evan said seductively. 'She could be a robber queen.'

'The tree won't hold us,' I said weakly.

Evan grinned. 'Sure it will. I've been up thousands of times.'

Naturally, he made me go up first.

I inched along the knobbled arthritic branches, with twigs and grey-green leaves sticking vindictively into my bare legs. Reaching the branch nearest the sewing-room window, I climbed onto the sill.

'I can't see anything,' I whispered, disappointed. 'She's left the light off.'

'Hang on. Let's have a look.' Evan swung past me onto the next windowsill, agile as a monkey. He glanced in and froze.

'Not that one,' I hissed irritably.

But he waved a hand frantically without taking his eyes from the window. I crawled across and looked in too.

At first I could see nothing, then the slow shadows took shape in the dim orange glow of the firelight. At once, I knew whose room we were spying on. No one but Mr Bracegirdle could afford coal.

There were two naked bodies on the bed. I knew what they were about. I leaned closer, my breath frosting the glass. There was something fascinating about the play of light on the pale flesh, the twined legs and sliding fingers. It looked to me as if the larger body was trying to absorb the one beneath it.

'Jeez,' Evan breathed. 'Jezus.'

I was shocked, but relished my mother's reaction when we told her old Bracegirdle had a woman in his room. That would be the end of him. I gloated at the downfall of the Meat Man.

'Mum'll have a breakdown,' Evan whispered. 'Poppy and the Meat Man. Jeez.'

And he went on talking, but I could hear nothing. The room behind the glass seemed red now, a window straight into hell, for even as he spoke the woman on the bed had turned her face to the window ...

I can't remember exactly what happened next. Poppy saw us, I think, peering in at her. She screamed and Evan fell off the sill in fright, breaking his arm in two places. I sat on the windowsill like a frozen gargoyle until Dave came and dragged me down by the scruff of the neck calling me a dirty little spy.

Poppy disappeared that night and Mr Bracegirdle left the next morning.

I saw Poppy only once after that. She came back to collect her things. I was sitting on the step with a stray cat in my lap. She did not look at me as she came up the steps and inside I heard the sound of an argument as she and my mother screamed at each other.

When she came back out, Poppy stopped beside me. After a long time I looked up at her. Her face was thin and twisted with bitterness.

'Don't be so bloody pious, Nicky. Who do you think has been feeding you? Who paid for your school books?'

When I said nothing, she shrugged and walked away carrying her little suitcase. The back of her skirt was grubby. It was not a thing I would normally have noticed.

For Poppy there were two worlds. Survival was important in the real world, but reality must not intrude on the other dream world of her imaginings. The dream world made the real world bearable. I had been more important to Poppy than I realised in keeping the two worlds apart. I had been a clean mirror for her to look into. I had seen Poppy the way she was in the other world: the world of her dreams and stories.

When I looked through Mr Bracegirdle's window, I smashed that mirror into a million cutting pieces.

A long time ago, Dave the opportunist told me that life was a game. 'You learn the rules,' he said. 'Then you twist them to suit yourself.'

I think life is more like the Monster game. You chase life, confident you're in control, that you're the monster. But you can't help looking behind just in case some other monster is sneaking up.

And maybe one day everyone turns around and the real monster is there, and you know his name when you look in his face, because he's you.

When I looked in that window, I destroyed the old Poppy who had built a fragile wall between the sordid business of surviving in the real world, and her world of make-believe.

But I did worse than that, I made Poppy look at the monster.

I wish I could apologise to her. I would say: 'Long live the giant who protects us from the monsters of reality, who keeps our dreams safe.'

CORFU

He had taken his bike then, and ridden for a long time, away from the housing commission area with its countless futile lives that hemmed him in. He rode up the highway and into town, passing its scaffolded dead centre which was destined to become the new Market Square and rise like Phoenix from the ashes. They had been at it again so he had slipped out. Escaped. There were times when he felt the fighting and screaming was all there was, and even when he was alone the voices went on saying the same old things inside his head: her martyred voice and Dave's low snarl.

Matthew backpedalled to slow up, and looked down the main street into the early morning. The sun had yet to rise but on days like this there were no splendid dawns, just a grey luminescence that got steadily brighter. The scaffolding of the complex looked like steel bones. Hard to believe there had once been streets in there and sidewalks and shops and parking meters. Now it was one dark building and even the tough kids avoided it and the temptation of vandalising it. That would come later, maybe. Matthew wondered what it was all for. The old streets had been all right. It was still the same old town, still a drab place where nobody important ever came or visited. A backwater.

He let the bike pick up speed again and a sweeper truck swished around the corner and gurgled off in the opposite direction. The street lights blinked off suddenly, like magic. Sometimes he and Sophie had pretended they were the only people left in the whole world. That was what the streets felt like now.

He came at last to the sea with a feeling of relief. The quiet rush of the waves and the faint whistling sound the wind made in the swings rose up to meet him. He coasted the bike to a stop and let the stillness come into him. There was a cleanliness to the world at that hour: a cold promise to the coming day. The sea was like liquid shadow and produced an oddly fetching gurgle as it moved along the edge of the cement car-park bordering the water. He chained his bike and walked further along where the cement gave way to a brief, grey stretch of sand.

Mostly he left early for the paper run, letting his mother believe it took longer than it did so he could have some freedom. Then Mr Murphy had made him head runner so he had afternoon runs when one of the other paper boys was sick. That meant he could get down to the sea some afternoons. The time he chose to come depended on his mood. Today was a morning mood because he felt the need to be alone and think.

At dusk the bay was a different place. There were people around and the city noise drowned out the waves. But at least the dusk stopped you seeing right across the stretch of water to where the industries belched out their filtered smog. And unless it rained and the fish took refuge in the deeps from the pounding on the surface, the old men would be there in the fading light, dressed in their shabby shapeless jumpers and baggy trousers, fishing off the end of the pier. At first he had shared the pier grudgingly with them, and mentally found himself echoing Dave's notion that all wogs should 'Go Home'. But he came to accept their presence, their queer-sounding English. And one day one of the men had spoken to him.

'Eh, boy! What you coming here every day only to stare? You no want to fish!'

It was the fattest of the group who spoke, a man with bright eyes and nut-coloured skin. He had introduced himself as Tony.

'I like watching the boats,' Matthew had told them, looking out at the horizon to where he had seen a hundred rust-blooded hulks drift across.

'Maybe you want to be a sailor then,' Tony asked on another occasion.

'No. I just want to travel. You know. See the world. I want to go somewhere where things are different.'

'Everywhere things are the same.' Tony smiled.

Matthew shrugged . . .

'You will have to grow up an' get rich then. Better if you be a sailor an' see the world.'

'Here is good,' said another of the men.

'I'm going to find my father,' Matthew said quietly.

'Where is he?' Tony started.

Matthew pretended not to hear and the silence grew. The old men were no fools. They understood.

'Well,' Tony said brightly. 'Well, I think he must be in Corfu for that is the best place in all the world. All sailors know the most beautiful place in the world. The sun never stops shining in the day and the water is warm like bathing water. Ahhh . . . '

A dark, rat-faced man snorted.

'What, Peter?' Tony demanded.

'An' the women,' he gasped, imitating Tony. The men laughed.

'Women are only a memory for him,' said another fisherman. 'Corfu is past.'

'Corfu does not go away,' said Tony. 'It is still baking in the sun.'

'All things change.' Peter smiled, and toasted Tony from a small bottle of brandy. 'Corfu is many miles away,' he said. 'Very far. Too far for fat old men. But not for a boy.'

Those men laughed a lot. More than people Matthew knew. They talked endlessly of Greece: their youth, villages, friends and relatives dead and alive and far away. Their lives were part of hundreds of other lives. Matthew felt his own existence to be curiously barren by comparison. He had no friends and only one aunt whom he had never seen living in Sydney. Apart from Dave and his mother there was only a faint memory of a grandmother and no memory at all of his father. Even while Matthew dreamed of freedom and independence he was drawn to the Greek men and their well-peopled memories.

Then he met Sophie. It had rained all day. He had known the men would not be there, but he went anyway to visit their ghosts. He was halfway down the pier before realising there was someone at the other end. He hesitated, but went on. When he reached the end he saw the lone person was a girl. At first he thought she had not noticed his approach. Her thick brows were nearly joined in a ferocious frown. What was she thinking? She looked up and there was no point pretending he hadn't been staring. She was quite plain with dark, frizzy hair.

'I know you,' she said simply, and without waiting for an answer, looked back out to where the factory haze was suffused with fading gold. 'I've seen you before. With the men. You know what they call you?' She flicked him a casual glance to see if he wanted to know. 'They call you the stowaway. They say you want to go away.'

She looked away again and Matthew followed her gaze. A bluster of wind brought the sea smell to him sharply fresh and strangely mingled with the smell of soap and oranges. He imagined Corfu must smell like that.

'I'm Sophie,' she said. 'Why do you want to stow away?'

'I want to get away from here.'

'What about your family?'

'You mean my brother and mother. I want to get away from them most of all.'

'Oh,' she said. 'And your father?'

'I don't even know what he looks like. There's a photo but . . .' He shrugged.

'I know,' Sophie answered. 'Old photos are just old photos. My family and relatives show me pictures of Greece. I don't know any of the people. I don't know what to say. It will be better once I've been there too.'

'You're going?'

'When I've finished school.'

He was entranced by her confidence.

'Will your parents let you?'

'Oh yes. They want me to go,' she said. 'But first they want me to finish school.'

Matthew thought of his own mother and her expectations. He wondered if she wanted anything for him at all.

'It's damp,' she said, sitting down suddenly. He sat anyway. 'Why do you want to get away?'

'My mother and Dave . . . ' He stopped. There hardly seemed to be enough words in the world to explain. 'They don't give a damn.'

'My father is ambitious for me,' she said. 'Sometimes I think my mother only goes along with him.'

'My mother works in a shop. When she comes home she just cleans the house or fights. She just works all the time.'

'But so does my mother,' Sophie said surprised.

'All the time she complains about how tired she is and how lazy I am. I can never say I'm tired or sick because she's always tireder or sicker. She's the tiredest, sickest person in the world. And she hates everybody.' He stopped, astonished at the things he had said. 'Once she told me her mother was a real slob. Her house was a mess all the time and when she got old she went mad. She thought everyone was stealing off her. Maybe my mother thinks the dust and the mess made her mad.'

He breathed in, his skinny buttocks growing numb unnoticed on the damp pier. He breathed in the smell of the girl and her serenity.

'And what about your brother?' she finally asked.

'Dave?' Again he hesitated. He thought of Dave drunk and Dave knocking him around. He thought of Dave yelling at his mother. There was not much to be admired in Dave and plenty to hate. Yet he did admire him. He was one of the world's survivors, leader of a gang, always just out of reach of the police. Dave had got out of school young and worked for a while in a supermarket. He had wanted to be a mechanic but after a while he just quit and stopped talking about becoming anything. 'He thinks I'm a creep.'

'Why?'

'I don't belong, so I'm a creep,' Matthew said, and there was something battered in his eyes when he said that.

'No.'

'If my father hadn't left . . . When I find him, I'm gunna ask why he went. I used to think it was because of me. My mother told me he didn't want another kid.' He looked at her. The gathering darkness made of her face a curious plain of light and shadow, almost not a face at all, yet he thought he saw a glint of pity in her eyes and was embarrassed for them both.

'Anyway . . . why do you want to go overseas?'

'To see the people and places I've heard about. It sounds so good. After that there are other countries.'

Her eyes on the bay were disparaging and Matthew could see the murky bay was no match for sunlit waters and green islands.

He had walked home with her after that, pretending it was not out of his way. Her father owned a fish and chip shop. He was a big muscular man with crisp hair and a wide smile. Sophie gave him a little parcel of chips, pretending to put money in the till. They grinned at one another, sharing the crime. After that first time they had met often, sometimes by accident but always on the pier after rain. The fishermen never spoke of her to him, so he guessed she did not mention him at home. In his turn Matthew did not talk about Sophie to anyone. He had an odd certainty that would change everything.

His mother called Dave's girls sluts, and Dave, who hated wogs worst of all, what would he say? NO. It was better to keep his secret. It was unlikely his friendship with Sophie would survive the touch of his family.

Two nights ago his mother had brought home a Sara Lee cheesecake and some chips for Dave's birthday. Dave had got home drunk and late with the help of a girlfriend and two mates. The visitors wolfed down the pathetic feast while his mother watched with tight lips. Matthew had been fascinated by the girl who was unimaginably thin with a home-made tatoo. He was struck by her eyes which reminded him of brown beetles scuttering madly.

In the play wrestling that followed, the remainder of the cake ended up on the floor with a broken plate. Later Dave passed out when the visitors had gone. In the morning Matthew heard his mother march into Dave's room and tell him to pack and go live with his animal friends. Dave sounded sluggish with his hangover and unresponsive. Matthew pulled the blankets over his head, knowing what would happen next. The door slammed open. She had been cleaning; he could smell the Ajax. She always scrubbed out the bath and toilet when she was mad. He sighed but lay still.

'Don't think I don't know you're awake,' she said.

Matthew jumped involuntarily.

'Huh?' he feigned.

'Don't think you're going to laze around here during the holidays like that brother of yours. He thinks he's so great! One day he'll go just like your father.'

'Jeez. It's the first day.'

'There's no holidays for me. I work here and then I go out to work.'

'No one asks you to,' Dave croaked in his hangover voice, passing the door on the way to the bathroom. He looked awful.

'Asked?' She seemed lost for words. Matthew was surprised to see the glitter of tears. 'No one ever asked what I wanted.'

'Look here, I said I was sorry about last night. I was drunk so I acted a bit off. So what? It was my birthday,' Dave said, his voice caught in mixed emotions.

'Sorry,' she snickered.

Matthew was vainly trying to look invisible. She glanced back at him.

'You try and get a holiday job.'

'Like me, Mum?' Dave asked. 'I got a job. You were glad of it then. Now I'm a no-hoper.'

They stared bleakly at one another.

'It was the least you could do ...' she whispered.

Dave shrugged and shuffled away. Matthew thought of her lugging the chips and frozen cheesecake home for his birthday. Even the good things they tried to do were somehow rotten and hopeless. He felt a rush of pity for his mother. What was there for her now? She was old and worn out, ugly and uninteresting.

There would be no other man for her. Even she knew that. Alongside her, Sophie was a radiant creature, full of laughter and promise. Full of dreams.

'And clean up your room,' his mother said as she went out.

He heard her follow Dave and start again. Matthew wished Dave would lose his temper and crack her head open or cave her face in. Anything to shut her up. He could not even take the responsibility for his own anger, yet he was aware his own fury held a capacity for violence far deeper than Dave's brief flares. His anger went underground and became a subterranean force, unseen and infinitely more ugly. It was a force as subtle and obscure as voodoo. Matthew understood that the ugliness was in him too.

'Are you listening to me?' she snapped.

Jesus God, thought Matthew, when will she stop? Then he heard the door slam and house was still. He lay there full of his impotent anger.

'You're a weak shit, you are,' said Dave easily, coming to lean in the open doorway. 'Why don't you stand up to her?'

Matthew curled his fingers tight. Dave was right. He was weak. He should have told her to piss off, like Dave did. He had felt a rush of loathing for himself that nothing, even the thought of Sophie, could erase.

'So ...' Dave said languidly, picking at a scab on his elbow. 'What are you gunna do?'

'Dunno,' he answered sullenly.

Dave always made him feel like that when he was unexpectedly friendly. Those occasions were so rare and brief it was better to ignore them. Yet there was a yearning despite everything, to end the barrier between them. To get somehow close enough to make it last.

'Dunno,' Dave mimicked. 'Well, Miffy boy ...' The nickname Matthew hated. 'I guess you'll never grow up. You'll be listening to her nag forever.'

Matthew ground his teeth together until they hurt. Shut up shut up shut up! he thought. Dave suddenly flung himself across the room, landing on him.

Matthew's breath came out in a barking grunt and he lay there winded. His hands were pinned under the blankets. Dave leaned close and made a mock swipe. His breath smelled foul.

'Yeah, that's about it too. You dog. You dog turd,' Dave sneered.

This was the way they fought. They liked it, he realised suddenly. They liked fighting because it got rid of the rage that burned a hole in you. And when it was over, they were always calmer. Dave paused, the leer fading. Matthew felt he was actually waiting for some response, like a secret code. Only I don't understand the game, he thought. He made a queer strangled noise.

'What?' Dave asked, looking closely at him. 'What?'

'Nothing! Nothing! Nothing!' He screamed so wildly that Dave jumped. Matthew felt a hysterical laugh in his throat but when it got to his mouth it was a strangled sob. Tears of shame and rage forced their way onto his cheeks. It was the final humiliation. There was a heavy silence and Dave let go. Matthew kept his eyes squeezed shut.

'You sure are a weirdo,' said Dave in a mildly surprised voice. 'You sure are.'

'I can't do it. I can't be like you two. I wish I could . . .' Matthew said in a low desperate voice.

There was a long silence again and finally he opened his eyes.

Dave was looking at a chink of sepia-coloured light where the curtain was crooked. He looked remote.

'You sure are weird,' he said again finally, but there was no mockery in his voice. 'I dunno how you came to be this weird. Maybe it's my fault. You were always such a mouse, such a little weed.'

For Dave, that was a long speech. Matthew saw then that Dave too had felt the barrier between them, perhaps been repelled by it. That surprised him and for a second the two brothers looked at one another like strangers just met. Matthew thought that Dave looked like a sort of warrior, tough and a bit war worn, but somehow still undaunted. A survivor.

'Maybe that's it,' said Dave the warrior. 'I thought you wanted to be out of it. I didn't know. I could've showed you how to get along better.'

Matthew saw himself being sized up as a raw recruit. Dave's eyes seemed to measure him.

'You take everything too hard. You gotta be cool. She's not such a bad old cow. But she's dumb, see? She thinks being honest and keeping the house clean is all there is. She's a pleb, y'know? Someone who thinks they're nothing. You gotta get the right way of thinking about things,' Dave said. 'She was better before the old man pissed off. She's just all soured up over that. Don't take her so hard.'

Matthew saw himself being gathered up and there was a sweetness in that, but there was also something frightening. But maybe that was what belonging meant?

'I guess you better come with me to Monk's this arvo,' Dave said, his eyes crinkling.

There it was at last. Matthew had not known until that second how desperately he wanted to belong somewhere. Yet he hesitated. Deep down he had always known that Dave and Dave's way must mean a submersion of him. He had said nothing to Dave then, but the offer was there and it would not come again. Somehow he knew that too. And when they passed Sophie in the street later that day on the way to Monk's, it was as if fate had presented him with its betrayal. A feeling of dismay came over him. Dave hated wogs and for the first time Matthew saw that Sophie was a wog.

He looked out at the sea. The paper run waited. He recalled how she had stepped back and the acceptance in her eyes: the smile fading and eyes flickering to Dave. Dave. In Dave's world there would be no place for dreaming and for watching ships come and go. Perhaps there had never been a choice, not really. He had been part of it all for too long. The voices were in his head forever. I'm not strong enough to fight the world for a dream, he thought. That's worse than any dragon.

His bike waited. He felt as though the last ship had gone. The bay was empty. But suddenly two seagulls flew overhead, their wings like big dark claws against the yellow sky. He watched until they had disappeared out to sea.

THE WITCH SEED

Riding back to the old neighbourhood felt like I had come a lot further than a few suburbs, maybe back in time. I found myself thinking of his mother, the witch queen, wondering if she would tell me where he was.

The familiar streets were oddly quiet around me. It struck me that neighbourhoods grew up too. Kids get older and leave home, parents just get old. No more kids yelling in the street on weekends, no more dogs barking, no more street games of cricket or water fights, and even the telephone box on the corner hasn't been vandalised.

No one knows I've come. It would be no good telling my mother. I tried to tell her once about the next-door neighbours, when I read in the paper Lily had died. She got that vacant look on her face and lit a cigarette in her quick fussy way, as if the cigarette was the only thing that made talking to me bearable. 'What can you do?' she asked. So I dropped it.

Our old house looked smaller.

Next door was the same brooding mansion with its frowning eaves and sullen drooping willows, still infested with her poisonous magic.

I was startled to see her sitting on the mouldy sofa on the porch, baggy old skin sucking at her big white teeth. All the better to eat you with, her eyes seemed to say: goblin dark and glistening as if they had been dipped in olive oil.

She watched me come up the overgrown walk with the suspicious malevolent look old people get after a while, as if they're looking through you, to make sure death isn't lurking behind your eyes.

The Eskimos had a better way of it, sending their old people out onto an iceflow to die quick and clean. Better than leaving them to go mad waiting for it, like my old gram.

On the way, I had seen a woman rummaging in the rubbish bin.

As I came level, she whipped her head up and stared at me, clutching an old tea cosy to her scrawny chicken's neck, 'Did you see my baby?' she asked.

I didn't turn around. I mean, she might once have found a baby in a rubbish bin, abandoned. Or put her own illegitimate baby there. I'd read of that kind of thing happening. A woman doesn't want her baby, so she puts it in the bin.

Some kids would be better off dying in a rubbish bin.

'What is it? What do you want?' Mrs Gedding asked in a scratchy, frightened voice. I could tell she didn't know who I was.

'I'm looking for Paul,' I said.

I think I have been looking for Paul for years, because the questions that fill me began with him. Underneath everyday things, I kept thinking about him and the others: Lily and poor Bo and Luke. Sometimes I wished I could get them out of my head, stop myself coming back and turning it all around, trying to understand. It's like I'm stuck in a groove, hearing the same line over and over. That's partly why I decided to come back.

My mother hated the old neighbourhood, blamed my father for our having to live there. She felt we didn't belong and tried to barricade us in with threats when she went off to work at night. She used to tell Bubba and me to stay inside or the welfare would get us. For years I thought the welfare was some sort of monster. Then later, when I was too old for monsters, I thought the welfare was a domestic spying service. I thought there was a whole government department devoted to watching our house, making sure we didn't go into the street at night. Kids believe anything.

I spend a lot of time trying to understand the why of things. My mother says I was born asking why and drove everyone crazy demanding reasons. Sometimes I had to be slapped to make me shut up.

That must have been why I started keeping things inside, turning thoughts around like a Rubik's cube, looking for clues. People are always comparing me to Bubba, wondering why I am so dull.

It was Bubba who told me my eyes were too close together. He said you were supposed to be able to fit an imaginary eye between your two eyes, like a cyclops. More than enough space for a third eye meant you were stupid, too little meant you were secretive.

I am secretive. I like knowing things no one else knows.

After he told me that, I used to imagine I did have a third eye that saw things ordinary eyes couldn't see. It would only work when the two normal eyes were closed. I spent most of my time looking through the secret third eye with its distorted truths.

My mother said I get the secretive aspects of my nature from Gram, whom I used to hate and often think of murdering. I hated my mother a little too, for her weakness in taking the old dragon in.

'She's old and she's my mother,' my own mother said defensively, as if I ought to take a lesson from that.

Gram was crazy. Sometimes she refused to eat because she was certain my mother was trying to poison her. And my mother would look hurt and try to cover it with smiling. I hated her for wasting the time, for wanting love from Gram instead of from me.

'Alex will be back to get me soon,' Gram would whisper, mistaking me for an ally. My Human Studies teacher told me it's called a Persecution Complex, and lots of old people get it. But I had never seen a mad man like that. Mad men murder and shoot guns and kill themselves or go to gaol. It seemed to me women suffer a different kind of madness. Something darker and more cruel. And being afraid is part of it.

Gram was always thinking people were watching her, shop girls, the milkman, bus drivers. Even if the phone rang or someone knocked at the door, she would get that hunted look in her eyes.

But maddest of all was his mother. Sitting on the porch, she was worse than Gram making my mother beg for love like a dog, worse than my mother for taking Gram in. But now she looks scared too.

And what makes them afraid? I used to think it was death. At the end of all the mad fears was the biggest fear of all. Gram keeping watch for the poisoner of poached eggs, the iceflow messengers, watching for death in all its guises. I reckon you ought to be glad to go when you're that old and ugly. What's the point of living when you can't do anything but be scared? And yet how they cling to life, sticking their cracked fu manchu nails into the crevices, hanging in there.

Mum used to go out to her meetings, Bubba disappeared with his pizza-faced mates, and I stayed home with Gram and her Persecution Complex. I was home on my own with her the night I first talked to him.

She yelled out, and I pretended not to hear, humming to myself, getting revenge for my mother. I waited just long enough for her to yell again, then I came in mid-bellow, and she huffed impotently, glaring at me.

'Mother, I'm sure she doesn't dawdle deliberately. You're being silly. You know what she's like – in a dream half the time,' my mother would say the next day when Gram reported me.

That night I had drawn the curtain, wading through the soupy yellow air in a room where the windows were always closed. She told me to pull the blind as well so no one could see in. Her teeth grinned wolfishly at me from a glass beside the bed. Flapping her lips together, she watched to make sure I closed it completely, shutting out the peeping toms and rapists and axe murderers panting to look in her bedroom.

I was about to leave when she started on my mother, started raving about how wonderful Alex was, and how he'd come for her soon, take her away.

Sometimes you can take it and sometimes you can't.

I turned around and told her the facts: that dear Alex, her only begotten son, couldn't stand her, had gone to the other side of the world to get away from her. 'No one wanted you. My mother took you because there was no one else. Like a stray cat you find on the doorstep.' Then I closed the door on her white face.

I was shaking and I couldn't bear to be in the house with her. I went out to the woodshed, hoping she would have a fit and die while I was out of earshot. I had sat there so often waiting to be let inside after fights with my mother, that I started to feel a sense of belonging. I had a store of candles, and I used to sit for hours, dripping hot wax onto my hand until I could no longer feel the slight burns, and the hand became a lumpy lurid paw in the flamelight.

My anger would ebb slowly, as the layers of wax built up, and finally I would sigh, looking at my leper claw with tired satisfaction. That night I lit the candle and started to drip away without thinking.

The shed was backed up to the fence and the Geddings' shed on the other side was a mirror image of ours. The fence formed the back wall of both sheds, and was a rickety barrier with feeble nails holding brittle grey boards together. Neither family could afford a new fence so it lived propped up on both sides by dozens of extra bits of wood. Clinging by its fingernails.

I was staring at the wax claw critically, trying to decide where to put the next drop, when I heard a scratching noise from the other side of the fence. I froze, imagining rats. Suddenly one of the fence boards rattled and slid aside. A green eye looked through the crack.

It looked at me, then it looked at the wax claw. I looked down, feeling embarrassed and weird, even though the eye had to belong to a Gedding.

If he had laughed or sneered, that would have finished the thing. Strange how so much can hang on one tiny action, or reaction. He looked up from the hand to my face. 'Got a scratch?'

I blinked, not understanding.

The green eye frowned half impatiently. 'Match?'

Wordless, I held the candle out. The board jerked again then slid further aside revealing a mouth, a nose and another eye. A dirty, bony hand put a cigarette between the lips and I held the flame to the tip. He puffed deeply with his eyes closed, then looked back at the claw. 'Does it burn?'

'A bit,' I said. I let the little reservoir of wax that had built up fall onto a gap.

There was quietness for a minute, then he held the cigarette out. 'Smoke?'

I set the candle down and he passed the cigarette carefully through the gap. It was awkward smoking with the wrong hand. The cigarette was moist against my lips and I shivered and pressed my knees together, thinking of it being between his lips.

I drew in a mouthful of smoke very carefully, then eased it down my throat so I wouldn't cough. It tasted like I had licked out an ashtray. Cancer, my mind thought in a dazzling little flare of fright.

I exhaled then, and was mortified to see nothing come out. I knew the smoke had gone in, so where was it now? Coating my lungs with its cancerous poisons? I swallowed, at the same time thinking it probably looked like I had faked a drawback. Humiliated, I passed the cigarette back.

'It's a bad habit,' he said kindly.

I shrugged. 'I always think of cancer and it makes me nervous.'

'I'm not afraid of dying,' he said. 'It's living that's hard.' He looked at me abruptly. 'Are you locked out?'

I shook my head. 'You?'

He gave me a hard suspicious look, then he sighed and smiled. 'I guess you can hear if I can.' There was a silence, then he said, 'Your mother sounds pretty fussy. I hear her yelling at you to clean up all the time. Even on Saturdays.'

I nodded. 'She's mad on cleaning and I mean mad. It's all she cares about. It's a sickness.' I looked at him. He was staring at the tip of his cigarette. 'I hear you sometimes. I hear your mother – ' I began, then stopped because there was no way to say the rest. To say I heard her holding their heads down the toilet as a punishment, flushing them, heard the choking and begging, heard the screaming and swearing, heard her say she would kill them, chop them into bits, burn them; didn't say: *I hear the witch.*

He shifted the board to make the gap wider and propped his knee against it.

Paul was the second eldest. Luke with his flat expressionless face and eyes like Morlock holes was the eldest, and after Paul came Lily and Bo. The father had left years before. Fathers were a touchy subject in our house, but my mother once said Frank Gedding had done the right thing.

It was Lily who attracted me most. She looked like something out of *The Great Gatsby*. Dreamy green eyes, pale wavy blond hair and a soft husky voice. I wanted to be friends with her the first time I saw her, but I didn't know how. I was too shy and dull to get anyone's attention, and Lily walked around listening to music no one else could hear. All the Geddings wore op-shop clothes. Not just the odd overcoat or jumper, but everything. Socks, pilled jumpers, old-fashioned skirts, maybe even underpants. But Lily still managed to look beautiful in them, like a princess in rags. That was how I thought of her too. A princess held captive by a witch mother. Only instead of just one captive, this witch had four.

'She's mad, you know. It's in our blood,' Paul said suddenly, as if he had read my mind.

We met often after that. Sometimes I had been locked out, but more often him. And sometimes we went there because we wanted to. The Doghouse he called it, and I adopted the name. We talked and laughed and were silent in the Doghouse, but if I saw him at school or in the street, he would ignore me, or even walk the other way.

'Why don't you talk to me at school?' I asked once.

'Because it might be catching,' he said.

I stared at him, wondering if that was the why of the Geddings. Maybe they had some terrible disease.

Paul started to laugh at the look on my face. 'I mean people might think you're like me. Us. The Geddings.'

'It wouldn't matter.'

He shook his head.

At Christmas I gave him a present. He blushed.

'I haven't got one for you.'

'Open it,' I said, excited.

He turned the carefully wrapped and ribboned parcel round in his big fingers as if it were a kind of animal that might bite.

'The present is inside,' I said pointedly.

He laughed shamefacedly and plucked at the string.

'Give us it here,' I said, and ripped the paper and ribbon off.

It was a lighter. I had bought it from a shop selling estate jewellery for the family of someone who had died. It had meant skimping on everyone else. I sent my father a card. He wouldn't care about not getting socks. He probably had a whole drawer of socks and ties and handkerchiefs still in their Christmas wrapping.

Paul held up the lighter with a kind of astonished wonder. 'Gold.'

I never dared ask him openly about anything, but I heard a lot of it anyway. Paul was a storyteller. He made up stories to tell me. Some were gruesome mysteries in which dozens of people were violently murdered, and others were funny gentle stories about make-believe creatures. Some of the real stories came through in both. Maybe a person can't stop the real things leaking in. There were often witches in his stories.

When Lily's head was shaved, he told me a story of an invincible magician whose power source was his long hair. One day a witch, wanting the power, shaved his head, leaving him helpless, an easy target for the robbers who killed him. And I wondered if there had been some power in Lily that her mother had wanted to possess.

Later Paul told me his mother had chopped off a bit of Lily's ear, in her rage to get all the hair. 'There were buckets of blood,' he said.

One time, not long before the end, I heard him calling while I was hanging out the washing. His voice sounded strange and croaky.

'Are you sick?' I asked over the fence.

He shook his head and put his hands around his throat as if he meant to strangle himself. 'My mother,' he said in a whispery voice.

He told me she had tried to hang him, pulling his jumper down to show the raw ribbed ring around his neck. She had made the noose from an extension cord, and tried to hang him from a hook on the back of the bathroom door. The nails had given way.

'But she wouldn't really,' I said. 'She was trying to scare you.'

Paul stared at me and I thought of a story my father had once told about a man who had taken his children into a dark wood where a cannibal witch had waited in a gingerbread house to eat them.

'What will you do?' I asked.

He shrugged wearily. 'She'll forget by tonight. It doesn't matter anyway.' He pointed to a spider web we had watched evolve over the last weeks in the gap between the boards. A strange spider had bumbled accidentally into the web, and was waving its other legs frantically. I reached a finger forward to free it, but Paul caught my wrist.

'You can't interfere with nature,' he said fiercely. The spider which owned the web raced forward and began to saw off one of the waving legs. Revolted, I stared back. 'That's probably one of the old babies from the last lot. They have hundreds, you know,' Paul added coldly.

A few days later I found him shaking the board, wrecking the web. The fat spider was frantically eating the pouch full of its eggs.

'See,' Paul said. 'It's not women and children first. It's survival of the fittest. All that building and planning and one day God makes an earthquake and it's all gone. I suppose that spider thinks I'm God.'

The Geddings were Catholics. Paul said Catholics drank blood and ate flesh as part of the appeasing of their violent God. I thought that maybe Paul's God was mad too.

I had never been to church except to be baptised. My mother was an atheist. I didn't know what I was yet. Sometimes I walked past the Catholic church and wondered if the police knew the place was run by cannibals.

The last time was like the first time. I was sitting on my own in the shed making a monumental wax paw. When I looked up, his green eyes were in the crack.

'Hi,' I said, preoccupied. It took me a minute to realise he hadn't answered. I looked up. 'What's the matter?'

'I have to go,' he told me in a low voice. 'If I don't, maybe I'll end up mad too. Maybe I'm already mad.' He was shaking from head to toe.

'What is it?' I asked. I reached my human hand through the gap and touched his arm.

It was like touching a live wire. A current ran shockingly between us, as if some energy in him was being earthed into me. He looked up with a strange expression of recognition in his eyes. My hands itched but I only understood later that another skin was waiting to be shed, that I was growing. That was how I saw growing, a process that happened in short violent bursts triggered by some catalyst.

He used my hand to pull me to the gap and leaned through it. I knew he was going to kiss me and my whole body felt light. I felt sick too, like the first time I had ridden a two wheeler, or the first time I had told a lie and been believed.

His lips were softer than I had imagined, brushing mine lightly as if he was testing the temperature, as if he thought my lips might burn him. Then he kissed me hard and it was nothing like the passionate movie-star kisses I had practised on my pillow. It was wetter, clumsier and more slippery than I had imagined. My heart juddered wildly in my chest. I could see that the wax claw had begun to crack and crumble away. There was a rushing noise in my ears like the sound made by the miniature ocean inside a seashell.

The fingers of my other hand were curled against his chest. His heart was pounding too.

He let go of me suddenly and shook his head. 'I have to go,' he said, as if I had argued against it.

'I hate her,' I said, and burst into tears. The tears leaking out of my eyes had tasted as warm and salty as blood. Dimly it occurred to me that tears were a kind of bleeding.

'You don't understand,' he said with finality. 'It's not just her.'

I was filled with anger that he could become so suddenly adult and lofty.

He relented and told me a story. 'When she was young, there was a princess and she married the handsome prince. She thought it would be all happily ever after. Everyone told princesses that was how it was. But she found out it was all a lie. There was only getting old and dying and having babies who would get old and die without ever knowing what it was all for. So she became a witch. The questions made her a witch.'

He was right. I didn't understand and I stared at him dumbly, seeing that he could love her in spite of everything.

'Will you ever come back?' I asked, trying not to cry again.

He only reached through the gap to squeeze my hand.

A few days later my mother told me Bo had been killed. He had fallen under a train, almost dragging his mother with him. It had happened the same day Paul left.

Paul had told me Bo often stood on the edge of the platform as if daring the train to sweep him under. I had even seen him once, teetering on the brink with his wild hurt grin making the other commuters nervous.

And so he had fallen, or jumped, or been pushed.

Last night Gram died, finally losing her tenacious hold on life. My mother had fallen asleep in the chair beside the bed, her mouth open slightly, snoring. I felt a rush of love for her sprawled so weary and sad.

I looked up and found Gram watching me. 'I'm dying,' she said softly, suddenly normal after days of raving. 'Nothing stops it coming. I wouldn't mind if I could have known why.'

'Why?' I echoed.

'What it was all for. The pain, the loving and losing. Living,' she said. Then she smiled, a sad, oddly beautiful smile.

Not long after, she died, life going out of her with a curious little regretful sigh.

Her words made me think of what Paul had said, about madness coming because there were no answers. I felt a sudden coldness, knowing the seeds of madness were in me too: the hunger for answers.

I thought of Paul, and finally understood what he had tried to tell me: that it was me as much as his mother that made him run away. He had recognised the potential for transformation in me, the witch vying with the princess. He did not understand that there were other choices, that I was evolving into something quite different with my third eye, something harder and colder than princesses, something braver than witches.

'Paul?' his mother echoed, sitting upright on the porch sofa. 'Paul?'

I had often wondered what became of him. Had he been too much of a Gedding to escape? Had he found his own platform to jump from? Or had he found a place to belong where witches and princesses would not torment and tear at him?

My skin itched suddenly, as if another was waiting to be sloughed away. I closed my eyes and let the third eye open, and understood that I would never know, and was content with not knowing.

I looked down at his mother, the witch queen. She was staring at me hungrily, questioning.

I turned and walked back to the bus stop.

SEEK NO MORE

'There he is!'

Noah bolted, cutting between two stone angels and grazing his knee. He dropped into a crouch, heart thundering. If he could get away from Buddha and his gang, he might just get back in time. There would be hell to pay if anyone discovered he had gone out today of all days.

Looking down at the fine black dirt, he was glad he had worn dark clothes, although Mrs Belfrey always tried to discourage him from wearing black. 'It makes you look anaemic, dear.'

He knew the darkness accentuated his pale skin and bone-white hair. Buddha and his bully boys had nicknamed him Spook because he was so pale. Noah told Mrs Belfrey dark colours hid the dirt but that wasn't the real reason he liked black; it wasn't the *main* reason.

The man in the dream was the main reason. He had white hair like Noah's, but it was long and flowing around his shoulders like a lion's mane. Pale skin too, but where Noah's eyes were grey, the dream man's were silver. He wore black, but he didn't look anaemic. He looked shining and somehow magical. Noah wore dark clothes because he wanted to look like the man who appeared in his dream the same night Buddha first beat him up.

He and another boy chased Noah from the bus stop, cornering him not far from Glastenbury.

'Look at 'im. He's got no blood,' said the other boy. Tall and bony, he had prodded Noah hard in the chest as he spoke.

'He's got blood all right,' big Buddha sneered, out of breath and red in the face from the chase. Then he'd punched Noah in the nose. The pain had been awful and Noah thought he must die from something that could cause so much hurt.

He grinned, thinking of the fuss Mrs Belfrey had made over the blood. The smile faded when he remembered how he'd been forced to retell his story in Mrs Bourquin's office. He had not expected the policeman to go straight after Buddha, turning a lone beating into a vendetta. Neither the orphanage people nor the police seemed to remember Noah had to keep on going to school with Buddha. It never occurred to them that he might want revenge.

Thinking of adults made Noah think of the Kendells and their daughter, *Katlyn darkhair*. Of course, that was not her real name; Noah had given her the name his heart whispered.

'*Names,*' the dream man had told him, '*contain great power, but only when they are truenames. Sometimes, the truename will whisper itself in that part of you where no lie can exist.*'

Take his name, pinned on the basket left on the orphanage doorstep. It fitted, but it wasn't his *truename*.

He wondered what Mrs Belfrey thought when she'd found him like that. It was the sort of thing that happened in stories, not in real life. He had read lots of books about babies found in mysterious places: on doorsteps, drifting downstream on reed beds, floating to shore on little boats. Those babies always turned out to be somebody important or special, like a king, or a great sorcerer.

Of course, Mrs Belfrey hadn't told him about being left on the doorstep. One of the wards had let it slip: 'Nobody wanted you, Noah. You were so ugly your parents left you on the doorstep.'

Noah peered cautiously round the edge of the stone angel, and was relieved to find the coast clear.

He edged himself out onto the path and stood up slowly, peering over the top of the gravestones. Buddha's gang was spread

out, but Noah thought he could reach the gate if he could get a
bit closer without being spotted.

'I see 'im!' a girl screamed.

Noah didn't wait to see who it was. He ducked down and
ran between two stone tablets and round the back of the stone
mausoleum, where there was a pile of rubbish: broken vases and
tins, faded plastic flowers and piles of weeds with little clumps of
dirt still stuck to withered roots.

'He went that way!' the girl shrieked.

'No he didn't. He ran along there! I saw 'im,' a boy yelled.
There was the sound of running footsteps and Noah froze in the
shadow at the edge of the stone house, sliding down behind a
clump of long yellow grass.

'He's gone to ground,' Buddha shouted. 'Spread out. One to
each aisle.'

Noah's heart slowed to a stumble because the voices were
moving away. A kind of exhausted drowsiness stole over him. It
was late afternoon but the air still shimmered with blistering
summer heat. A hot North wind blew, stirring the dust and the
dry yellow grasses. Noah guessed the Kendells had reached Glas-
tenbury and wondered if his absence would make them change
their minds about him.

At Glastenbury there was always talk about adoption, even
though most of the kids were State wards and couldn't be adopted
because they already had parents. The wards sneered at the idea
of being adopted, and boasted about the very parents who put
them in the Home, but Noah wondered how much of that was
sour grapes. Those who could be adopted dreamed of being taken
home to parents who would love them and give them everything.
None of them had been at Glastenbury as long as Noah.

There were some things everyone understood. It was harder
to be adopted the older you got, and harder still if there was
anything the matter with you. There was nothing wrong with
Noah but he was so small and pale that it put prospective parents
off. He'd been happy growing up at Glastenbury, fed and fussed
over by Mrs Belfrey and her husband, Stan, and occasionally
scolded by Mrs Bourquin, the Head of the Orphanage.

Family life, according to the wards, sounded awful: fights and beltings, screaming arguments and trouble with the police. Yet, for all their horror stories, the wards were always running away from the orphanage, trying to get back to their families.

Even so, Glastenbury seemed a calm refuge in a world of madness. Noah loved the big sprawling stone buildings and outhouses all classified by the National Trust because they were so old. The dark dormitory rooms and cement corridors were chilly in winter but lovely and cool in summer, though Noah spent most of his time roaming in the huge grounds surrounding the orphanage. There were only a couple of flower beds. The rest of the grounds were green, smooth lawns planted with huge gnarl-trunked trees and low spreading shrubs you could get right under. Best of all, Noah liked the rows of pine trees along the drive and around the fenceline. They were like a barrier, protecting Glastenbury from the rest of the world. He would sit on the great mats of dry orange pine needles beneath them, smelling the bitter pine-sap smell, and listening to the murmur of the wind in the branches.

At Christmas, that year as every year, they had gathered pine cones, painting them gold and silver and tying them in bunches with red ribbons. A small pine tree had been chopped down by Stan, and on Christmas Eve, those who wanted to decorated the tree, singing Christmas carols to the radio and drinking Mrs Belfrey's frothy yellow egg-nog.

Christmas always went so quickly. The tree had been taken down that morning, ready to be chopped into firewood, fuel for the fire they would light that night. It was not cool enough to warrant a fire, but they would all sit there in shorts and T-shirts out under the stars, slapping at mosquitoes and toasting marshmallows. 'For luck,' Mrs Belfrey would say, as she did every year at the Christmas tree bonfire.

Noah had watched the decorations being wrapped in newspaper and packed in familiar cardboard boxes that morning with a queer ache of sadness in his throat.

From where he was hiding behind the mausoleum, he could see the cement tower and mentally saluted the giant buried beneath and within it. That giant knew a lot about being chased and hurt by people. Noah had told no one what the white-haired man in his dreams had revealed about the giant, but now, he seemed to hear the gentle voice inside his head.

'*Before the Age of Man, the Old Ones ruled the Earth: sorcerers, witches and all manner of faerie folk. The Age of the Old Ones passed, but even today there are those born of the ancient faerie bloodlines. Those who know the truename of their faerie bloodline have great Olden powers. But some are born who do not know what they are. One such was the giant. Persecuted and tormented for his unnatural size, he thought himself a freak. He lived and died a lonely broken exile. If he had known the truename of his faerie bloodline, he might have used his power to save himself.*'

Noah sympathised with the giant. The other kids called him freak and albino, and he had no friends either, except Mrs Belfrey and Stan.

The white-haired man told Noah how people found the giant stiffened in death, one arm stretched out immovably. They buried him and encased his outstretched arm in a cement tower.

The day after the dream, Noah asked Stan about the water-tower.

'Lord, but that's no grave, kiddo!' Stan had chuckled. 'It's just a water-tower, plain and simple.'

But Noah knew in the part of him where no lie could exist, that beneath the tower lay the giant. And staring up at the tower, he sensed that the white-haired man told the giant story for a reason. With strange clarity, Noah understood that he, Noah, was one of those born with Olden blood. In that moment, he knew the dream man told the story of the giant as a warning to him, to show what would happen if he failed to find out the *truename* of his faerie blood. And then despair rose in a great wave, for how could Noah learn his *truename* when he didn't know who his parents were? Surely their name must be his *truename*.

Oddly, Buddha again marked the way, chasing Noah into the cemetery he would never otherwise have entered. Hiding there, Noah had listened to Buddha's mates baulk at going after him so close to nightfall.

'It's near dark an' me dad'll kill me if I'm late home again!' one of the boys groaned.

'There's vampires come out after dark,' the other boy quavered.

'Ya pair of bloody cowards!' Buddha had snorted. 'Ah let the vampires have 'im. Spooks to the spook.' Then they all went off making fake moaning noises.

Less scared of the cemetery than of Buddha, Noah waited a while, just in case they had not really gone away. To pass the time he wandered along the rows reading the gravestones in the fading light.

Alia St Claire 1938-1961. That made Alia twenty-three when she died. The next grave read: Alfredo Grabble 1845-1938. Alfredo had died the same year as Alia was born. He had been ninety-three. That seemed a better age to die. Noah wondered fleetingly how his own parents died, for he was sure they were dead, else they would have come back for him.

Another grave a little further along read: Elene Calthorpe 1959-1960. Elene had been only one year old. Then a queer feeling came into Noah's bones: a feeling he now thought of as his Olden blood stirring in him. He'd looked up at the giant's tower, then little more than a dark shape in the dimness and at last, he knew.

He had often wondered why the giant held his hand out at such an extreme angle, what gesture he had made to last until his bones crumbled. Sometimes it seemed to Noah the giant's hand must be shaped into a plea for mercy or understanding. Other times he imagined the giant died with his hand clenched into a fist of rage, a vow of hate.

But that day staring up at the tower, he understood that whatever the giant had meant, his upraised arm had become a beacon to those of his kind. Staring round at the cemetery, Noah's skin prickled with the realisation that the giant was not the only one of his kind buried there.

On that day, Noah first felt the slumbering magic beneath the cemetery and he saw at last where he might search for his own faerie bloodname. For where else would his parents be if they had died, but in this cemetery, among their own secret kind?

From that day, Noah spent more time at the cemetery than in the grounds of Glastenbury. The other orphans and wards thought him more queer than ever, and even Mrs Belfrey disapproved of what she called his morbid search. He had been made to talk to the visiting counsellor, and some perverse whim had made him tell the wizened little man everything about the Olden power and his faerie bloodline. Naturally, the counsellor thought he was making it all up.

Everything had gone on that way until the Kendells came to Glastenbury. He could remember the first time they came. They'd eaten lunch with Mrs Bourquin in the dining hall, and Noah assumed they were her friends. But when they came back, this time with their daughter, everyone knew they were looking for someone to adopt. That was when Noah gave Kate Kendell her *truename*.

'Now don't get too excited,' Mrs Belfrey cautioned them. 'Most of the people who come to Glastenbury don't return. That isn't because they don't like you. It is more often because their own circumstances have changed, or because they give up once they find out what is involved in adoption. We don't give our precious children to just anyone, you know.'

She made them sound like prizes in some sort of complicated adult game, but Noah hardly listened because he never thought of himself being adopted.

Then the day arrived when Stan came looking for Noah in the grounds. He'd been sitting in a pine tree re-reading one of his favourite books when a green sedan came up the drive. Mr and Mrs Kendell got out, followed by their tall daughter. A third visit meant the Kendells must want to meet someone in particular. Turning back to his book, Noah wondered fleetingly who it would be. It didn't occur to him to connect Stan's calls for him with the Kendell's arrival, but a moment later he was being ushered into Mrs Bourquin's office. Seeing the Kendells, he stopped dead.

'Come right on in, Noah,' Mrs Bourquin said, a trifle impatiently.

'Noah,' Mr Kendell greeted him in a deep voice, his eyes full of questions. Noah sensed a frustrated sort of anger in him. 'This is my wife.'

The slight woman seated beside Mrs Bourquin had golden blond hair that floated in a feathery cloud of curls about her jaw. Her eyes were blue and she smiled at him, holding out her hand.

'Noah,' she said tenderly, making of his name something it had never been before. 'I'm so glad to be able to meet you at last.'

'Jane . . . ' Mr Kendell murmured warningly. He set himself between Noah and his wife and introduced his daughter.

'Kate,' he barked. *Katlyn darkhair*, Noah echoed the girl's *truename* inside. He turned to stare into the deepsea blue eyes and found them remote and watchful. Wait and see, her eyes seemed to say.

Mrs Bourquin prompted Noah to talk, and then went to supervise lunch. By the time she returned, Noah and Mrs Kendell were seated knee to knee, deep in conversation. Noah thought her the most wonderful person he had ever met. Her eyes widened when he told her about the time he'd been trapped up the tree all night. She laughed at his description of making nests from pine needles and she looked excited at the idea of seeing his collection of treasures. When he told her his favourite books, it turned out she'd read most of them too. She said she would get one he recommended out of the library. Shyly, he offered to loan his copy to her.

All the while she held his hand and her golden curls floated between them and against his cheek, smelling sweet and clean.

Every now and then, Mr Kendell had stopped his restless prowling to put in a question.

'Do you like sport?' he said gruffly. Noah was tempted to lie because he knew parents liked you to be good at a sport. That was one of the questions they always asked. But the look in Mrs Kendell's eyes made him tell the truth.

'I'm not very good at sport,' he offered sadly.

'I *hated* sport at school,' Mrs Kendell confessed. Mr Kendell grunted and went back to his pacing.

Lunch came and went, but Noah hardly ate. He had never talked so much in all his life. When Mr Kendell announced that it was time to go, he had been sorry and he thought Mrs Kendell was too. She held his hand right up to the last moment, and waved until the car was out of sight.

Adopted, adopted, adopted, the pine trees whispered exultantly.

'Don't get your hopes up. It's better not to think about it at all,' Mrs Belfrey had advised. Sometime before dawn, it occurred to Noah that he'd forgotten to lend his book to Mrs Kendell. It wasn't until the next day he remembered the cemetery and his search for his *truename.*

His heart told him he must find out his parents' name before the Kendells took him away. (If they took him, warned Mrs Belfrey.) If he failed to find his *truename,* he would never reach all the things he sensed locked in his chest: all the powers that surged in their cage.

And now it was the last day. He had sneaked out, climbing over the back gate, holding onto the chain to stop it rattling, and hurrying through the blazing heat for one last search of the cemetery.

He had hardly been there any time before Buddha and his gang turned up. Unlike the first time, they got hold of him before he realised they were there. Maybe they had been watching and waiting for him. He hadn't tried to struggle because there were too many of them. He let his arms hang limply, waiting for the two holding his arms to relax too, and give him a chance to pull free.

'We've come for you, Spook. We've come to put you in your place,' Buddha leered, his face shiny with sweat. The two boys holding Noah started to walk, dragging him between them.

'Where ... what are you doing?' he'd asked warily. He was always a bit afraid Buddha would get carried away one of these times and really kill him.

'We're taking you home,' said the bony boy he saw most often with Buddha.

'Yeah, home,' giggled a girl with dull brown hair and flat eyes.

Suddenly his two guards stopped.

'Home,' Buddha announced.

Noah looked at him uneasily, and followed his gaze. Then his heart started to gallop because Buddha was looking at a freshly dug grave. A big pile of dirt was covered with some green fake lawn, and a stiff green plastic lid concealed the hole for the coffin. The North wind breathed its hot fetid breath in Noah's face.

'What are you doing to do?' Noah asked.

'You like it here so much, freak, we're doin' ya a big favour. We're gunna make it so ya never have to leave again.'

'We're gunna plant ya!' the bony boy announced with a half hysterical giggle.

'Lift that thing off,' Buddha ordered and the gang obeyed, heaving the grave lid to one side. They all stepped forward to stare into the dense darkness of the hole, struck by the rich earthy scents and the depth, struck by the idea that this was where it all ended.

The moment gave Noah the chance he'd been waiting for, and he twisted violently to free himself from the loose grasp of his guards, running straight for the old part of the cemetery where the gravestones and monuments would give him some sort of cover.

'He must be here somewhere, keep looking,' Buddha yelled, and Noah's heart nearly stopped. He'd been daydreaming like a fool and they were all around him. He could see Buddha and it was a miracle Buddha didn't notice him. He was too scared to move and by the time Buddha shifted away a bit, Noah was wet with sweat.

It had been too close for comfort. He got up cautiously and made his way round the edge of the building and back onto the path. There was no chance of him getting to the gate or even the fence now, but there must be a better place to hide. He slipped between two graves and walked in a silent crouch. In this part of the cemetery there were no fresh flowers. The graves were old and weathered and hardly anyone went there any more. He came to a whole row of graves with monuments shaped grimly like the real coffins buried underneath. Noah noticed one of the false stone coffins was cracked. He assumed the big squares would be solid, but he could see through the crack that the mock stone coffin was hollow.

He climbed up on the cracked tablet and began to tug frantically at the broken bit. He was pretty small and if he could just budge it a bit futher, he could slip inside and lie there safely until Buddha had gone. Better to get back late than bloody and beaten up.

'Hey!' One of the gang spotted him. 'Hey ... ' he said less certainly, as he saw what Noah was doing.

Another boy skidded to a halt behind him. 'Is 'e ... ?' He stopped, staring at Noah crouched on top of the grave, fingers in the crack.

Buddha came thundering up to them. 'What are you two standin' here like stunned mullets for? Get 'im!'

'He ... 'e was gettin' in 'is grave,' the first boy said, looking sick.

'He was,' the other confirmed faintly.

'What?' Buddha asked incredulously. The rest of the gang arrived and they all stared at Noah, still crouched atop the grave.

'He was gettin' in 'is grave,' one of the boys told them.

'He *is* a spook,' a girl whispered nervously.

'Maybe 'e's a vampire,' someone else said in a high-pitched, frightened voice.

Noah stood up suddenly, and they all jumped. He held his hands up to the sky and looked down at them.

'So. You know. But I'll make sure you don't tell anyone the truth about me.'

It was broad daylight, but the sun gleamed oddly on Noah's pale form and his body appeared to shimmer insubstantially in the heat haze. Unwittingly, some of the gang stepped back. One of the girls started crying.

'Bullshit ... ' Buddha said, but his face was pale. He took one step forward.

At that moment, a black shadow that had been creeping fractionally across the cemetery all afternoon reached Noah, and his pale dazzling form fell into darkness.

'Run!' one of the boys screamed, and they ran, scattering like leaves before a stormwind. All except Buddha.

'Buddhaaa . . . ' Noah moaned, then he gave a low cackling laugh. That was enough for Buddha. His nerve broke and he turned to race after his disappearing gang.

Standing in the shadow, Noah was trembling from head to toe partly from fear and partly from triumph. He had frightened them off. Him.

But that shadow . . .

He looked up at the giant's tower, a silhouette in the fading gold of the afternoon, and a strange feeling seemed to flow up into him from the grave under his feet. Slowly he turned to stare at the message inscribed in the stone, and his skin rose up into goosebumps.

Seek No More.

His eyes moved up, and he read the name above the message.

Kate lifted the hair from the nape of her neck, wondering what sort of weird kid would hang around a cemetery on a boiling hot summer day. First they had been delayed in traffic coming through the city, and then they had arrived at the orphanage to find Noah missing. The orphanage woman who met them offered to get him, but her father had to volunteer Kate. When the woman said he was bound to be at the cemetery, her father had given her mother a pointed look.

Noah was a weird kid all right. She hadn't even noticed him the first time they brought her to Glastenbury, until her mother had pointed him out. Of course, Kate hadn't paid too much attention hardly believing they would really adopt someone.

Adoption had been her father's idea to help her mother get over having a baby who was born dead, and not being able to have any more children. Funny how they reversed positions after one visit. Suddenly her mother was keen on adopting and her father wanted them to wait. That was because of *who* her mother wanted to adopt. They hadn't been able to meet Noah straight off because of raising false hopes in him, but they had gone to look over the merchandise a couple of times.

'He looks like an albino,' her father had murmured in the car on the way home. Kate pretended to be asleep so they would go on talking. 'I might have known you would choose the sickest looking kid there. You always choose the runt of the litter at the pound!'

There were lots of visits after that. On one, they had spoken to some psychiatrist. 'There's nothing wrong with him physically,' her mother had said afterwards in a low tense voice, peeling potatoes. In the hallway, Kate had stopped to listen. Eavesdropping was the only way to get uncensored information.

Her father had been boning a fish. 'You heard the psychiatrist. He's mentally disturbed. It's probably some kind of hereditary thing.'

'He's not crazy.'

'I didn't say he was crazy. Don't be so defensive. You're obviously far too emotional to make a sensible judgment over this. Why can't you pick an ordinary kid?'

'I don't want an ordinary kid,' her mother had said angrily. 'And I can't see that fantasising he was found in a basket makes Noah crazy.'

'He thinks he's some sort of wizard or something,' her father had spluttered. 'He thinks he's got special powers!'

'Shh, Katie will hear. Jack, he's a lonely little boy who daydreams and imagines he's special. What's so terrible about that? He's got a good imagination and he reads a lot. Maybe he's finding it a bit hard to separate what's real from the stories, but we can fix that.'

Her father said flatly, 'Is that what this is all about? He's sick and you think you can cure him?'

'Jack, if anything, I think he can cure me.'

That seemed to be that and the adoption went ahead. They told Kate a watered-down version of Noah's daydreaming, though they did condescend to tell her Noah had made up a name for her: Katlyn darkhair. She liked the sound of that.

Her eyes were drawn by the medieval-looking water-tower in

the paddock, its shadow falling right over the cemetery.

As she approached the gates, a gang of scruffy-looking kids came hurtling through into the street. The heat seemed more intense once she was inside and Kate squinted against the sun. At once, she spotted someone towering above the graves over to one side near a stone crypt.

She frowned and blinked in astonishment, then she realised she was only looking at Noah who was standing up on top of a grave. She shook her head, thinking the sun must be getting to her, or the cemetery. For a minute she would have sworn she saw a tall, darkly dressed man with flowing blond hair right where Noah was.

She hurried over to where he was now squatting, staring at the headstone above the cracked grave slab.

'Anyone you know?' she quipped.

Noah turned quickly, his face tense as if he were expecting someone else. Then he smiled.

It was the sweetest smile Kate had ever seen in her life on a human being, and all the smart-alec jokes flew out of her head.

'Hullo,' Noah said, an echo of the smile in his voice. 'Are we leaving now?'

Katlyn darkhair nodded.

THE PHOENIX

'Princess Ragnar?'

Ragnar turned to William and tried to smile, but her hatred was so great that it would allow no other emotion. She did not feel it as heat but as a bitter burning cold flowing through her, freezing her to ice, to stone. Driven by such a rage, a princess might unleash her armies and destroy an entire city to the last person. She might command the end of a world.

'Princess? Are you cold?'

She barely heard William's words, but when she shook her head, before he turned away to keep watch for Torvald, she saw in his pale-green eyes the same blaze of devotion that had flared three summers past when he had pledged himself to her.

Her mind threw up an image of him making that pledge, the words as formal as the words from an old Bible.

'Princess, I, William, am sent by the Gods to serve and guard you in this strange shadowland, until we are shown the way home by such signs and portents as I am trained to recognise. I pledge my life to you.'

Twelve years old, with one slightly turned eye, a broken front tooth, ripped shorts and a too large cast-off T-shirt advising the world to 'Be happy', and here he was pledging his life to her.

He had a collection of T-shirts abandoned by the drug addicts and drunks who came to stay at Goodhaven to dry out. The weird thing was that those T-shirts always seemed to have something pertinent to say about what was happening when he wore them, and in the end, she came to see them as signs, just as William saw as signs a certain bird flying overhead, or a particular rock resting against another.

Hearing his absurd pledge, she had experienced a fleeting instinct to laugh out of nervousness or incredulity. That would have changed everything. Life could be like that sometimes – hinging on one tiny little thing or other. But she hadn't laughed because underneath the urchin dirt and crazy talk, she had seen a reflection of her own aching loneliness.

'Are you sure you have the right person?' she had said, instead of, 'Are you crazy?' But it was close. They even started with the same words.

'You are Princess Ragnar,' he had said.

Those words sent a shiver up her spine, even after so much time. Because she had never seen him before. Then there was *how* he said her name – as if he was handling something infinitely precious. No one had said it like that before in her whole life except maybe her mother, though perhaps that was just a memory born of wishful thinking.

'How do you know my name?' she had demanded.

He had grinned, flashing the chipped tooth that she later learned had been broken when he'd happened on a drying-out drunk who had managed to drink a whole cupboard-full of cough medicine. The Goodhaven people stocked up on everything because they thought the world was going to end any day now and they wanted to be prepared. Though how a hundred tins of baked beans and a cupboard full of cough medicine was supposed to help you survive the end of the world was beyond Ragnar. The drunk's back-handed slap had left William with the chip in his tooth that his aunt called God's will. In fact, that was what William had told her when she'd asked what had happened to his front tooth.

'It was God's will.' As if God had slapped him one.

The chip was wide enough to make him talk with a lisp, but since he could still use his teeth, fixing it would have been cosmetic and his aunt and uncle eschewed worldly vanity, believing it to be one of the things that brought most of the human debris they called Poor Lost Souls to Goodhaven in the first place.

Besides that, William was simple and it would hardly matter to the poor addled child that he had a chipped tooth when his brain was all but cracked clear through.

Those words came to her in William's mimicked version of his aunt's high-pitched folksy voice. That was how she explained him away to occasional government visitors and fund-raising groups concerned about a child being exposed to the sort of people who came to Goodhaven.

'Oh, he has seen much worse than anything he could ever see here,' William had mimicked his aunt. 'Why his brain cracked under the pressure of seeing his mother and father murdered before his very eyes. He was there all alone a good two years before someone found him wandering around mad as a hatter.'

William had been looked after by the same people who had murdered his parents, though no one could figure out why they would bother. Maybe it was because he was so young. He was four when his relatives had agreed to take him on.

He was no simpleton. Ragnar had seen that right off, but he was sure as heck one strange piece of toast, and no wonder. Seeing your parents murdered would be enough to make anyone a little crazy.

Of course, she had known nothing at all about that the first time they'd met.

She had been swimming and had come out of the water wearing nothing but her long red hair. There was never anyone around during the week and she had been pretending to be the mermaid; trying to make up her mind whether the love of a prince would be worth the loss of her voice and the feeling that she was standing on knives every time she took a step. Especially when her father said love did not last, or else why had her mother run off and left them?

She was trying to figure out where she had left her clothes when William walked out carrying them. He had his eyes on her face and he did not once let them drop. He just held out her

clothes and she snatched them up and pulled on jeans and a
sloppy paint-stained windcheater, her face flaming.

Then he had suddenly fallen to his knees.

Her embarrassment evaporated since she was clothed now and
anyway the boy clearly had no prurient interest in her nakedness.

She put her hands on her hips. 'Who the heck are you?'

'The gods have seen that you are lonely, Ragnar, and so I was
sent to be your companion.'

Anything she would have said was obliterated by astonish-
ment. For she was lonely beyond imagining. Her father had for-
bidden her to let anyone at her school know they were living
illegally in the boathouse, which made it easier to have no friends
than to make up believable lies. They had been squatting since
the owner had moved to America, having told her father he could
use the boathouse for his dinghy if he kept an eye on it. Her
father took the dinghy out maybe three times a year and she was
always convinced he would drown because he never took any of
the things you were supposed to take like flares or lifejackets. He
didn't have to fish since his Sickness Benefit paid for food and
cask wine. He worried her sick when he went out, and she could
never understand why he did it. It wasn't even as if he ever caught
anything big enough to be legal or good eating.

Once, while they were keeping vigil for his return, William told
Ragnar matter-of-factly that her father fished because he remem-
bered when he had been a real fisherman.

'He was never a real fisherman,' Ragnar snorted. 'He was
some sort of mechanic.'

'In his past life he was a fisherman and he slept with one of
the goddesses. She took you away with her, but because you were
part human, the gods made her send you here. As a punishment
to her because she broke the rules.'

'Seems to me the gods and goddesses do nothing but break
rules. Look at Prometheus and Pandora.'

'They are lesser gods,' William had said with a lofty kind of
pride. 'My princess comes from an older and greater race of gods.

And if he was not a fisherman once, then why does your father fish?'

As usual his habit of suddenly circling and darting back on an argument left her gasping like a fish out of water. The thing was she did not know why her father had brought them here to this spit of flat sand between an industrial wasteland and a whole lot of salt pans and wetlands. Nor why he fished.

Ragnar had known no other life. Not really. She sometimes remembered a mother who did not seem to have much to do with the mother her father muttered and cursed about. William had an answer for that as well. He thought that she was remembering not her mother in this life, but the goddess mother of her other life.

'Then how come my father remembers me being born?'

'The gods can make anyone remember or forget. They made your father remember his wife having a child – and maybe she did have a baby.' His eyes flashed as he warmed to this theme. 'Maybe she took their real child with her and the gods just stepped in and put you here, so he would think she left his baby. So he would take care of you and keep you out of the eye of the world.'

William was as worried about the eye of the world as her father. William, because of his uncle and aunt's fear of negative publicity that might affect Goodhaven's funding sources, and her father because he did not want to be thrown out of the boathouse, or have Social Security people poking around. Sending her to school worried him because if he didn't They would be after him – They being the Government – but if he did, people would find out where they were living. He had solved the problem by sending her to school, but telling her that if anyone figured out where she lived, she would be taken away to an orphanage and locked up. That had frightened her so much she said so little at school that people thought there was something wrong with her. Fortunately integration policies, and her own consistently normal marks, kept them from trying to send Ragnar to a special school of the sort William told such horror stories about. His relatives had tried a whole lot of schools before he had managed to convince them he was too far gone for school.

'I like people thinking I'm crazy. It's easier and I know what I am inside so what they think doesn't matter.'

Of course as she grew older, Ragnar's fear of the authorities was diluted to wary caution, but her father sealed her silence. He said they would never allow her to take Greedy away with them.

Greedy was a crippled seagull William had rescued and given to her as a gift, saying that in the realm of the gods, the seagull was her personal hawk. It was so devoted, William told her solemnly, that it had followed her to this world, but in order to come to her the gods offered the proud hawk only the form of a lowly scavenger. He told her the hawk's real name was Thorn, but secretly she nicknamed it Greedy, because it was.

'Thorn is hungry because in his previous life he was starved by the gods to try to make him forswear his allegiance to you,' William had told her reproachfully the one time he heard her calling the bird Greedy.

William had an answer for everything. Truth was, he was a lot smarter than most of the kids and the teachers at school, at least in ways that mattered. He did not read, but he could tell stories better than any book, and he had built around the two of them a fantasy that was far more wonderful than life could ever offer. In the years since they had first met, he had been her companion and everything else she had wanted – slave, brother, confidant, friend. He had shed blood to seal his pledge though she had not wanted or asked for it, and he had promised to serve and obey, honour and protect her – with his own life if necessary.

He had watched her for a long time to make sure she was truly the one, he told her earnestly one time as they were baking mussels in a battered tin pot of salty water on a small fire. The water had to be salty or the crustaceans tasted vile.

'But how did you know in the end?'

He shrugged. 'I found a sign and I knew – a ring of dead jellyfish on the beach in the shape of a crown.'

It was easier to obey William's odd instructions than to try to understand why he thought a toilet brush in seaweed was a warning that you were being discussed, or how walking a certain way round an overturned shell could avert an accident. It was very rare that he wanted her to do anything troublesome, though once when he said they must walk along the railway lines for so many paces, she worried a lot because, if they were caught, they would end up in the children's court. But they had done it and William claimed that was what had stopped a council van coming down to Cheetham Point to check out rumours of people living there.

Did he manipulate events as he claimed? Mostly, Ragnar figured not, but it never hurt to take out insurance. Because there were many times when William knew things he could not know. Sometimes she would be going to catch the train and he would tell her that she would miss it, so he would wait for her in their secret place. And the train mysteriously would not come. Other times he would tell her it was going to rain when she was dressed lightly and, sure enough, by the end of the day, it would be pelting down.

Coincidence? Maybe. Ragnar did not believe she was a princess in exile. Not really. Though she did feel as if she had been born for more than this bit of barren land. One part of her looked at her father when he was drunk with his mouth open, a thin ribbon of drool falling from his lips, and knew she had been born of nobler blood. Sometimes when she was sitting in class, knowing the answers, but never speaking out because being too smart could bring you into the Public Eye even more than being too dumb, a little voice would whisper to her that she was special and destined for greatness, just as William said.

Sometimes when she and William sat at the very end of the land watching the sun fall in a haze of gold into the ocean, he would ask her if she felt the magic, and she would nod, lifting her chin and holding back her shoulders as regally as a princess, proud even in exile. Greedy would shiver on her lap, as if for a moment remembering his life as a mighty hawk hunter, bane of mice and small birds and even of cats.

It had been through such a sunset of molten gold that Torvald came to them. The day was uncommonly still and a sea-mist was shot with bloody gold and red lights as the sun fell. Ragnar saw something shimmer and all at once could see a young man with golden hair flying in the wind, and a proud handsome face, coming on his boat out of the mist, and her lips had parted in breathless wonder. Then she heard the whining stutter of the speedboat engine and realised he was coming across the water to Cheetham Point from the Ridhurst Grammar School jetty.

She felt foolish the way she always did when she entered a little too deeply into William's world of myth and magic. Just the same, sitting in the back of the boat with one hand lightly on the tiller, long pale hair about his face, there was no denying he looked marvellous. She wished she could see what colour his eyes were, for her daydreams, but of course he would turn back before he reached the Point because of the shallows.

Only he did not turn. For a moment she thought he had miraculously managed to sail over the sandbar even with the tide out, but then he had come suddenly to a grinding halt, beached until the tide rose again. After making some useless attempts to get the boat off the sandbar, he looked back, obviously concluding it was too far to swim. Then he turned to face the Point.

I will always see him that way, Ragnar thought. Him turning that first time to face them, so tall and handsome, the sky all gold and glorious behind him.

'We must help him, Princess,' William had announced.

Ragnar had been shocked, because one of the rules was that they should never seek out the Public Eye or any other eye. During the holidays when boat people came, they stayed away from the Point during the day, mostly within Goodhaven grounds. And they always stayed away from the rich spoiled Ridhurst students who would do anything for a dare, including tormenting a small boy.

'He's from Ridhurst,' Ragnar hissed, remembering how William had shivered when he told her how a group of students had ridden around and around him in ever smaller circles on their roaring motorbikes.

'He is one of us,' William had announced, though he looked paler than usual.

Ragnar stared at him incredulously. 'One of us?'

'Aye, Princess. He is the golden-haired voyager from over the sea whom you are destined to wed. His coming is a sign that the way will open soon for us to return. We must save him because there will only be one chance for all of us to cross.'

'William, he is not from over the sea. He came from Ridhurst ...'

But he was running across the sand and shouting to the young man to wait and that they would help him. The handsome stranger waved back, and sat on the edge of the boat.

'We'll get the Longboat,' William cried out over his shoulder.

The Longboat was a slim wooden boat to which its owner hitched his larger boat when he came to the Point each Christmas. It was bolted to a post outside the shed that housed his bigger boat, but William discovered that with a bit of wriggling you could get the chain off in spite of the lock. They often used the Longboat to fish or to go for short jaunts, but never in broad daylight.

'William, stop, I ... order you to stop!' She only used her Royal prerogative to stop William from his most dangerous schemes, because it did not seem fair to take advantage of his illusions that way. But on this occasion he seemed not to hear her. He was wriggling the chain out from its bolt and dragging it towards the water, straining his skinny arms.

'Oh, for heaven's sake!' Ragnar muttered, then bent and helped him. The sooner they got this over with the better. They rowed out to the sandbar and up close Torvald was as handsome as he had been from the distance. His teeth were perfectly straight and white and his eyes as blue as the sweetest summer sky. He was a picture-book prince, which may have explained what happened next.

'Hi,' he said, smiling right into her eyes. 'Thanks for the rescue. No one warned me about the sandbar.'

Ragnar had melted at the sound of his voice, deep and soft, with just a touch of an accent. But she managed to say, 'It wasn't me ... I mean, William got the boat.'

'I meant thanks to you both. William, is it?' He held his hand out but William bowed.

'I am William and I am the pledged protector of Princess Ragnar in her exile.'

Ragnar could have died. Her face felt as if it had third-degree burns.

'Really? Well, I am Torvald the Curious from over the seas,' the stranger answered and bowed low to William and then to Ragnar. 'I am pleased to make the acquaintance of the beauteous Princess Ragnar.'

William gave Ragnar an 'I told you so' look as Torvald the Curious stood up and smiled at them both.

'Come aboard our humble craft, my Lord Torvald, and we will bear you to shore and give you what humble sustenance we can offer in this place of exile until the waters allow you to depart,' William said.

Torvald's smile deepened and without further ado, he gave their boat a push to free it from the sandbar, and climbed in. William rowed them back and Ragnar looked steadfastly towards the shore, refusing to look at Torvald whom she could see staring at her out of the corner of her eye.

The humble sustenance turned out to be her leftover school lunch and a rather shrivelled looking trio of apples that was William's offering. Torvald lowered himself to sit in the sand, stretching his long legs out in front of him, and when William solemnly offered him their picnic, he smiled a little and chose one of the apples.

'It looks as if you were expecting me. And this ...' He held up the apple. 'This seems appropriate, somehow.'

'Truly,' William agreed. 'Eve offered the apple of knowledge to Adam, and Aphrodite offered an apple to Paris.'

'Ah, but he should have taken the apple from the Goddess of Wisdom, shouldn't he?'

'Perhaps,' William said. 'But some things are cast in the stars and love is one of them. It will have its way, no matter what tragedy it calls in its wake.'

Torvald's smile faded properly for the first time then. Perhaps that was the moment he realised this was no game to William. His eyes shifted to Ragnar questioningly, and she forced herself to meet his gaze with no expression, because to show what she felt would be to betray William, and to act as if she believed what William believed would be to betray herself. Also if she started talking, this golden-haired young man would begin to ask questions.

Torvald's expression of puzzlement grew more intense. 'So . . . you are both in exile?' he said at last.

'Truly your name fits you,' William said.

Torvald looked confused until he remembered the name he had announced himself with. 'I am afraid I am curious to the point of rudeness. My father said I will never make a politician unless I learn to tell lies sweetly.'

'No,' William said. 'You will not be a politician.'

Torvald frowned at him. 'You think not?'

William shook his head. 'Politicians cannot afford to be curious. You will always be a seeker of the only true beauty which is truth.'

Torvald blinked, much as Ragnar thought she must have done the first time she encountered William the Sage. That, he told her, had been his role before he was sent to her. He had been a seer of things to come. A Merlin.

'You are a strange boy,' Torvald said. 'Do you live here?'

Ragnar plunged in hurriedly. 'No. We just came down for the day. We live over in Calway.' That ought to put him off since it was a Housing Commission area.

'That is a long way. Did you walk?'

'We came around the beach.' She pointed vaguely to the route she walked after catching the train from town on school days.

'Past Ridhurst?'

She nodded. 'You go there, don't you?' Better to turn the talk back on him. She found that a useful way of dealing with curiosity.

But he just nodded and said, 'You are brother and sister?'

'I am the servant and protector of Princess Ragnar,' William said calmly.

Ragnar wanted to strangle him. 'We're friends,' she said.

'I have that honour also,' William agreed.

Torvald looked from one of them to the other.

'Your father is a politician?' Ragnar asked, somewhat desperately.

'He is a politican of sorts. A diplomat.' His eyes crinkled deliciously into a smile again. 'He lies for his country rather than for a political party.' Now his eyes were on William and they were serious. 'But why did you say I will not be a politician? It is what my father wishes and I am not averse to the idea. He sent me here so that I will make important connections for the future. The sons and daughters of many influential people come to Ridhurst but it seems to me they worry about cricket and parties and the right clothes more than important matters. But perhaps I misjudge them as trivial and shallow because I arrived only last week. When I know them better, things might be different.'

'Maybe,' Ragnar said, thinking of the young women in their pale uniforms lifting their brows at her high school uniform when she got off the bus at their stop. The trouble was it was the closest stop to home, and even then it took a good half hour to walk round the beach to Cheetham Point.

Somehow, she had managed to get him talking about his father the diplomat and his appointment to Australia. His father was in Canberra but he had decided to send Torvald to the highly recommended Ridhurst as a boarder, at least until his mother, a doctor, followed a year later.

Ragnar was relieved when William announced suddenly that they must go back out or the Ridhurst boat would float free of the sandbank without him.

The trip back was conducted in relative silence, but as Torvald climbed out of the boat, he smiled at them both. 'I thank you again for saving me from sitting like a fool in the boat until now. No doubt that is what was intended by the students who suggested I might enjoy a boat ride across to Cheetham Point.'

'It was our pleasure to help you thwart your tormentors, Lord Torvald. Farewell.'

'Perhaps we will meet again?' Torvald's eyes shifted to Ragnar and she felt the blood surge in her cheeks.

'I don't think so,' she said. 'Come on, William.'

'As you will, my princess.'

Ragnar cringed.

She thought that would be the end of that, but Torvald proved true to his name. He waited on the path a number of days and even wandered around Calway in the hope of bumping into his two off-beat rescuers. She, having some inkling perhaps, had gone a roundabout way through the wetlands to avoid the walk by the school, but one afternoon came home to see Torvald and William deep in conversation in the dunes near the boathouses.

Her heart lurched in sick fear.

'Princess Ragnar,' Torvald said, getting to his feet.

Ragnar's fright was swamped with rage at the thought he was mocking William.

'What are you doing here?' she snarled.

William looked worried. 'It is well, Princess. Truly. He will bring you no harm. He is your ...'

'What do you want?' Ragnar demanded, cutting off whatever William would have said for fear he would start talking about future weddings.

'I am Torvald the Curious.'

Ragnar did not know what to say in the face of that, especially with William sitting there beside her looking stricken. She calmed herself because maybe he had not said anything to this Ridhurst student about where they lived. Though it must look queer for them to come down here again like this.

'My father owns a boathouse and we were planning to camp out for the night, but it's not allowed. I'm sorry if I snapped at you.'

'William is right. I mean no harm to you, Princess Ragnar.'

'Don't call me that!'

'Being noble-born you may address the princess by her name if she is willing,' William interpreted.

Ragnar sat down, speechless.

'Then I shall call you Ragnar and you will call me Torvald, or Tor. I prefer the latter.'

'Thor . . .' William muttered.

Oh great, Ragnar thought. She glared at Torvald and asked William to leave them alone for a moment.

He rose at once, saying he would look for Thorn.

'Thorn?' Torvald asked.

'A crippled seagull that William thinks is a reincarnated hawk. Just like he thinks I'm a princess and you're some sort of lord,' she said angrily. 'What are you doing here sucking up to him and pretending to believe what he says? Are you going to write a paper for Ridhurst on the local feral kid?'

'William is a very interesting boy. I think he can see into the future sometimes. It's often the way with those society deems to be mad or simple. They see what most people do not. You are angry because you fear I will harm him, but I am not a student with a motorcycle and no brains or compassion.' Torvald's voice was mild and serious.

'He told you about that?'

'He told me many things, and he was right when he said I will not harm either of you.'

Ragnar was frightened again. 'What did he tell you about me?'

'Nothing that I would ever use to harm you. I swear it on the honour of Torvald the Curious.'

'Don't mock him!'

'I do not mock. You mistake me. I have honour and I have sworn by it. And who is to say that William is not right?'

'What?'

'He says we are destined for one another, and that my soul was the soul of a god who loved you, and has followed you into exile.'

Ragnar's face was burning. 'You don't love me.'

He did not answer for a long moment, but only let his eyes hold hers. Then he said, 'How do you know I did not fall in love with you the first moment I saw you coming towards me in that little boat, your red hair gleaming like molten copper and your face as fair as any goddess's? How do you know that the moment I saw you all the hungers and longings of my life were not answered?'

Oh, his words were as beautiful as his face, and they had gone through her defences like a hot knife through butter. And in those months that followed she had come to love him body and soul; she had come to believe that William saw a different reality and in it, she was truly a princess and Tor her destined love.

And then two nights past, she was on the train dozing, catching the late train home from school because she was rehearsing for a school play in which she was one of the King of Siam's lesser wives. She woke out of a deep sleep to hear Tor's beloved voice, and for a moment she revelled in the sweetness of it, until she realised she was not dreaming and his words were anything but sweet.

'I am telling you, Rosco, you or any of your friends mess this up for me and I will throttle you. I have a sweet set-up for myself and that red-haired peach is ripe and ready to drop into my hands. I gave her romance with a capital R and she ate it up along with her ferrety little friend.'

'Should've run right over the gruesome little creep, cursing us, and two days later I broke my arm and Tristam fell over and slipped a disc.'

'Yes, well, I think William the Wacko loves me enough to kill for me. He thinks I am some sort of king which means he has class even if his brains are scrambled.'

'Just so long as you're not getting soft on them. If it wasn't for you playing the girl out, I would've reported the soak of a father for living in the sheds weeks back.'

'Idiot.' Tor's voice held a serrated edge of scorn Ragnar had never heard before. 'I said the girl pleased me. I did not say I would introduce her to my parents or bring her to a school dance. She is a pig, but I prefer her in her shack where I can get at her – until I am bored. After that you may have what revenge you want on the boy.'

'After you finish shacking up with the Pig Princess, eh? Ha ha ha.'

Torvald had laughed too. Hard cruel laughter from a Torvald

she had been too blind to see. Ragnar sat there in her corner as the train pulled up, praying they would not spot her. She stayed on until the East Potter stop, and then walked the seven kilometres back along the highway to the Cheetham Point turnoff, driven by the viciousness of her self reproaches and taunting echoes of William's words.

'I loved you the first moment I saw you ...'

'She is a pig but I prefer her in her shack where I can get at her ...'

'I will never harm you ...'

'I would not introduce her to my parents ...'

She might not have told William, but he was waiting for her in a T-shirt that said 'Shit Happens'. It does, she thought, savage and half-mad with despair. She let William encircle her with his thin hard arms, and told him everything. And when there were no more tears, and the ice had begun to form over her emotions, she looked up into his face and found his pale eyes curiously blank.

'He proved too weak to withstand the darkness of this world and we should leave him to it. That would be the greatest torment for such as he,' William said distantly. 'Yet he is one of us and he must be punished for a betrayal that must make the gods weep when they learn of it. As they will when we return.'

'Return?'

William nodded. 'It is time. Two nights from now when the sun sets, a way will open to the realm of the old gods by their grace. This once and once only. I have dreamed it and I have read the signs. If we turn from it, we will be trapped here forever in this land of cruelty and darkness.'

Ragnar had been too distraught to really listen. All she understood was that William had a plan that would punish Torvald for his seduction and betrayal.

'What do you want me to do?'

William asked her to send Torvald a message to come over the water to them on Sunday afternoon. It was Friday and normally he would not come on weekends for fear he would be spotted and followed by Ridhurst students who might discover the truth. Or so he had told her, she thought bitterly. William told her to write that the tide would be high enough for him to negotiate the sandbar in the Ridhurst dinghy.

Coldly Ragnar wrote the note and slipped it into the internal mail box in Ridhurst after dark while her father snored in his bed. She had not known what William planned then or now. She didn't care as long as Torvald suffered.

'He comes,' William breathed.

Ragnar squinted through a rising sea-mist and saw Torvald launch the heavy school boat. She sat, stiff-backed and still as a statue as the boat came over the water and William ran to meet him and bring him back to where a picnic feast was laid out.

'Ragnar, my love,' Tor said and bowed as he always did. But now Ragnar saw the gallant gesture for the mockery it had always been and her hatred weighed in her stomach, heavy as a stone.

'Tor.' She forced her lips to shape a smile but there must have been something wrong in it, because instead of smiling back, Torvald frowned questioningly at her. He would not ask aloud what was wrong though, because of William. He would wait as always until William withdrew and they could speak freely.

Ragnar bent her head to hide the rage bubbling within her and stroked Greedy with fingers that trembled. He would not settle – no doubt he sensed the turmoil in her.

'Now we shall drink a toast, my lord, for this very night the way opens to the realm of the gods from whence we all came,' William said, and passed a chipped enamel mug to Torvald.

'What?' Torvald asked.

'Drink,' William said and handed a plastic mug to Ragnar, who was staring at Torvald with such longing and loathing that her soul felt as if it were curdling in her breast.

'Tonight we drink to the joy of William the Sage, who returns to the realm of the gods where he is an honoured Merlin.' William drank and, like an automaton, so did Ragnar. Torvald shrugged and drank.

William spoke again with an almost hypnotic solemnity,

holding up his own jam jar as if it were a jewelled goblet.
'Tonight we drink to Thorn the mighty hunter as he returns to
his airy realms ...' He drank again and so did Ragnar and
Torvald.

'Tonight the Princess in Exile returns to claim her
kingdom ...'

Ragnar drank her father's cheap red wine, and found her head
spinning because she had barely eaten for the last two days. But
Torvald had not taken another drink.

'You are leaving?' he asked worriedly. 'Would you go without
me?'

'I am not finished, my lord,' William said sternly. 'We drink
the bitter dregs to you for a betrayal that will sunder you forever
from the princess. We might have let that be torment enough,
were you a creature of this dark world. But you are of the
golden realms and so your treachery is too deep for us to let
you live – even here in this shadow world.'

'What?' Torvald asked, but his words slurred so badly they
could barely understand. 'Princess Ragnar?'

Ragnar's confusion over William's words dissolved in a
boiling lava of bitter despair. 'Don't you mean Pig, Tor? Don't
you mean Ragnar the Pig whom you would never introduce to
your parents or bring to a dance?'

His eyes widened in shock. 'But, Ragnar ...' His eyes clouded
and he fell forward, catching himself on one hand. He stared at
the spilled wine seeping into the pale sand. 'The ... drink?'

'Not poison but enough tranquilliser from the Goodhaven
store to kill a horse, or a lord who betrayed his true land and his
deepest love,' William said sadly.

Fear flowed over the handsome features, then acceptance.
'William ... I do not blame you for this.' He looked at Ragnar. 'I
was trying to divert Roscoe and his friends from reporting your
father when I spoke ... as I did on the train. They would ... never
be held back by compassion or ... honour, so there was no point
in speaking of such things to them ... had ... had to ... to play
their game.' He coughed and fell forward onto his elbow, twisting
his head so that he could look into Ragnar's horrified eyes.

'Had to play ... a cruel game they could understand and sympathise with. Even admire. I ... did not want to tell you the truth until I had thought of a ... solution. You see, in a way, I did betray you. They ... they followed me, you see ...'

'Torvald!' Ragnar screamed and gathered him into her arms, her terror too deep for words. Surely William had been joking. Surely he had only been trying to frighten Torvald.

'I should have told you the truth sooner ... my love. Shouldn't have tried ... being a hero ...'

His eyes fell closed. Ragnar shook him and knelt to press her head to his chest. She could find no heartbeat nor breath in him. She tried mouth to mouth resuscitation, letting herself think of nothing but the rhythm of breathing and pushing on his chest. How long she tried she could not have said but when William's hand fell on her shoulder and she sat up, her head spun.

'Bring him to the boat, Princess. They will be able to revive him perhaps in the sunlit realm of the old gods where all things are possible.'

Ragnar stared at him hopelessly, thinking that she had let one of the two people she loved in all the world kill the other. It was not poor battered William's fault, for he had never known any sort of normality. It was her fault Tor was dead, her fault William was a murderer.

'I have made you a murderer ...' she whispered, stricken.

But William's eyes met hers steadily. 'Tor's is not the first death at my hand in this dark world.'

'What?' Ragnar whispered.

'I killed my father. He was trying to scalp my mother when I woke. So I took the gun he had thrown down and I killed him.'

All the horror of the night coalesced around the bleak dreadful image of a small boy forced to shoot his father, and Ragnar's heart swelled with pity.

'Ah, William ...' she whispered, blinded by tears. 'What are we going to do?'

He reached out and took her hand in a surprisingly strong grip. 'I have never lied to you, Princess. We belong to a world where there is hope and this is a world where there is none. Only come now, and help me get Lord Torvald's body into the longboat.'

Ragnar stumbled to her feet and took Torvald's feet as William instructed. She did not know or care what he wanted to do. She had brought him to murder. Now she supposed they would dispose of the body.

The body. They half dragged Tor over to the side of the Longboat which was anchored close to the water and, straining and pushing, heaved him over the edge. Ragnar felt sick at the thumping sound his body made as it landed in the bottom of the boat. She climbed in beside him, gagging at a queer acrid smell as she lifted Torvald's golden head onto her knees.

'Thorn!' William called and Ragnar looked up in time to see the seagull stagger hippity-hop over the sand to his feet with a creaking caw of delight. He scooped the bird up and put it in the boat then pushed it off into the water and climbed in beside them. Ragnar stared up at him as he lifted a plastic bottle from the bottom of the boat and tipped what looked like water over Torvald's unconscious form. Greedy squawked as he was drenched, and the smell was intensified as William sprinkled it over Ragnar's legs and dress.

'What is it?'

'It is the test,' William said, emptying the last of the liquid over himself and the boat.

Ragnar watched him throw the bottle into the water and rummage in his pockets, before withdrawing something. 'A test?' she asked dully.

William lit a match that flamed the colour of the clouds on the horizon all shot through with the bloody brightness of the sun's death, and smiled at her.

'Do not be afraid, Princess. It is the last test of courage required by the gods – to know that we are worthy to dwell in their realm.'

'William . . .' The clouds in Ragnar's brain dissolved as the match fell onto Torvald's body. Flame made a feast of him, but he did not move because he was beyond pain.

She watched the flames play over him and William came to

sit beside her. He took her hand, sticky with tears and petrol, in his own thin strong fingers and kissed it reverently.

'What comes will be a moment of pain before the gods pluck us from the crucible.' He looked down at Torvald. 'Love was first born where we journey, Princess. Hold fast to that, for all love in this world is but the palest shadow of it. Where we go, love has magical properties and there may be a way to bring him back.'

'We will die . . .'

'No. It only seems so, else there would be no testing. But hold fast, Ragnar, for you are a princess and the gods are watching.'

Ragnar wondered if she was mad but as the flames tasted the petrol on her dress and licked along the hem almost teasingly, she felt a surge of hope, for it seemed to her she could hear the brassy call of a horn, peeling out an eldritch welcome for a long-lost princess.

She stroked Torvald's face as flame licked flesh, and steeled herself not to scream, for she was a princess among the gods, and she was bringing her beloved home.

As flame rose around them like a winding sheet, Thorn the hunter lifted himself on crippled wings and flew.

PART 3

THE
WORLDROAD

*'The worldroad led everywhere, even home,
if you walked it long enough.'*

LONG LIVE THE GIANT

You! Come over here. I want to tell you the story of death and of the fairies at the bottom of the universe.

My name is Forever.

No, you will not get into trouble for listening to me. Student groups are always brought to this wing because I am here and they think I am harmless. Like a friendly bear in the zoo, which will permit itself to be petted. The nurses are happy to have me to amuse those who come through, for it leaves them free to do their hair or call their boyfriends. They think that I am tame, but they are wrong. Oh, you need not be afraid that I will bite or froth at the mouth or tear my clothing off and caper naked before you. But I am dangerous just the same because I may cause you to think too much. You can die of that.

Oh yes, you can die of anything – of lonesomeness or homesickness, of a broken heart. You can even die of stupidity. And in the end, if you haven't died of anything else, you die of life.

Yes, you are right. I am old and I talk too much. I will take your advice and get on with my story.

Is it a true story? Forgive me smiling. I know it looks as if I am laughing at you, but I am only amused by the irony of your question, for once my mother asked it of me in that same suspicious way. Or not quite. Her exact words were: Is that true or is it a story? You see how she used the word *story* as if it were the word *lie?*

I had told her, you see, that I was late home because the fairies had got hold of me and kept me prisoner. I created that story to make amends for having come home so late. I had not meant to deceive her so much as to offer her my story as a gift, little knowing how prophetic it was. The truth seemed a drab sparrow of a thing, and so I brought her a gorgeous plumed exotic instead.

She slapped me, and in the pain of that slap was an important lesson: no matter how wondrous a story is, if there is no truth in it, it is ugly. But truth is complex and rarely comes in the form of undiluted fact. Stories are facts with soul, and stories that have no truth in them are indeed lies.

The nurses here call me a liar, you know. They say: *The woman in Room 304 tells lies.* Just as they say of the woman in Room 303: *She has Alzheimers.* (She is dying of forgetfulness, I tell children, and they nod their little tousled heads with a wisdom that humbles me.)

Why am I here? I suppose you could say that what ails me is the opposite of what ails the woman in the next room. I am dying of too much knowledge. I am distended with truth, bloated with stories, while the woman in Room 303 is almost an empty husk, the knowledge of her life all bled out of her. I have told her many a story to try to nourish her shrivelled soul, but they leak out of her as fast as I put them in.

The nurses would probably tell you I am dying of lies, which they call senility, or of old age. Lies do come more easily as death approaches. They form a barricade against the tidal wave of fear that roars at me when I think of dying. Behind that flimsy barricade, life is piercingly sweet.

Stories give me the courage I need to keep my promise, and to laugh. I will tell you later of the promise.

My grandfather was a liar, you know. *She probably gets it from your father,* my mother used to whisper to my father, as if lies were hereditary. *Perhaps she is a throwback,* my father would respond, to dissociate himself from our bad blood.

My grandfather liked to answer questions with stories. *How can she learn if you tell her such outrageous things?* my mother would ask him in exasperation.

When a drunk driver annihilated my grandfather on a wet road one night, my mother shook her head and said it was a pity, but in her eyes I saw a certain satisfaction, as if he had got his just desserts.

One of the stories my grandfather told was this:

We were passing the city cemetery. Adjoining it was a field occupied only by a couple of amiable and moth-eaten horses, and a grey tower. I asked what the tower was for. My grandfather answered that it held a giant's arm.

(I have told this more than once before. But I cannot tell *this* story without it. It shapes the two great preoccupations of my life – truth and death.)

In answer to the clamour of questions this tantalising titbit about the giant evoked, my grandfather explained that some eons past, humans had stumbled on a giant's body in a field during a cross-country trek. *In those days this area,* my grandfather had said in a dry aside, *was completely deserted.* This accounted for no one knowing the giant existed or noticing the body sooner.

Human doctors came to examine the enormous corpse and found that the giant had died stretched out flat, except for one arm. Rigor mortis had set in, and the arm was fixed in that position. The doctors could not shift death from his bones long enough to lower it, and even the engineers and builders had no luck with it. Finally it was decided to bury the giant normally, except for the offending arm, which would be encased in a stone tower.

This would also serve as his monument.

I do not know if it still exists. I never leave this place now. As a young woman I would avoid the cemetery and the field with its mysterious tower. It frightened me, that monument to death. But now, when I am afraid and my courage fails, I picture it in my mind and whisper: *Long live the giant!*

Oh, I was afraid of death after my grandfather died. I loved him and his loss grieved me. But the thought of him mouldering under the ground with the worms in his eyes haunted me. It drove me to seek out truth, for I had got it into my head that truth would save me from death – that somehow truth and immortality were the same thing.

Yes, I am laughing, but I am not so far from sorrow or terror. I laugh to give myself the courage to keep faith with the giant. I laugh because truth is a wild beast with teeth that rend.

I abandoned the magic and fairytales of girlhood to investigate the source of life in a search for truth that would fill my every waking hour. When the test-tubes and chemical equations of my prime yielded no answers, I turned in grey-haired middle age to philosophy. I was called wise and brilliant, but let me tell you, what lay at the bottom of all that studying and thinking and talking up a storm was my fear of dying.

At the last, I made up my mind to take the initiative with death instead of having it stalk me through the years. I was tired of waiting and it had come to me that perhaps death and truth were the same thing.

I walked out the front door of my house to the nearest bridge and jumped without bothering to leave a note or think twice.

One minute I was flying through the air towards the cold and stinking river with its rotted black teeth of stone; the next I was hovering in the air, surrounded by golden light.

The fairies had got me after all.

Oh, listen. That is not the end and it is rude of you to turn away when the going is rough. A story is a road and you have your feet upon this one. Kindly walk it to the end. This is the hardest bit, I promise you. It's all downhill from here.

Now where was I? Oh yes, flying through the air and then – floating. For a minute I thought I was dead and truly it was something of an anticlimax. I had been taken up by a molecular refractor, though you might as well call it fairy dust. I woke naked in a cage of woven sunbeams, neither dead or even mortally wounded. I was pretty shocked I can tell you. Nothing had prepared me for this turn of events.

The creatures who had got hold of me were humanoid: their heads were devoid of hair, but they possessed two great chilly liquid eyes, two slightly pointed ears, flattish noses and lipless mouths. They were much bigger than we are – as big as a two-storey building. Truly giants. We talk of giants, but you can't imagine what it was like seeing their great faces peering in at me, their pores open like little gasping mouths. I fainted straight away and several more times until I got used to the sight of them. And even when I began to study them, I could not like their hugeness for it dwarfed and utterly diminished me.

It was some time before I looked at them well enough to note that they were different in another aspect from humans. *They had wings.* Not glorious enormous feathered things such as medieval angels might wear, nor even gleaming transparent wings of butterfly gauze, or I should have noticed them sooner. Their poor shrivelled little wings of flesh had forgotten how to flap.

Seeing the wings, in spite of their smallness and weakness, I understood that what I had said to my mother all those years ago had come to pass. Fairies had indeed got hold of me, though they did not call themselves Fairy but Vaeri.

There was no visible way of differentiating male Vaeri from female. They were telepathic, though often they spoke aloud as well. They moved in a languid, sinuous way that always reminded me of seaweed waving in slow motion under the ocean.

The biggest difference between our races, though, was not their size, or their wasted wings, but their agelessness. It was impossible to say from their faces if the Vaeri were young or old, yet their eyes seemed immeasurably ancient. When I understood that they were immortals I gave up lethargy and disbelief and began to try to communicate with my keeper, wondering if here, at last, I should find truth.

Of all the Vaeri, my keeper alone seemed able to display emotion, and at first this was so subtle as to be imperceptible. Gradually I became aware that he was pleased when I responded to his overtures. He was the only one of that giant race who tried to reach me with words and pats and small fumbling kindnesses. His name was Borth Jesu H and he named me Awen-du.

I learned the language of my captors with extraordinary rapidity, and only later understood that the potential for this language, indeed the memory of it, was buried in my genetic make-up. At the time I thought it was my own brilliance that enabled communication with these alien beings.

My life among the Vaeri fell swiftly into routine. There would be great periods of time when Borth would ask me about my life. In particular, about my suicide attempt. I was more interested in finding out if the stories of fairies on Earth had been planted by his people, and what it was to be immortal. He always managed to turn the topic to his own questions, though. If I asked too persistently where I was, or why, or even how I had got there, he would simply go away and leave me alone.

In between our long conversations and being fed the tasteless paste which Borth said cost much effort to prepare, I would be bathed in ion rays that separated all grime from my flesh, and taken to an enormous room with a great vaulted ceiling open to the stars. This was a sort of circular amphitheatre around which sat rank upon rank of white-robed Vaeri facing a small central stage where I was made to stand.

My first trips to this room were frightening simply because I was afraid I was to be killed and eaten, or sacrificed.

But no one even addressed me, though the speakers would often point at me. As I learned their language I came to understand that the word they called me, Uman, meant monster. Once it would have mortified me to be called that, but since the Vaeri themselves could not help being aware of my likeness to them, I assumed it could not be my form in general that repulsed them.

I know now that this likeness of human to Vaeri was the very thing that made me a monster to them. Then, I decided it must have been the result of some action of mine. And since they had taken me from my suicide, I decided I must be on trial for that, for I had become convinced this was some sort of galactic enquiry.

'You are not on trial,' Borth had assured me when I asked.

Humanity then? I had guessed, but he would not answer. I decided that must be it – Earth was on trial and I was an example of my race. Poor Earth, I thought.

I did not understand the trial procedure at all. Individuals of the Vaeri spoke in a sort of high oratory when they addressed those gathered in the dome, and their words were so abstract as to be nonsense.

These alien rites were fascinating to begin with, then dull, then worrying; for as time passed, I began to fear for my own fate. Whether I was on trial or not, this strange enquiry centred somehow on me.

Why, you might reasonably ask, should someone who had been quite content to abandon life altogether be concerned about anything that happened thereafter? But now that life was forced on me, I had rediscovered an interest in it.

The end of the trial came quite without warning. One day Borth did not come, and another Vaeri brought me to the dome. Then Borth was brought there also and stood beside me. I had not previously thought of him as anything but my keeper, but now I saw that I had been wrong.

'You, Borth Jesu H, chosen above many to study Creation, are charged with creating monsters,' said one of the Vaeri.

I was shocked to realise it was Borth who was on trial. But the mention of monsters puzzled me greatly. The Vaeri had called me a monster – were they saying Borth had created me?

I did. Borth sent the words to my mind. I realised he had taken the question from my thoughts.

'I do not believe my creations are monsters,' Borth said aloud. 'How could they be when I modelled them upon our own forms?'

'You admit you made images of the Vaeri from Murmi clay, always intending to breathe life into them?'

'I did,' Borth said. 'I do not regret it.'

What is Murmi? I thought loudly, hoping Borth would hear.

I hear, he sent.

Then he told me this, in thought, so it came to me swiftly:

There are many sorts of clay. At first, students of Creation are given Ramo to practise on – a coarse and short-lived clay which will hold no life. This is intended to develop dexterity and aesthetic taste. In time, we progress to Pya, a softer, finer clay that allows greater subtlety of form and develops delicacy of touch and restraint. Everything created of these clays is destroyed lest something imperfect accidentally be given lifebreath.

Only in the final stages of study are students permitted the use of Murmi, an actual form of Porsoul. Of all the clays, only these two are dense and complex enough to contain and hold sentient life. Murmi starts out as Porsoul, but at some point before maturity, it

*is flawed and begins to decay. Use of it gives the students a feel for
the real thing, but its flaw prevents it keeping hold of lifebreath.
Whatever is formed of it will degenerate as the lifebreath dissipates.
Used Murmi is taken far away and dropped onto a barren planet,
and there, certain rites are performed to ensure that all potential for
life is extinguished.*

'From the very beginning I was fascinated by the Murmi and
its inability to hold lifebreath for more than a short while,' Borth
was saying aloud to his accusers. 'The creations I made of it
became more and more beautiful and elaborate as I attempted to
induce the clay to cling harder to the lifebreath I put into it, but
in every case my creations ceased after a time to function.

'The more I thought of it, the more curious I became as to
what this flaw would do to a life that bore it. How would an
exquisite form react to the fading of lifebreath? How would it
degenerate? How would it understand its degeneration? I wanted
to try – to breath lifebreath into my Murmi creations. I spoke of
this desire to the other students and my teachers. They were
horrified and I was forbidden to think of it.

'I bided my time. I was a model student for a millenium
or so, and only then did I dare volunteer to journey with a
crew that disposed of Murmi. The load we had was unusable,
of course, but I had some fresh Murmi in my pocket and in
secret I spent many hours locked in my shiproom labouring
over my creations. I made the most exquisite forms I had ever
made, modelled on the Vaeri. Of course they were much tinier,
for I had scant clay and nowhere to hide lifesized creatures. I
did not bother with the wings, for they no longer served a
purpose in my own kind. When I was finished, I wept to see
how beautiful they were.

'I called my creatures Ur-lings.'

In human words that would be translated as Little People, Borth
sent to me.

'When we reached the place where the clay was to be thrown
out, I pretended to be lost so that I could put my Ur-lings on
the ground and breathe life into them. Then I left.'

'Did you ever return?' one of the Vaeri asked.

Borth inclined his head, having picked up my habit of using body language to enhance speech or thoughts.

'Twice. I did not dare come again for fear I would be tracked. But the time I spent among the race arisen from my Ur-lings made me see the decadence and staleness of the Vaeri. The Ur-lings are neither smug nor complacent. Their lives contain pain and anger and sorrow, and they strive and yearn for beauty with every fibre of their beings. Life is infinitely more beautiful and precious, and even those who seek death, such as Awen-du, worship it as much as they fear it.'

Of course, by now I knew that the name Borth had given me meant Forever, but only now did I understand why.

It was your radio and television emissions and satellite launches that attracted the attention of the Vaeri at last, Borth sent to me.

An expedition was sent and it was not difficult then to trace the source of the Murmi-based life forms back to Borth.

I am charged with creating monsters, he sent, coming the full circle.

What will happen if they find you guilty? I thought.

I do not know. They will devise a punishment, I suppose.

He did not look too worried. I suppose it is hard to worry about anything when you are immortal.

'How can you have condemned these creatures to Murmi fate? Have you no guilt for the wrong you have done them?' asked a Vaeri. 'Porsoul is mentally programmed for immortality. By using Murmi instead of perfect Porsoul you have condemned your creations to futility and despair. It is cruelty beyond imagining to make creatures into whose essence is woven the understanding of immortality, but to make them from a clay which will not hold lifebreath eternally.'

I felt a stab of pure terror as I understood at last what the trial was about. A dozen different bits of information slid into place. Porsoul was immortal. Murmi was an imperfect form of Porsoul which, though it could capture the lifeforce breathed into it by its creator, could not continue to hold it. Borth had created humanity of Murmi.

In short, Borth Jesu H had given his precious creation mortality.

'This monster race cannot be allowed to go on,' said another of the Vaeri, and I felt sick.

Borth spoke then, with greater eloquence than I had ever heard in his kind. So might a mother plead for the life of her baby.

'I do not care what punishment you bestow on me,' he said at last. 'But these creatures I have made deserve to live. Come with me and move among them. You will see then ...'

'I have seen how they live and what they make of the little lives you have bestowed on them, Borth Jesu H,' said a grave, stern voice. 'These Uman are greedy and violent. They rape their world and one another. They dwell in poverty and squalor, in hunger and despair. They live for instant gratification and exist in terror of death.'

'But that is the thing,' Borth said excitedly. 'Don't you see? In spite of all that, they create, just as we do. They create beauty in their music and their words, in paintings and buildings and sculptures. They make for themselves a bittersweet immortality. Think of it! *No other race we have created, creates!*

There was a long, strange silence at this.

Borth rushed on. 'It is their fear of death, and their knowledge of its inevitability, that gives them such transcendent power. When Awen-du jumped from that bridge, she thought death was truth. She was prepared to give up her short and precious life to learn this single truth. Would any of us do such a thing? Would we have the courage or the greatness? These Ur-lings have a fleeting second — a minute lightness between birth and death which is their lives — yet they exist like a nova exploding in the infinite darkness of space. Our lives are dim candles beside theirs, for we have no passion, and our creations are as cold and perfect and lifeless as we ourselves have become. When we gave up death, we forgot to use our wings. We forgot to fly. In giving my Ur-lings mortality, I gave them passion and beauty. I gave them love and hate and desire. *I gave them wings.*'

I began to laugh then, for I saw that this was the truth I had spent my life searching for. That broke up the proceedings because the Vaeri, who do not laugh, thought I was having some sort of fit.

The last time I saw Borth was as he waited for his sentence to be pronounced, for of course he had been found guilty.

They are going to send me to Earth, his thoughts floated into my mind.

Why? I thought fearfully, wondering if they would simply bomb the Earth and destroy both the creator and his creation.

No, Borth sent. *They cannot unmake. It is forbidden and has been since my people discovered immortality. They mean to expose me to sun crystal which causes Porsoul to become Murmi.*

I did not understand and he was forced to say it more plainly.

I will be mortal there. They have elected to give me the gift of death. They have told me that I may move among my monsters and instruct them on the joys of death and mortality.

I was aghast for him, but he seemed unafraid.

I go uncaring. The Vaeri are a dead race – decadent and sterile. They became ghosts when they gave up death. If they saw your world and your people as I have, they would know that. Perhaps this is why they despise you so.

What will they do to me?

They will sent you back as well. Borth hesitated. *They mean to offer you immortality and, through you, humanity. They have discovered a way to reverse the process of degeneration.*

We stared at one another for a time, as the other Vaeri began to assemble.

Good luck, I thought. Maybe I will see you on Earth.

I do not think so, Borth sent. *I wish you luck, Awen-du. And I hope immortality pleases you. But before you take what they offer, look upon the Vaeri and then upon your own race, and see who lives more sweetly.*

And his eyes asked a thing of me.

I returned to Earth. Borth was right: I did not see him again. I took the pills the Vaeri gave me, and these gave me immortality; not constant immortality, because I am made of Murmi, but a temporary immortality which could be extended infinitely by taking one pill after another. These pills prevent the degeneration from progressing. My life was immortal only by their grace, but the Vaeri told me that any offspring I had would be of unflawed Porsoul, so long as I was taking the pills at the moment of conception, and that these children would bear the seed of immortality.

Through me, humanity could grow to deathlessness.

I wanted to think, so I travelled. I grew no older outwardly, but inwardly I aged hundreds of years as I went about trying to see what path death played in our lives, and whether immortality would heal the ills of humanity.

In all that time, I let no man fertilise my ova and spawn a race of immortals. Whenever I saw something that made me consider it – a great man or woman dying, a great beauty fading – I thought of Borth's face, and the cold, dead eyes of the Vaeri.

Yet I could not resist it. I told myself I needed to live just a little longer to experience enough to ensure I would make the right decision.

But the ages I lived began to weigh heavily, and with them came at last the truth of Borth's words, for with immortality had come deadness to my soul ... a numbness and an emptiness. Worst of all, sometimes, when I looked into the mirror, Vaeri eyes stared out at me, and I was chilled.

So at last I did not take the pills, and now I grow old.

Oh I pray that I am mad enough and brave enough to do what I know Borth wanted, and that is to die. I am still afraid of it. Though I am old and creaky and withered, life is sweet to me, it has a beauty that brings me to tears. Sometimes it has such radiance that it fills my soul and pains me sweetly.

That is something the immortals can never know or feel.

Wait. Before you go, there is one last thing. It is my theory that laughter, which the Vaeri never understood, is the answer humanity has evolved to cope with the gift of Borth Jesu H. Thus my own much-maligned flippancy is an answer to the ultimate truths that I am privy to.

Borth? Well, I have often wondered what he found among his monsters. There had been talk of setting him back in time for some technical reason or other, and of course I cannot help but wonder if, by some strange chance, his is the body buried underneath the tower in the field next to the cemetery.

There is poetry in that thought.

If it was Borth buried under there, the only thing that nags at me is a desire to know why his arm was thrown out. Perhaps at the last irrevocable second, like any mortal, he feared death and flung up his arm to his brothers, the gods, in a futile plea for mercy.

Or maybe – and this is what I like to think – maybe, at that last minute, he felt the same great sweet sadness as I do to know he must lose his life and face the mystery of death, but his courage did not fail him. I picture him in my mind, lifting his arm and laughing as he gave his brothers the finger.

Oh yes. It pleases me to think our creator died laughing. I am you see an incurable romantic, and I like endings of all kinds to come with a flourish.

That is a very mortal thing to wish for. The Vaeri have no stories because they have no concept of endings – and stories must begin and end if they are to fly. But the Vaeri have forgotten how to use their wings. How dreary for them, poor things.

THE PUMPKIN EATER

I ride this day upon the Worldroad, alone, except for Courage, who rides on the pommel of my saddle fluffing his feathers. I did not dream of journeying thus as a child. Maeve told me that women did not travel unaccompanied, especially not beautiful princesses who must wait for their prince to come for them.

Not that I am a princess any longer, nor beautiful enough to make them catch their breath at the sight of me.

I wear the trews and knee boots of a man, and the wind blows my hair wild about my shoulders. I have split ends and chafed lips and my legs and arms are muscular and strong. I have left curling tongs and perfume and silk behind.

Maeve told me a woman was either beautiful or ugly, but I have learned to be something else altogether. No doubt it is fearsome in its strangeness, though, for a commonwoman in her pumpkin house peers out at me with a kind of dread, and her man waves his hoe at me and makes the warding sign to keep off evil.

When I was a princess, they bowed and smiled to see me go by, dazzled by my beauty, relieved to see a man riding with me: my keeper.

Now, a pedlar glares at me and gives me a wide berth in his wagon. He does not know what to make of a woman alone riding the Worldroad. I am neither commonwoman nor princess, but some strange new hybrid. Worst of all, I am manless.

'What will come of it?' I hear him mutter. 'If one rides alone, will not more ride after her?'

I remember drawing the card of long journeying the year my firstblood came, and the bird of my heart, caged for so long, beat its wings against my breast.

I knew it could mean either a physical or mental journey, but this was the third time it had come to me. To draw a card three times is a trine, and summons all the meanings of the card. So then, a mental and a physical journey. I did not know how long that journey would be, and that not all of it would take place on the road.

I had focused my mind and summoned the earth magic that belongs to women, willing it into my hands as I drew again to see what the journey would entail. I remember the spread as if it is before me now.

Under the significator, I laid the four permitted explanatory cards, face down, and crossed them with a fifth. I kept one ear on the door, not because of Maeve at her chutneys and sauces in the kitchen, singing tunelessly even though she swore she didn't, but for fear my mother would come and catch me.

She might well take the cards and fling them out the window, or tear them up. Worse still, she might just give her cold, cawing laugh, and the Seerat would be forever tainted with her sneers and black mocking glances.

My mother was more silent than not, and bitter-mouthed when she spoke. Sometimes I thought she was insane. I could not imagine how I had come from her, for it seemed to me we were not alike in any way. She was dark, lean and spiky and sombre as a winter tree, and as a child, I was blond and plump. I decided I must be more like my father. I did not dare ask how he had looked, but I knew that he had blue eyes – mine were blue too – and I extrapolated the rest of him from my own features: shorter than my mother, with smooth creamy skin and pale hair like buttery down.

He had died fighting in the dragon crusades when I was

still in my mother's womb. I knew this only because Maeve, who had come with my mother to the edge of the world afterwards, had let it slip after drinking fermented berry cordial. I learned that the rare indulgences in this small vice offered the best opportunity to wheedle information from her. That and eavesdropping were the only ways I had of learning anything. I did not know what a crusade was, and she would say nothing more about it other than that it was to do with fighting and was therefore the business of men.

For Maeve the world was divided into nobles and commoners, men and women. I believed her, but I had no intention of letting any of her categories shape me. I would be my own thing, I thought blithely, never knowing that this would be the hardest thing of all.

'Men's business? Fools' business,' my mother had snarled at her, overhearing us speak of warring. I was glad she did not know how the conversation began. A sort of madness had seemed to come over her the one time I made the mistake of asking about my father. She began calmly enough, telling me he had ridden up to the tower on a white horse and called her to let down her golden hair so that he could climb up.

'He was fair as a dream with his eyes full of clouds, and his hair slicked down by his mother's spit. When he looked at me, it was like being swallowed up by the sky, drowning in that endless blue.'

'Was that love then?' I had asked eagerly, and then wished I had not, for the black glitter in her eyes seemed to stab out at me.

'Love? Who spoke of love to you?' she hissed.

Maeve, shivering in her boots, confessed. 'She had to know,' she added defiantly. 'You think bringing her here will keep her from it? Love will come riding on a white horse for her, and she will go, just as you did.'

My mother gave a crazed howl of laughter that froze my blood and Maeve hustled me out, clucking under her breath.

'Why did she bring us back here?' I asked, when all was quiet, and Maeve came down at last to give me supper.

'Because of love,' she said with weary sadness. 'Without your father, the palace, the dresses of precious watered silk, the sweetest summer wines, were meaningless. You see, love is like the sun. It makes everything golden, but when it sets, all is darkness and shadows. Then there is nothing but a tower of one sort or another.'

I understood from this that my mother had brought us back to where she was born at the edge of the world, because my father had died. The death of her love had acted upon her like the bitterest winter frost which bites to the very soul of a tree, so that it never grows true again.

Why else would she choose this draughty lonely tower, from which her prince had rescued her, over the summerwine and watered silk she might still have possessed in his palace, though he was gone?

I did not know what watered silk was any more than love, but I imagined they must feel the same: the touch of cold water in the stream on the bare secret places of my body mixed with the feel of petals from the wild brambles around the base of the tower.

I had played at love in the forest after that, in a dress of watered silk, but by the time my firstblood came, I had tired of making believe, and became strangely restless.

Sometimes I felt as if my head was a great echoing space barely occupied by the few things I knew – the tower, the forest, the Worldroad, the domestic secrets Maeve taught me when she was of a mind – how to iron a seam flat and how to remove a stain from white cloth.

I longed for my own prince to come and take me adventuring throughout the world with him. I imagined us riding together, but we would not go where the crusades were, and the wars and killing. I did not know why men were drawn to such things, but it seemed fighting and bloodletting sang to them as the Worldroad sang to me. But I would keep that deadly music from his ears and we would make a song of our own and he would be grateful to me for saving him.

That was what my mother should have done, instead of

letting my father go off alone to be killed like that. She should not have listened to the stories that said a woman does not travel. She should have defied the stories for love.

I did not tell Maeve of my notions, for I knew she would call me a fool and lecture me about the duties of women who must stay in their pumpkins if they were commoners, or in their palaces and towers if they were princesses.

I would not argue with her, but I knew my prince would not leave me behind. He would understand the hunger in my heart to see the world and know that it must be fed. He would be glad for me to ride with him, for if he loved me, would he not want me with him?

I pushed my mother's voice out of my head, and imagined what I wanted to see in the cards I had laid out – the knight of wands coming across the desert bearing the cup in his hands, and perhaps the ace of cups otherwise known as the house of the true heart. And what for the third? The ten of cups, or better still, the lovers.

A journey with a prince who would offer me true love. Maeve told me once that I was a true princess, though my mother had been a commoner before her marriage. A prince must be a prince by blood, but a woman could be raised from commoner to noble by a prince, if she was beautiful enough to make him love her.

I turned the first card over.

Woman in trammels, surrounded by swords. My mother had got into the reading after all, for wasn't it her that I wanted to escape? Her with her swords and binds.

What else? The Beast – a friend in unexpected guise who might even seem to be an enemy. I did not know what that might bode. There was no one in my life but my mother and Maeve. Only a pedlar who came each year when the leaves changed colour.

Could the pedlar be the Beast?

Each year I managed to convince myself before he came that he was less smelly and silent and unpleasant than I remembered, and would happily take me with him to see the world for the price of my two silver hair-combs. Then he would come, fetid of breath and foul of tongue, his eyes sly and shifty, and I would change my mind and remember I was a princess and must wait for my prince.

Yet the Beast card gave me pause, for sometimes the prince did not fetch the princess in Maeve's stories himself but sent an emissary. I could not think a prince would send someone so ugly to fetch his beauty, but sometimes a prince or more often, their mothers, tested a princess. Maybe I was supposed to pierce the superficial ugliness of the pedlar, and see the beauty of his heart underneath. In stories, princesses always saw and felt things more deeply and truly than other people.

I frowned. The pedlar could not help his looks and it was uncharitable for me to judge him by them. I would be nicer to him when next he came, just in case.

I turned the next card. The moon with its sickly glamour, and the dogs howling at it – illusions and deceptions. I did not know how that fitted with my journey.

The final explanatory card was the Fool: innocence and ignorance. I shrugged – representing me, no doubt. Well, I was not ashamed to admit that I knew nothing. Ignorance was lack of knowledge, not stupidity. How could I be anything but a fool when no one had ever told me anything? I had never been anywhere but the woods surrounding our tower, and a little way down the Worldroad, (so named, Maeve said, because it leads to everything eventually).

I turned the last card, crossing the rest.

It was the bleakly beautiful Veiled Empress – guardian of mysteries, of secrets yet to be revealed, of wisdoms in waiting. A good card but in that position, it represented what lay in the way of what I wanted. It meant I had to find answers to secrets if I would ever journey.

Later that day I found the egg. I almost left it, because the shell was broken and though I could see the chick in it, I thought it must be dead. Then I saw its tiny thorn of a claw flex fractionally and I stooped to take it up. The poor wee mite, featherless and blue with cold, was already flyblown, but its life beat, feeble as a whisper, under my fingertip.

I took it inside and peeled away the shell. I washed off the maggots, dripped sugared water into its thin beak and put it in my handkerchief drawer. It grew a ragged down, pecking milk-sodden bread from a saucer, and slept on the pillow by my head when it was too big for the drawer. When it was a full grown bantam rooster, and Maeve had stopped talking about roast whitemeat and begun to feed him little messes when she thought I was not looking, I decided it was safe enough to name him.

I invoked the cards and drew the Lion of Courage, which speaks of inner strengths and the ability to endure. I took this as an omen, and with Courage on my knee clucking softly in avian contentment, I gazed out of my high turret window at the Worldroad, dreaming patiently of my prince who must surely come before the spring ended.

On the festival of Beltane, we lit the sacred fire and sang the ancient songs thanking the goddess for her bounty, and praising the earth mother. That night, Maeve told me another of her seemingly endless store of stories about princesses. This one was about Cinderine, whose prince found her dirty and cleaning a scullery, terrorised and enslaved by her relatives. He had taken her away to his castle and made her a princess. He had loved her greatly, Maeve said, and could not bear for her to grow old and ugly. He sealed her up in a diamond so that she would be young and beautiful forever.

That night, I dreamed I was trapped inside a diamond, suffocating and silent. I woke screaming, and wondered if Cinderine had allowed her prince to lock her up for the sake of love. I would not have let him shut me up, I thought with a shiver.

That night, for the first time, I thought about beauty. It was a vital ingredient of the princesses and would-be princesses in Maeve's stories, fair or dark, tall or tiny, sweet or cool. Beauty even granted social mobility to commoners. My mother had been a commoner but men had swooned at the sight of her. Because of it, the prince had brought her away to his palace and wed her, transforming her into a princess. But then he had gone away to war.

With the sweat of my nightmare cooling on my skin, it

seemed to me suddenly that beauty was a coin with two sides. It was also the reason the women in stories – commoners and princesses alike – were locked up by their fathers and brothers and husbands; as if beauty was a sort of wild thing that men feared might escape and run away, or tear their throats out. No doubt the men who had swooned at my mother's beauty had not liked her any more for it when they woke with a bump on their heads, feeling foolish.

I climbed out of my bed and crossed the cold stone floor to stare into the dark mirror over my dressing table. Was I beautiful? I did not know. I had only my mother and Maeve to compare myself with. I did not think Maeve, with her sagging breasts and big feet and hairy eyebrows, was beautiful, and my mother's beauty had surely died long ago.

I did not know whether to hope I was or not. Beauty was clearly dangerous to possess, yet one could not be loved without it. And the only alternative, Maeve said, was ugliness.

If I was ugly, something terrible might happen to me, too. The ugly sisters or stepmothers in stories often fell into terrible fits of jealousy and either tried to murder the beauty, which was ridiculous because beauty cannot be killed, and they would end up getting their heads chopped off; or else in demented attempts to render themselves beautiful, they would hack off a heel or a toe, and bleed to death.

At the very least, lacking a beautiful sister or cousin to drive me mad, ugly, I was destined to be unsought, unloved, unsung. No one would come to take me journeying on the Worldroad. Without beauty I would be stuck in the tower forever.

I suddenly remembered a thing my mother had once said.

Maeve had been scolding me for playing in a mud puddle. 'Now you are ugly,' she snapped.

'Would that she were,' my mother had whispered in a voice that shivered my soul. 'Men will kill and die for it, but they cannot bear it once it is theirs. It burns them.' And she had turned her face away from me.

The pedlar came when the leaves had already fallen and the days had grown short and cold. He stared at me as he had not done in other years, until Courage flew at him and pecked at his ankles. I decided I had made a mistake in trying to be kind to him. My instincts had told me he was ugly right through, and I should have listened to them. He leered and offered to buy Courage for his cooking pot as I backed away.

I was glad to see him go, but I understood for the first time that there would be others like him on the Worldroad, and I was glad to think of a prince riding with me, to protect me. No wonder women did not travel alone, for who would protect them?

The first snow flew and then it was too cold to swim in the stream, too cold to dance in watered silk, too cold to drink anything but hot milk. The three of us sat in the tower room as close to the fire as we could, working on a tapestry stretched between us and covering our knees.

'I don't know why I bother lighting that fire,' Maeve grumbled, rubbing her swollen fingers. 'That wind steals the warmth before it does any good.'

I looked into the flames and thought the illusion was better than nothing at all. I did not look outside for the ground was not white with snow, and the Worldroad had all but vanished. No one travelled in winter. I had set my hopes on spring.

Courage shifted and resettled himself under my feet.

Maeve, then, facing the window, was the first to notice the solitary rider.

'Look,' she croaked, nearly swallowing the pin between her lips.

I looked and saw the cloaked figure on a horse and understood that my prince had come at long last. My mother rose and crossed to the window. Coming up behind her I saw that she had driven the point of the needle deep into her palm and three drops of red blood fell into a snow drift by the window. The sight of that blood against the purity of the snow made me want to vomit.

The rider's name was Peter. He had dark hair, sherry brown eyes and a smile that started in them. He was handsome, but he was not a prince.

'My prince has sent me to bring you to this palace,' he said, in a voice that was like the first sun after a dark long winter, and something in me thawed and became liquescent.

'A pedlar spoke of a rare beauty in a tower, guarded by a wicked witch.' He coughed apologetically and Maeve shrugged. She knew stories required poetic licence.

'When my prince heard that you were the fairest maid in all the lands he had travelled, and a princess of the blood as well, he swore he would have no other to wed. I had thought to arrive in the spring, but it is much further to the edge of the world than I'd realised.'

And he knelt at my feet and paid homage to my beauty. I knew then that I would travel after all, and I smiled down on him in purest joy. He did not swoon, but he did stagger slightly.

Maeve fussed over him and tut-tutted at his wet cloak, insisting he come and sit by her cooking fire to dry while she dished him up some leftover stew from our lunch. It was not proper for a commoner to go up to the tower where my mother was, she whispered, when I said the fire upstairs was nicer. I blushed, feeling like a bumpkin, and he kindly pretended not to notice.

If he had come in spring, we would have left almost immediately. But it was winter, and snow fell and fell, flattening the land's contours so that the trees were nothing more than skeletal shapes etched blackly against all of that whiteness. I chaffed at the delay, and when Peter apologised for his lateness saying that other than the distance, there had been storms and forest fires and even a tornado in his path, I understood that the very forces of nature had conspired against me, and that all was as it should be. Forces were always arrayed to keep the lovers apart in stories – but inevitably the obstacles would be overcome.

I felt foolish at having gaped at him like a common girl when he first arrived, imagining him to be the prince, and so I treated him haughtily during the weeks he stayed with us in the tower to make up for it, and managed to avoid him by staying in the tower with my mother. To my surprise, she did not try to talk me out of going, but she told me one night in a soft voice that she had wanted to go with my father to the crusades, but that he had waited until she was carrying me to decide that he would travel.

'First it is love of them that catches us, then love of a child that binds us forever. Do you understand what I am saying?'

I nodded, but understood nothing.

It seemed a long winter. But at last the snow began to melt, and we left. Maeve went and bade me be a good girl and to wear my long underwear in winter because palaces were even draughtier than towers. My mother would not come down, so I said goodbye to her in her tower room. I kissed the pale cheek she offered, and she told me to remember that the Worldroad led everywhere, even home if you walked it long enough.

I shuddered inwardly at the thought of coming back.

'Goodbye,' I whispered, as the tower with my mother's face at the window and Maeve's plump figure by the door receded and was swallowed up by the whiteness.

It was a long journey to the palace where my prince was waiting, and after trying to maintain a chilly silence for several days, I gave it up, and asked Peter why the prince had not come for me himself.

'He was hunting and then there was a siege he had to attend,' he explained.

I frowned, for it seemed to me he was saying that these things were more important than me. But I consoled myself with the thought that he had not actually seen me yet, and so he could not strictly be in love.

To begin with, I rode on the back of Peter's grey horse, with my bag tied on the back of the saddle and Courage nestled in my bodice near my breast. Maeve had insisted I leave him, saying princesses do not carry fowl in their bosom.

I had pretended to give in, but I would not have left him, even if he had let me. There was some slight trouble the first time we stayed at an inn and the matron there discovered the little bantam when he flew at her from under my pillow.

Peter looked startled then amused when the wretched woman taxed him about me keeping dangerous animals in my bed chamber, but somehow he smoothed things over. He accomplished much with his soft voice and warm brown eyes and I found myself thinking of them a good deal too much. Petting a palfrey he had bought for me in one of the bigger towns, I imagined what it would be like to have him gentle me in that way. I blushed with shame at my thoughts and hid my confusion in admiration over the mare which was sweet and white as the finest sugar, and that was what I called her.

When we left the next day, he asked me how I came by the rooster. With as much dignity as I could muster, I explained. He did not laugh but seemed to find it remarkable that I had bothered saving its life.

'Why shouldn't I?' I asked him wonderingly.

He looked suddenly sad. 'When you get to the palace, you will not be able to keep Courage.'

'Why?' I asked, shocked, because I had thought I would be free of rules when I left the tower.

'Princesses do not keep such things as pets. It is not seemly. You must have a cat with green eyes and sable fur, or a golden nightingale to sing to you from its cage. Even Sugar will be exchanged for a finer horse, for she is just a travelling beast. The prince would be embarrassed if you had less than the best.'

And so it went. Bit by bit, I learned that my prince was proud and demanding and had been much sought after as a husband for these qualities since the woman he chose must be, by definition, perfect. He had refused to wed until he could be sure his bride was the fairest in all the land. He rode the fastest, finest horse, and collected the most beautiful things to set about in his palace. His gardeners had instructions to bring him the finest blooms and fruits only. If an apple had a single mark, he would fling it from him.

Why should he not have the most perfect woman for his bride?

I said, hesitantly, that perhaps the prince would find a blemish on me, and turn me away.

Peter had blushed and said in his soft voice that there was no blemish on me. His eyes stroked my cheeks and said that if I were his to love, he would find the most perfect pumpkin and make it into a golden coach for me, so that I might dream of travelling the road in it.

But it would still be a pumpkin, my heart whispered. And you would leave me for the song of blood that only men hear. That night, I dreamed I was a nightingale, singing its heart out behind golden bars.

Then there came a night which Peter said would be our last. The next day, we would reach the palace and I would be handed to my prince. It was nearing the end of spring again but the nights were still warm. On impulse, I asked Peter if we might not sleep outside by a campfire.

He had agreed reluctantly.

'But you must not think of such things after this night,' he said in a troubled voice. 'A princess cannot camp out like a gypsy, nor go about barefoot.' He looked pointedly at my toes. 'There will be fine dresses and glass slippers. The prince will not want anything that might hurt you or mar your perfection. He will want you safe. The windows will be curtained, so you do not freckle, and fires will burn in every room even in the summer so you will not catch a chill.'

At length, he curled up in his blanket and slept, but I could not sleep.

I stared up into a sky ablaze with stars – the diamonds of heaven – and wondered when I would see them again if the windows of the palace were curtained. The breeze fanned my cheeks, and I thought how hot rooms would be where no breeze was allowed to blow. The trees whispered their secrets in the air around me, and life rustled in the leaves and undergrowth. Courage had made himself a little depression in the ground, but he was not asleep either. The sounds of the night seemed to make him restless. His black eyes caught the fire and offered it to me, and I wondered what I would see the next day in the eyes of my prince.

Love and watered silk?

I only knew that I would never be the same again. Love binds beauty, my mother had said. I would never be free to camp outside, or dance in the forest in my bare feet, or swim naked in a cold stream. Sugar and Courage would be lost to me forever, and I would never ride the Worldroad again.

Just as my father had done, my prince would possess me and snare me with his love, and leave me with his seed growing, to ride away to blood and glory. And like my mother, the maggot of love and loneliness would gnaw into my heart and soul. I would love and I would hate, but I would never be able to leave because love was the one snare that could bind the wild beauty of a woman.

It occurred to me that none of Maeve's stories had explained what happened after the princess was taken to the palace by her prince, and I thought again of Cinderine trapped in her diamond, imprisoned by love. Now at last, the Veiled Empress had revealed her secret.

I got up very quietly, scooped Courage into my arms, crept to the tree where Sugar was tied, and slipped away.

That was the first night I rode the Worldroad alone, and the beginning of my true journeying.

Sometimes, I hear my prince searches still for his vanished princess, but I know it is the dream of beauty he seeks, and not a real woman. And me? I do not regret the loss of love or watered silk and summer wine. Each day I ride feeling the sun on my face, or the rain, and am content. The Worldroad is long, and each bend brings some new thing to me. My mind is now filled with the wonders I have seen, all stored as stories. I keep them safe, because the Worldroad comes to all things eventually, and so I know that one day it will bring me to the Tower where my mother sits.

I will put my arms around her and kiss her, and tell her I love her. I will show her all that I have seen, and I will tell her that I have learned one need not be ugly or beautiful, princess or commoner. One can be something else, if one has courage enough to ride alone.

THE RED SHOES

Amerie was reading a book her mother had left her. On the flyleaf was written: *To my darling daughter, Amerie, on her birthday.* Amerie had found the book in the back of the bookshelf still wrapped and she was trying to understand what it could mean.

Andersen's Fairy Tales Revisited by Ander Pellori was inscribed across the front page in swirling important looking golden letters. And all around the golden letters, goblins and fairies and sprites cavorted and danced in a frenzied celebration.

Amerie could remember little of her mother whom her father said had left them both.

'She left us just before Amerie was five, and she broke our hearts,' her father said whenever anyone asked. And that was all he would say.

The first time she overheard her father say that, Amerie worried that she had not been treated for the heart that was broken when her mother left. She did not mention it to her father because his heart was wounded too. She felt a kind of deep ache whenever she thought of her mother, and imagined that there was a dribble of blood still leaking out of her heart. It seemed to her that talking and thinking of her mother reopened the wound, and so she did not speak for her father's sake. For he brooded darkly and rarely smiled.

Once she had heard him tell her teacher that she was too young to remember her mother, but that was not so. It was true that she did not remember her doing the sorts of things other girls' mothers did. She had no memory of her mother ironing or pushing a trolley in a supermarket or going to have her hair done. She had no memory of her mother stirring a pot, nor even of her dressed in a business suit and carrying a briefcase the way Raelene's mother did.

Amerie's memories were anything but ordinary.

The reason her father thought that she did not remember her mother was because she never spoke of her. That was partly to save him pain, but mostly because the memories were so strange she had kept them secret and silent inside her.

One of the memories was of both her parents arguing.

'I'm sick of this . . .' her father had growled through his black beard.

Her mother had said in her soft cooing voice, 'Shh, Jon. You'll wake the baby.'

'If you were not so flighty . . .'

'I do what I must do,' her mother had said in a pleading voice. 'You know that. When we married I warned you how it was with me and you said you understood.'

'I did not know it would take you away from me so often, or that you would consort with those creatures . . .'

'You are jealous, and there is no need. I do not love my companions as men. They are like me and they understand how it is to be possessed by . . .'

'Nothing and no one will possess you but me,' her father had said in his heavy voice. 'You belong to me.'

'I will not let you cage me . . .'

There the memory broke off suddenly. The talk of flight and birds and cages had shivered Amerie's soul because of another memory. The most secret memory of all.

Her mother came to her wrapped in the shadows of the night, and stroked her face and kissed her as she lay drowsily in her bed.

'I will come back to you soon . . .'

But her mother had not been entirely human in that memory. Woven through her dark lustrous hair were sleek black feathers, and Amerie's hand felt them on her breast and shoulder as well. As if she had not quite changed all the way into a bird yet.

There was only one other memory. Amerie's favourite. Her mother's hair was out of its usual bun and flowing all around her shoulders and Amerie was permitted to brush it. A black feather fluttered out onto the floor. The wind caught it up and tried to whisk it out of sight, but Amerie jumped down and ran lightly across the floor to catch it in her hand. Her mother laughed softly when she brought back her treasure. Looking around to be sure they were alone, she closed Amerie's fingers around the feather and said, 'You are half me, little one, and one day you will fly. I see it in your movements. You are light as a feather.' Then for a moment she looked sad and proud all at once. 'You will long for the red shoes as I do and no price will be too high. You will fly because it is in your blood . . .'

Amerie did not remember her mother going away. Nor even which order the memories had happened in. She had not understood all of the memories, but she had known from them that her mother *was not entirely human.* She was a thing of lightness and dark feathers, and music could move her to dance as the wind moves a feather. Part of her yearned to fly even when she was in human form. Amerie had often seen her dance and sway on her toes, flinging her arms out like wings. She did not look entirely human either. She was not round and soft and comfortable like the mothers of other girls. She was very thin and her legs and arms were bony and hard with muscles. *From flying,* Amerie knew now.

And Amerie was like her mother. Much as she ate, she was not heavy and solid like her father. She was slender and light-boned and her feet were narrow like her mother's though they lacked the queer calluses that must come to her in her bird form.

Once she had heard a neighbour tell her father after a visit that she ate like a bird.

But more than her body, she knew what she was because sometimes she would feel a strange yearning for something more than life could give. Something nameless and demanding and wonderful would dance through her blood, heady and intoxicating. Her fingers and feet would tingle and she would realise that she was on the verge of shapechanging, as her mother had done. But she was half her father as well, and she realised that the fleshiness of him weighed her down and caged her bird self, just as he had wanted to cage her mother.

Amerie had never been able to bear to see birds caged after she realised the truth. Outside pet shops, she would watch them, and they would look into her eyes and know she was part bird and understand her longing to free them. If no one were watching, she would slip open the catch and the birds would fly away.

Some did. Others just crouched against the bars in fear because they had been caged too long. Even shaking the cage would not make them fly because they had forgotten how.

That frightened Amerie because in those terrified birds she saw herself trapped forever. Too frightened to fly. She understood from this that if she did not learn to fly, there would be a day when the urge would leave her and she would come to accept the cage.

After this for a time she sought out and opened every cage she could find, hoping that if she could free enough birds, she would free her own birdself. Because she felt sure her mother had not left her willingly, but only for fear of her father's cage. She must pray for me to fly to her, Amerie knew, pray that her daughter would come to her birdself in time.

Oh, how she longed to fly away from her father's thick angry silences and his black thorny beard. His hand was hard and sometimes when he hugged her, she felt he was trying to make a cage of his body and put her inside it so that she would be trapped there forever beside his great red beating heart, fluttering and fluttering in despair.

In the end a pet-shop owner caught and shook her, asking if she did not understand that the birds were safe when they were caged; that other bigger birds and cats and all manner of predators would eat them now she had let them go, because the poor birds did not understand the danger of freedom.

'They are tame birds and tame birds must be caged!' the pet-shop man had said, giving her a final shake and warning her that if he saw her near his shop again he would call the police.

Walking away, shaken to her core, she understood that to accept the cage and to forget to fly was to be tamed. While to fly was dangerous freedom. Her mother had chosen to fly away because her father had wanted to tame her. He had wanted her to forget to fly and swoop and sing. He had wanted her safe in a cage, just as he wanted Amerie safe. He held her hand when they walked in the street in his big tight grip to keep her safe.

But to be safe, one had to be tamed, and being tamed meant you would never fly again.

And the predators? Amerie thought of them seriously, cats with flashing wicked eyes and who knew what other sinister beasts waiting to eat up freedom. But then another awareness came to her so powerfully that she stopped in the street and stared in front of her with fear and wonder, because she understood at last how her mother's sadness could have joy in it.

If it was in her to fly, she must fly! She *could not choose* to be tamed and safe in a cage because freedom was in her blood and would never permit it. Though she might die by the teeth or under the wheels of a car, she must fly. The urge was so strong that it was like a beast inside her, roaring to be free. She must fly, else that inner beast would tear her to pieces with its own teeth. She would be alive, but she would be dead inside.

She tried not to open any more cages after that. Her father frightened her when he was angry and he would be very angry if he knew what she had done. All the more because he would know at once why she was releasing birds from their cages. If she gave the slightest hint that freedom raged through her veins, he would find some way to cage her. He must never know, and so she was careful to pretend she was tame.

Instead of dancing around the room or singing, which brought his heavy glowering gaze to press her down to the earth, she would sit quietly and read.

That seemed to please him and he would lay his great hand on her head and say that she was a good girl. He did not understand that while her body was still when she read, her mind flew far and wide. She would only dance and swirl and let her bird spirit move her body to music when her father went out to church on Sunday evenings. That was the only time he left her alone. Only then, as she dipped and leapt, did she dare to pray to her mother to help her learn to fly before it was too late.

And now, the book. Her mother must have flown back in secret to hide it, knowing that searching for books on her own shelf in her father's library, she would find it. Her eighth birthday was only a few days away. Amerie held the book tightly against her chest, understanding that she had been given a warning. If she did not fly before her eighth birthday, she would be too heavy and the urge to freedom would be tamed.

Her heart pounded against her chest, the mended crack aching with the force of it, as she opened the precious gift.

The hair on her neck stiffened because the first story was called 'The Red Shoes'.

Shivering with excitement, Amerie began to read.

It was the story of a girl who longed for a pair of red dancing shoes so desperately, she forgot to care for her dying grandmother. She dreamed of nothing but the red shoes and eventually stole money to buy them. But when she put them on, they danced her until she was exhausted. They would not be removed for they had grown to her feet. They danced her into a ragged urchin, and finally a woodcutter offered to chop them off her. 'So that you may be still and quiet at last.' The girl was frightened because it meant he must chop off her feet as well, and she would not ever dance again. 'I will carve wooden feet and strap them to your legs so that you can hobble around. You will never dance again, it is true, but look where dancing has brought you. Let me chop off your feet and you will be safe.'

And the girl had bowed her head and wept as she agreed.

Amerie closed the book, frightened by what she had read. Her mother had once told her she would fly when she wore the red shoes, but here was a story of magical shoes that would not be removed unless your feet were chopped off as well. Her mother's message must be riddled into the story, and she would have to fathom it.

That night, she slept with the book under her pillow. She lay awake for a long time, thinking of all the magical shoes she had encountered in stories. Puss-in-boots had boots that carried him seven leagues at a single step, and that was a kind of flying. And Cinderella had been given glass slippers by her Fairy Godmother, and in them she had flown to the heart of her prince. Then there were the red shoes Dorothy had got from the Wicked Witch of the West, which took her anywhere she wanted if she clicked the heels together . . .

When Amerie slept, it was to dream that she was the girl wearing the red dancing shoes, whirling and dancing and leaping herself to exhaustion, and yet, though she was half dead, her heart laughed and danced inside her and freedom flowed through her soul like a river.

The woodcutter came to her big as a bear in the moonlight. He had a black beard and a red mouth, and he carried a silver axe with two cruelly sharpened edges.

'I will make sure you don't fly away. I love you and I will tame you.'

Amerie was frightened, but the delight in her blood ate up the fear and she danced in a circle around the great heavy wood-cutter. 'I will not let you cage me.'

The woodcutter made a lunge for her, but she danced out of his grasp and ran until she came to her own house in the middle of the dark woods. Somewhere a wolf howled as she threw open the door and ran up the stairs. She could hear her father's feet on the veranda. The front door slammed open.

'Come to me,' his voice boomed. 'Let me cut off the red shoes and you will be safe.'

Higher, the shoes whispered.

But there was no higher. Except . . .

Amerie turned to look at the attic stairs. Her father had

forbidden her to climb them. The roof is dangerous and unstable and you will fall through it, he had said.

Higher, the shoes whispered urgently.

She ran up the wooden steps, light as a bird on the snow. Up and up and into the roof. It was dark and the roof slanted deeply. Moonlight streaming in through the dormer window lit up boxes and cases and heaps of clothing; it silvered a lace of tulle and a dressmaker's dummy festooned with spider webs.

'I know you are up there. I will kill you before I will let you leave me again ...' cried her father, and now his feet were thunder on the stairs. 'If I cannot have you, no one will have you.'

Higher, whispered the red shoes.

There is no higher, Amerie thought.

Then you will be tamed and you will die ... the red shoes whispered.

'I love you!' roared her father, his boots clumping on the wooden attic steps, shaking the house.

Amerie woke up.

Her face and hands were slick with sweat as she reached under the pillow and took out the book. The cover was cool and velvety as a puppy's belly under her hot hands, and she lay there until the sun rose, holding the book tightly to her, trying to think what to do. She must get up into the attic and find the red shoes that would show her how to fly. But her father would not leave her alone until Sunday and that would be her eighth birthday and it would be too late. She would be trapped forever.

She must get into the attic, but her father had forbidden it. She must get him to leave her alone. But how?

'Are you all right?' her father rumbled that evening. She had sat very quietly all day, not even reading.

'I feel sick,' Amerie said in her palest voice.

Her father's black brows pulled together over his dark eyes and he took her chin in his big hand and lifted it so that he could look into her eyes. Amerie prayed he would not smell the talc on her cheeks.

'You look sickly, my little one. Perhaps I should bring you to the doctor tomorrow.'

Amerie's heart thumped. 'Maybe if you give me some of the tonic you gave me last time, I will be better by morning.'

He frowned again, then shrugged. 'We will try it.'

He went to the bathroom, but the bottle was empty.

'That is strange. The bottle is finished. I will go and buy some more. You had better get into your bed.'

She gave him a docile nod, and went up to her bedroom. A moment later, she heard the front door close. She ran to the attic steps and hurried up them, and just as in the dream, there were boxes and a dressmaker's dummy with her mother's slender shape, and in the corner near the dormer window, a froth of gauzy tulle.

But no red shoes.

Her father would only be away a little while and she must find them and return to her bed before he came back. Frantically, she began to search. Under clothes and dresses and a suitcase of silky woman's clothing. There were lots of shoes but none were red. She opened the top of one of the boxes and found letters.

One began, 'My dearest Winter, Jonathon must understand that you need to dance, surely. Did he not first see you soaring on the stage? Does he think you can just stop as if you were a secretary typing letters?'

Winter was her mother's name, Amerie knew, setting the letter aside. She had obviously left all of her letters and clothing behind because in her bird form she had no need for them. Her father had told people she had gone away because he wanted no one to know he had married a shapechanger.

But where were the red shoes? Surely that was what the dream had meant. She opened another box and another. She had no idea how much time had passed, but she had not heard her father's tread on the steps yet, and so she decided to take a few more moments to search.

Help me, Mother . . . she whispered.

Her eyes fell on the silvery tulle, and she noticed a black feather caught in it. Her heart leapt.

Then she heard her father's boots on the wooden veranda.

She pulled at the tulle; there was masses of it. It was a kind of dress, and though white and silver, the bottom of the hem was thick with darkness, and there were black and white feathers stuck there. And there, under the tulle were dark slender dancing shoes with long silky tapes. They looked black, but the moon made red look black, she reminded herself. Without thinking, she pushed her feet into them. There was a crackle and a roughness inside, as if someone had put red paint in the shoes as well as on the outside, but they fit her perfectly in the heel. They are too long, but I will grow into them, she thought dreamily.

'Amerie?'

Her father was on the second floor and it was too late now to go down and get into her bed because he would see her. She listened to him going into her bedroom as she tied the tapes round and round, making a neat bow at the rear.

'Amerie. Are you up there?' her father growled. He was at the bottom of the attic steps.

She stood up, thinking she must hide. Perhaps, then, he would think she had gone out and go looking for her. And she would come down and pretend she had ...

His boots clumped purposefully on the steps.

'Amerie, I know you're up there. I told you never to go up there. I warned you and you would not listen. You are just like your mother ...'

Amerie heard an axe in his voice and was frightened, but the red shoes filled her with joy. *I must hide*, she thought.

He will find you, whispered the shoes.

Amerie thought of the dream and whirled to the dormer window. It was open and she could fit through. Outside the moon shone like a bowl of silver water.

Higher or you will die ...

Amerie understood then, and she hesitated and looked down at the shoes. They looked black, but surely they were the red shoes. In this darkness she could not tell. But she felt them growing onto her, filling her with feathers and the urge to fly. She looked down at the book her mother had sent as a message.

The gold lettering was silver now and winked at her as if to say she must choose now and forever.

And she laughed. *I cannot choose, for I must fly, it is in me . . .*
And she flew.

THE KEYSTONE

for Jochen

'Speak, daughter. Unburden your heart and mind.'

The ritual words ought to have been comforting, and yet there was a coldness in Signe. Her eyes went beyond the older man to the violet sky, reflected in green hill pools.

I have lived my life for this moment when I will stand as Keystone of the Riftgate, she thought. Can any life have been so shaped and wrapped in purpose? I tell myself I am lucky to have a purpose. Yet we know nothing of the world into which the Valoria has fallen, other than that the rift between our world and this one is nearly wide enough to permit an adult. We few will soon pass into that other world: I, the Keystone, Savid the Watcher, and the Searchers who will locate the lost Valoria so that we may bring it home at last.

But the Dakini will follow, and they will bend all their efforts to prevent the Valoria being returned to its own world, for that will mean the loss of their savage domination.

It will be up to me to hold the Riftgate open long enough, but even if I give myself entirely to this purpose, it might not be enough. If I fail, my people will never be free.

'I am afraid,' she said at last. 'It is almost time.'

'It is past time and yet a thousand aeons before the moment of your passing, daughter. Do not fear time, for it is eternal and loops back on itself. What has been will be again. What is past is yet to come. A moment is the same as a million years. We swim in the river of time, driven by our perceptions, limited only by our vision.'

Mystic words. Beautiful and incomprehensible; in a way, irrelevant to her fear. And yet it was true that time was fluid and *bendable. She was young, and yet she felt ancient sometimes. Fear drained her as the Riftgate would.*

'Sing with me, and become one with the rift, for it is time and you must not fight it. You must let it flow through you.'

'Who was *that*?' Ricky asked.

Old Mrs Robbins squinted through the shop window. 'Said his name was Jurgens. Foreigner of some sort.'

'German,' her husband said out of the side of his mouth. 'He's ... '

'No, I mean I've seen him somewhere!' Ricky's eyes widened. 'I remember. I saw him on television. He goes all over the world exposing fake stuff. Gerhardt Jurgens his name is.'

'Magic,' Mr Robbins said. 'The television said he exposes fake magic. He's after them lights in the desert east of here. Witchlights the papers call them. Harry up the weather station said he'd been asking if there'd been any earth tremors.'

'What've earthquakes got to do with magic?' Ricky asked, absently popping the top off his coke.

All three gazed out to where the man was climbing into his four-wheel-drive. An errant breeze whipped the fine desert dust into a red spiral. When it cleared, the car was receding in a rusty cloud spewed up by the knobbly tyres.

'Man like that don't believe in nothing and can't bear no one else believin' either,' Mrs Robbins said softly.

Her husband did not dispute her. The man's eyes had pressed against his face like questing fingers. He wondered what would drive a man to spend his life so hard looking for nothing, because that's what it amounted to, didn't it?

In the car, Gerhardt was not thinking of the witchlights rumoured to shine in this godforsaken place, but of a drive across another shimmering red desert almost two decades past and half a world away.

He could summon up the exact moment his long search

began. He had been sitting in the foyer of the Las Vegas Hilton, having picked up his older brother's interpreter from the airport. They were waiting for their rooms to be made up, and he had challenged her to live up to his brother's claim that she could read nationality from body language alone.

Raven Campbell did not smile, though she was amused. That was partly the job. Interpreters were not supposed to react to the words they translated. You learned to suppress your responses. But an interpreter was not simply a cipher, translating word for word. A language was the vehicle for the culture that spawned it. You had to be able to interpret not just words, but also the nuances of gesture and tone, the body language that enhanced and amplified, and which sometimes concealed, meaning. She was very good at her job.

'Try them,' Gerhardt prompted, nodding towards the entrance to the foyer.

Raven turned to see a tall man with dark, greyflecked hair pulled into a ponytail usher a slight blonde girl to the reception desk.

Their clothes were elegant and expensive, but subtly foreign. No doubt this was why Gerhardt had fastened on them. Raven did not recognise the cut of the clothes, but in any case such things were deceptive. She turned her attention to their body language, seeking the subtle clues to nationality revealed by manner and mannerism. The man was solicitous of the girl. No. More than that, protective. She was not famous – Raven would have recognised her, but perhaps she was some sort of obscure royalty. She was beautiful and poised enough to be a princess.

As the pair crossed to the elevator, Raven became aware of tension in their movements – a precision that made her suddenly certain they had come to Las Vegas for something more than gambling in the casinos. Or perhaps they had come to gamble everything they owned on one roll of the dice. One might look that way then.

'Well, what nationality?' Gerhardt asked.

'I don't know,' Raven murmured, intrigued.

The lift bell chimed and the couple entered. The door closed and Raven watched the little arrow move and then stop at the sixth floor. The lift came back down.

'Well, I guess even my brother's interpreting angel can't be entirely perfect,' Gerhardt was saying in his oddly accented but very good English. His brother sounded much less German, but there was something rather innocent and forthright about this young man that his brother lacked. 'You know, I was actually a little afraid of meeting you. Kurt sang your praises so highly that I felt you must disapprove of a drop-out physics student.'

Raven looked at him with her own direct gaze. 'Not a drop-out surely. Kurt said you were taking a year off to travel. That sounds very wise to me. I wish I had done it. What is it?' she asked, as he frowned.

'I am trying to imagine what you were like as a student. You don't look much more than that now. I was surprised at how young you looked.'

Now she did smile. 'For an ancient thirty-two-year-old, you mean?'

He flushed and she was reminded again of his own age. Twenty-two, Kurt had told her, and very serious about the world. That was young in a woman, but younger in a man. She should not tease him.

'I did not mean that you were old, only that you look younger than your years,' he said earnestly.

An attendant finally brought their keys over. 'Your bags will be brought up. Your rooms are on the sixth floor, overlooking the strip.'

In the lift, Gerhardt asked her about dinner. 'Las Vegas is not a place for eating alone.'

'It's awful,' Raven said.

But she was thinking of the way the town had looked as they'd approached it in the hire car. Through the golden haze of sunset, it had been like some mythical city. Of course, it had been some trick of the light or mind. Or perhaps only a mirage, for as they came closer, there were the endless rows of fast-food outlets clustered along the highway, and the heavy cement buildings with their garish facades, and endless neon exhortations to gamble and win.

It was said there were no clocks in Las Vegas; when you were inside the casinos, there were no windows to let in outside light, so you would never know the time. The whole town was designed to disorientate. Everything but gambling was streamlined. They had even passed a powder-pink chapel offering five-minute weddings.

Hideous. A gangster's Disneyland.

'It is truly ugly,' Gerhardt agreed. 'But Kurt has a meeting here and that is all he cares about. You and I are here at his behest, but perhaps there is a reason for it that has nothing to do with my dynamic brother.'

Raven lifted her brows at him, genuinely surprised. 'A fatalistic physicist? Isn't that a contradiction in terms?'

'Maybe that is why I am taking a break.' He smiled crookedly as the lift hissed to a halt. 'What about dinner?'

'I suppose I have to eat,' Raven said distractedly, then bit her lip at her ungraciousness.

'Have I managed to make myself so disagreeable already that dinner with me will be such a punishment?'

'Of course not. It is Las Vegas that I find disagreeable.'

In her room, Raven sat on her bed with a sigh, wondering how every hotel in the world managed to look and smell the same. Expensive sterility. The thought startled her because usually she found the anonymity of hotel rooms soothing.

Three doors away, Gerhardt unpacked loose pale trousers and wondered what had possessed him to ask the woman out to eat. He should have left her to her own devices.

The trouble was that he had expected an efficient and starched dragon after his brother's description. Instead he was faced with gypsy eyes and a coarse bramble of undisciplined black hair. In spite of her air of control, he sensed she could not be entirely tame with hair like that. The drive across the desert had produced a queer intimacy of the kind that sometimes grows between strangers thrust into close company, but she had revealed nothing of her personal life. That was probably exactly why he had suggested dinner. He grinned ruefully at his whimsy.

Three doors away, Savid bowed deeply to the blonde girl who stood facing him.

'Lady, I will go to see how the Searchers progress. I am certain there is no danger in this place, but it would be as well if you remain here.'

Signe inclined her head slightly. Even that was an effort. She had not imagined the dreadful draining of her meld with the Riftgate, the feeling of being devoured. It was taking all of her self-control not to scream and beg for mercy.

Please let them find it quickly, she thought, as the door closed behind her protector.

When Raven and Gerhardt came outside some hours later, they were both surprised at the warmth of the wind blowing in from the desert. After the chill of efficient air-conditioning, the heat made them both relax out of their intended formality.

The city skyline blazed around them, encrusted with diamond bright lights. Raven was reminded of her first fleeting glimpse of Las Vegas, and the momentary thrill she had felt at the fairy spires and pale shimmering towers her imagination had wrought. A mirage, and yet, just now stepping out of the hotel into the dazzling night, she felt she had entered that briefly imagined place.

'You know, when I was a kid, I used to make up these magic spells,' she said in a soft, low voice Gerhardt had to strain to hear. 'I remember one night . . . just for a second, it seemed like everything trembled on the brink of changing. As if I'd got the spell almost right – but I had spoken a moment too soon, or too late. Or I had got one word wrong.' She fell silent, remembering how the magic had seemed to respond in some subliminal way to her.

Gerhardt thought of how that scrap of memory had transformed her face, infusing it with life and a wistful longing that reminded him of his own childhood. And yet, one had to grow up and get on with the world, didn't one? One had to put away childish things and accept there was no magic in the world, and that honour and trust and love that lasted forever belonged in books, not in real life.

'We will cut straight through the Treasure Island Casino, and go out the other side,' he said. 'The restaurant is just past it.'

They were approaching the side doors when they opened suddenly to disgorge a gesticulating crowd of Arabs. Gerhardt reached out and caught Raven's hand, drawing her to one side.

'Rude bastards,' he said mildly.

Raven waited for him to let go of her hand, but he did not. She felt uncomfortable but did not want to seem foolish by overreacting to what had been no more than an instinctively protective gesture. Inside the foyer, she forgot her discomfort in amazement at finding herself in the jungle. The enormous foyer was filled with trees, ferns, sinuous vines and lush orchids drooping their heads and exuding a heavy languorous scent.

A small sign at the beginning of a golden marble path leading into the dense greenery offered arrows to Tiger Palace and Pool Bar, or Reception Desk.

Gerhardt considered the directions.

Taped jungle noises increased the impression that they really were in the jungle, and when they passed an immense waterfall backlit with green and blue lights, Raven thought that when make-believe and pretence were on such a scale they transcended themselves, and became a kind of magic. The only jarring notes were the people and the electronic siren call of poker machines. The path wound for some distance before bringing them to a clearing where, behind a thick wall of glass, two white tigers paced on the terrace of a lavish white marble palace. A bathing pool surrounded by pale pebbles was filled with iridescent blue water, and one of the tigers padded to the edge and immersed itself.

There was a crowd of watchers pressed up against the glass, and they sighed at the sight of the swimming tiger.

'Just shows what money can do,' one man said in a twanging midwestern accent.

Raven was appalled. It was awful to see the creatures, who were real and surely rare, caught up in this frozen false world, and yet, still, there was a sense of the incredible about the extravagance of the illusions brought by money. No wonder people gambled their lives away here.

Feeling vaguely suffocated, she made her way towards an exit door half concealed by a curtain of creepers. It led to a darkened pool area where the only light was a jewel-blue glow from dim submerged lights. The door closed, and the hum of talk and music was cut off as if a switch had been thrown. Hot wind rustled the foliage, and the sound of traffic beyond the wall sounded far away.

Gerhardt was abruptly aware that he was still holding Raven's hand. Her fingers seemed hot and heavy in his. He felt a flicker of fear at the thought that he might have got himself into something that was going to be hard to get out of gracefully. But as if she sensed his discomfort, she slid her hand free, and pushed through the foliage to stare into the pool. A cloud of blue butterflies, disturbed by her movement, erupted, and for a moment she was enveloped in an azure spiral.

Gerhardt thought she looked like a pale goddess rising from a cloud of attendant butterflies.

She is much older than you, he told himself sternly, and in more than years. Look how little concerned she had been when you held her hand, he thought disapprovingly. Contrarily though, he now wished he was still holding it. There had been something exciting about being afraid.

He wondered what she would do if he kissed her. Maybe she would like him to kiss her. Maybe she would laugh and he would feel foolish.

Suddenly she stiffened. 'Did you hear that?'

Without waiting for his response, she darted around the pool and into the foliage on the other side. He heard her cry out, and arrived at her side just in time to see two men grasping the arms of a man, while a fourth buried a knife in his chest. The wounded man crumpled at their feet and lay still.

Raven gave a frightened moan and one of the men moved towards them, but the man who had the knife grunted and made a chopping gesture with it. The three turned and ran into the trees.

Gerhardt's heart battered at his chest in a mixture of fear and anger. He wondered wildly if he should try to follow the muggers or call for the security guards.

Raven had hurried to the injured man and was feeling for his pulse. 'He's alive . . . Oh!'

The prostrate man had grasped her hand. 'Lady . . .'

'You . . . you've been stabbed.'

'Hear me,' he interrupted. 'Find Signe . . . warn her . . .'

The moon cleared a patch of cloud and they were startled to see that it was the grey-haired man who had brought the blonde girl into the hotel earlier that day. His eyes held Raven's, pleading.

'Help me . . .'

'I'll get a doctor,' Gerhardt said.

'No,' the man rasped. 'It is too late. The dagger was . . . poisoned. Please. Find Signe. Tell her the Searchers are dead. The Dakini killed them all . . .'

The man sucked in a laboured, rattling breath, then slumped, fingers sliding off Raven's arm.

Gerhardt felt faint, but the urgency in the man's voice had wakened a sense of apprehension in him. 'We . . . must get the police . . .'

Raven visibly collected herself, but she could feel the dead man's hands pressing her arm. 'I don't think we should go to the police first. If we do, we'll have to go to the station and it might be hours before they believe we didn't kill this man ourselves. I have a feeling that girl he was with is next in the line of fire. We have to help her.'

Gerhardt gave way before the blaze of purpose in her eyes. 'How will we find this girl? We do not even know her surname . . .'

'The sixth floor. They got off at the sixth floor.'

There were three hundred and forty rooms on the sixth floor, and it took them half an hour to find the room, through the simple process of splitting up and knocking on doors, starting either end of the building and working their way towards one another. This took some time, but when they were separated by ten doors, to their amazement, one opened and the blonde girl they were seeking stepped out into the hall. Only she was not a girl. They had been mistaken about that. She was about twenty, and looked confused as she started towards the lift.

Raven reached out without thinking and caught her by the wrist.

'I'm sorry, but you are Signe, aren't you?' she said.

The young woman merely blinked at her, then tried to walk on.

'We found your friend,' Gerhardt said. 'The man with the ponytail and the grey suit. He was attacked . . .'

The woman moaned and her eyes widened. 'I knew. I felt something was wrong. It must have been the Dakini . . .'

Gerhardt looked at Raven, registering this was the name the dead man had uttered. She shook her head minutely, ushering the shaken young woman to her room.

'These Dakini – are they some sort of gang?' Raven inquired gently.

'Savid is dead?' she asked, and when Gerhardt nodded, all the anguish and sorrow of a moment past were wiped from her expression. 'His spirit swims in the river of time.'

'I'd better call the police,' Gerhardt said, and Raven nodded.

'No.' Signe's voice was silk wrapped around a steel blade.

'What do you mean? Your friend has been murdered.'

'He was not my friend.'

'He was killed and apparently these maniacs who did it have killed some other people too . . .' Raven was indignant.

The blonde woman started to her feet and swayed, shock enlivening her pallid features yet again. 'The . . . the Searchers are dead as well?' She moaned like a wounded animal. A terrible twisted desperate sound.

'No one will find you here,' Gerhardt murmured, thinking she must be afraid for her own life.

But she laughed. A horrible raw sound. 'No one will look for me. The Dakini know that without Savid and the Searchers, I am helpless. The rift is increasingly unstable as is the nature of such flaws in the walls between worlds as they widen. Eventually it must collapse. The cost of holding it open is high and I have no strength left to search for the Valoria as well.'

Gerhardt and Raven looked into one another's eyes, thinking the same thought.

'We will get some help for you,' he said gently.

The woman turned cold teak eyes on him. 'If you would aid me, find the Valoria. It is a small stone which contains the power to subdue the invading Dakini hordes. We lived in peace and the barbaric Dakini also, until it slipped through a small rift into this dimension, and they reverted to their former selves.'

'Dimension ...' Raven echoed carefully, because the poor creature obviously believed what she was saying.

'Such cracks between worlds and even times are not uncommon. They occur naturally in all worlds. They are small to begin with, then they widen until the pressure collapses them, closing the gap. The rift into your world was minuscule, so my people have dwelt in exile and terror for two generations, waiting for it to widen enough that Searchers might retrieve the Valoria.'

'But, if this thing fell through a ... rift so long ago, it is probably buried under a building or even under the ground,' Gerhardt said, thinking the man Savid must have been a psychiatric nurse.

'Time here and in my world does not flow as one. But in any case the Valoria would not allow itself to be buried. Its power is shaped to repress violence, even to itself. That is how it controls the aggressions of the Dakini. It will not be hard to find for wherever it lies, it will affect magic. This entire place is infused with its power, although your people have disguised the true magic beneath false glamours. But the closer to the Valoria, the more real the magic will be, and as the rift widens, this effect will spread.'

'Poor thing,' Raven said, closing the bedroom door quietly.

Gerhardt sighed. 'She is disturbed, but that bodyguard *was* killed. We had better talk to the hotel manager to see what is the best way to proceed.'

Descending in the lift, he collected himself for a confrontation with American hotel bureaucracy. When the doors opened, he was astonished to find the pristine hotel foyer filled with shouting men and women, all of whom appeared to be trying to check out.

'What's the matter?' he asked one of the liveried attendants.

'Dunno. All these folks came running in and yelling about escaped wild beasts.'

Gerhardt thought of the white tigers in the glass and marble enclosure. Could they possibly have escaped? Another time the thought of that would have delighted him, though another part of his nature deplored the carelessness of such an incident. He shook his head reminding himself that he had other things to concern him. The manager proved to be a great urbane slab of a woman in an expensive grey suit. Her toothy smile vanished as Gerhardt explained what had happened.

'Is this some sort of joke?'

'Of course not. We saw a man stabbed to death by a group of men in the pool area of the Treasure Island Casino. There is certainly nothing funny about that.'

The woman scowled. 'All I know is I've heard more wild stories today than in my whole career. People telling me the sky is purple or that they saw a mermaid in the fountain. Guests complaining that other guests are trying to murder them, or that they saw mermaids in the lavatory. I have no idea what all this craziness means, but I don't need the aggravation. If you really did see someone murdered in one of the other hotels, I suggest you see the police, sir.'

'What a place . . .' Gerhardt said, as Raven opened the door. Then he stopped because she was as white as a sheet.

'She . . . you were gone for so long.'

He nodded. 'I spoke to the manager, and then I went to the police, but this whole city seems to have gone mad today . . . These crazy Americans. What's the matter?'

'I . . . when you were gone so long, I went in to check on her. She . . . you'd better look yourself.'

Signe was sitting up on the bed, her back to the door.

'Excuse me,' Gerhardt said, beginning to back out. He had thought she must have killed herself from the way Raven looked.

Then she turned.

Gerhardt felt as if someone had hit him in the stomach. It was the same woman, but she was old. Ancient. Her cheeks were still high and pronounced but the flesh was sunken and ravaged, hair grey and lustreless. There was a brief flare of hope in her eyes, and then it was gone. Incredibly, she laughed. A dreadful, hopeless wrenching sound.

Gerhardt felt Raven's hand on his shoulder. He felt as if his blood had iced up, leaving his limbs cold and stiffly unresponsive.

'This is not possible,' he said, when the door was shut again.

'You think she made herself up to look that old?' Raven snapped, taking refuge in anger. 'She hasn't moved out of that room – I've been here!'

'But ... what can it mean?'

She looked at him incredulously. 'What do you think it means? It means she was telling the truth. She said that holding this rift open between her world and ours was costing her time.'

'That is absurd.'

'What other explanation is there for a woman who ages decades in a matter of hours?'

'Some sort of stigmata ... perhaps.' He stopped.

Raven shook her head decisively. 'I think she was telling the truth and if we don't find this Valoria so she can go back where she belongs, she'll turn into bones and dust right in front of our eyes. Look at her. She is alone and she needs our help.' Again Raven seemed to feel the dead man's fingers tightening on her arm. 'I know it can't be real, Gerhardt, but I am suspending my disbelief as of now. If I'm wrong, someone will have a good laugh at my expense.' She was far calmer now than when he had arrived, as if she had come to some decision. 'You said the city had gone mad?'

'There are people downstairs demanding to check out of the hotel because there are supposed to be wild animals in the streets, and at the police station there was a woman trying to report fairies in her hotel swimming pool. I told them there was a dead man by the pool and they all but yawned and told me they had been getting reports of bodies all night long. Seven so far, and it was obviously a hoax because the bodies were not there when they investigated. I guess the other bodies were the ones Savid mentioned. The Dakini must be disposing of them. I gave up trying to explain because probably they have already shifted Savid's body, and those police looked like they wanted to gaol me.

'Well, if the police won't listen we'll have to . . .' Raven's eyes blazed wide. 'Of course. If the magic is manifesting itself in real ways around the Valoria, all we would have to do to find it is look for real magic rather than illusion.'

Gerhardt did not know what to say. It was incredible and yet in a mad sort of way, it fitted. But he was a physicist. He didn't believe in parallel dimensions and magic. There must be some logical explanation for the way in which Signe had aged.

His eyes flickered to the bedroom door, and Raven shuddered. 'Every minute we stand here talking, she's dying. I have this horrid vision of going in and finding her lying there dead and withered. I have to try and find this thing. You can stay here if you want.'

'We will go together,' Gerhardt said.

It was a night of black velvet, soft and warm with the moon a mere sliver of silver. They stopped at the bottom of the steps to let a fat man with a beatific look on his face walk past. The woman following him looked puzzled and annoyed.

'What do you mean you saw the grail, Ernest?'

Raven and Gerhardt exchanged a look and they turned in the direction from which the pair had come. At the front of Treasure Island Casino, Gerhardt stopped, remembering what the manager had said about the wild beasts. Maybe it was a sign that the magic was here. Even the name of the place seemed to offer a coy clue. After all wouldn't treasure island have a buried treasure?

'It has to be somewhere where nothing has changed for years,' Raven murmured, as they entered the foyer, 'after all Signe said the stone wouldn't let itself be built on.'

Gerhardt glanced at an ornamental pool and was flabbergasted to see a small greenish face look up at him and grimace.

'I suppose it will be pretty small given that they had to wait all these years before the rift was big enough for people to come through ...' She looked up when Gerhardt made no response. 'What's the matter?'

Gerhardt had grabbed her hand and pulled her back behind a bank of poker machines. 'Look.'

It was the man they had seen stab Savid: a Dakini. It occurred to them both simultaneously how broad and heavily muscled the man was, and how long and flat his face. Raven was reminded of pictures she had seen of the ferocious Mongolian tribesmen commanded by Genghis Khan, but the thought of Signe's pale desperation made her square her shoulders purposefully.

'At least we know we're in the right spot. Signe told me they would not be able to touch the stone or even get too close, because it would begin to exert the same pacifying influence over them as it did in her world. She said they would probably guard it from a distance to make sure no one else gets it either until the rift collapses.'

Gerhardt frowned. 'What exactly do you suppose will happen when this rift collapses?'

'I don't know, but we don't have much time before we're going to find out. Come on.'

They went carefully, weaving in and out of people and poker machines. There were less people than usual, and most were staring at their cards or machines with glazed concentration, unaware of the clouds of butterflies that fluttered about over their heads, or of the wildlife roaming along the carpeted aisles. Some sort of antelope was rubbing the velvet off its horns on the edge of the bar, and a monkey was seated on a stool beside the poker machine. The man on the machine alongside was punching in coins, oblivious to the nature of his hirsute companion.

They passed a roulette table where a man was swearing that the dice had changed their spots in front of his eyes.

At last, they reached the rim of the jungle again. 'We found Savid just out there,' Gerhardt said. 'Logically that suggests ...'

'It definitely can't be here, because the Dakini killed Savid here and the stone is supposed to suppress violence.' She frowned. 'Unless it has to be close to affect them, or they might need to be around it for a long time to be affected from a distance,' Raven said.

'I think these animals ... Uh-oh.' Gerhardt had spotted another of the Dakini on the other side of some blackjack tables. The man turned as if he sensed their attention.

'Run!' Raven cried.

Sprinting towards the jungle path, they heard a shout from the other side of the foyer. They could hear pounding footsteps close behind. Without warning Gerhardt almost wrenched Raven's arm out of her socket, pulling her sideways into the bushes and pushing her onto the ground so hard he winded her.

'Sh!' he hissed urgently as she gasped for air.

She pressed her lips together, hearing boots clump by. She thought two men had run by, but there might have been more. She made herself relax, letting her lungs fill with air. More boots.

'They must have gone through,' someone growled in a flat gutteral accent, frighteningly close. 'We must keep them from the witch egg, else they will take it to the sorceress and she will bewitch us again.'

They departed and Raven turned to look into Gerhardt's face. 'Bewitched?'

He leaned close so he could speak softly. 'Signe said the Dakini invaded their land and that they were violent and blood-thirsty. So her people made this thing and used it to pacify them. I guess that qualifies as bewitching from their point of view.'

Raven frowned. 'Signe's people were simply protecting them-selves the best way they could. Look how much smaller they are than those brutish Dakini. They didn't kill them.'

'Maybe if Signe's people had used their magic to communi-cate with the Dakini instead of pacifying them – they would have had the opportunity to grow beyond brutes.'

'Maybe you're right, but we can't let them just slaughter Signe's people. Maybe we can get this Valoria and give it to her on the condition that she agrees to try and find some other way to deal with the Dakini.'

'Let's get it first.'

'But the Dakini ...'

'Can't go near it apparently. We need a distraction to clear the way. Wait here.'

He pushed his way through the bushes, heading back towards the gambling area.

Fifteen minutes later, they sat watching from under a rubber plant on the fringe of the jungle, as uniformed police and SWAT men poured in through the doors. Some of the gamblers noticed, but the majority kept on playing until police roused them.

'Did they say how many bombs?' one policeman asked another.

'Ten, set to go off in half an hour.'

'But we can't possibly do a full search of this place in that time. My god, we'll barely have time to get the people evacuated.'

'Our instructions are to evacuate the building. These damn Mafia have gone too far this time. Hallucinogenic gases to make people crazy so they'd keep the authorities occupied, and they could plant the bombs. The FBI are on the way now ...'

They moved out of earshot and Raven turned to look into Gerhardt's eyes with admiration.

He grinned and tried to look modest. 'There were so many calls and alerts I thought they would take no notice unless it was something big enough to explain everything else. I thought they would jump at a logical explanation. Look!'

Three SWAT men appeared dragging one of the struggling Dakini.

'How did they know to go for the Dakini?' Raven whispered.

'I said they looked like foreigners and I described them as savages in suits. It's not like they blend in exactly.'

The Dakini's muscles bulged with his efforts to free himself, and the SWAT men were swearing and looked as if they were on the verge of calling for reinforcements.

Gradually the hall emptied out and when the coast was clear, Gerhardt and Raven made their way silently to the exit door. Outside, the air was alive with butterflies diving and swooping in jewelbright swaths amongst the foliage surrounding the pool.

The water seethed with creatures that were demonstrably not human.

'It's got to be somewhere out here,' Raven said.

'No,' said a deep voice behind them, and they whirled to find another of the enormous Dakini emerging from the bushes, his eyes bright with malevolent intelligence. Like the others, his hair was cropped close to his skull and his hands clenched and unclenched at his sides. 'The Valoria is with the catbeasts. So does the witch egg protect itself. But you do not have such protections.'

'Wait!' Raven cried as he drew out a great serrated blade. 'We want to help you . . .'

The man smiled showing filed teeth. 'I need no help from you.'

'It's no good,' Gerhardt said in a low voice. 'I'll distract him and you get back inside and get the stone. It's our only hope. Once you have it, bring it out and maybe it will start pacifying him. It obviously needs to be closer in this world than in theirs.'

Raven nodded once, then pretended to lose her nerve and darted away into the bushes. The minute she was out of sight, she dropped to her knees and backtracked. Peering through the bushes, she saw the Dakini lunge at Gerhardt. If the Dakini had any sense, he would simply have guarded the door, but his aggressive instincts would not let him wait passively.

Reaching the wall, she inched her way out of the bushes towards the door. Unfortunately, Gerhardt's eyes flickered to her for a split second, and the Dakini whirled.

With a gasping scream, she wrenched the door open and threw herself inside.

She could not let herself think of what was happening outside. She had no illusions that the slender young German, for all his height, would be a match for the Dakini. Approaching the tiger enclosure, she stopped dead.

The white tigers were both stretched on the ground *outside* the enclosure. Had they been outside when she and Gerhardt had run by only moments before? It was a wonder the creatures had not attacked them. Now they merely watched Raven unblinkingly through impassive, lovely eyes. She had the strange feeling they knew exactly what was happening. Surely there must be some sort of magic about creatures like these. Their blood must resonate to the tingle of enchantment in the air, just as her own bones vibrated with an awareness that this was what she had spent her whole life waiting and longing for, without ever knowing it.

Somewhere in the jungle, a concealed bird let out a raucous cry, and she started violently. Twin pairs of ice-blue eyes watched her unblinkingly as she took a step towards them. Her hands were wet and she felt sweat crawl down her spine.

Now she could see into the enclosure. The butterflies were so thick they were like a storm of white blossoms. She looked back at the tigers and her heart lurched, for they had risen.

Her legs felt watery and she had a horrible vision of those great gleaming ivory teeth closing in on her, the spurt of blood and a moment later, the crunch of the bone.

Then it occurred to her. The stone suppressed violence, and eating her would be violence to her, so – perhaps she was in no danger. Unless eating did not qualify as violence . . .

She took a deep shaky breath and took another step. It brought her face to face with the tigers, and for a second, she could see her own reflection in four pale-blue eyes, feel the heat of their breath on her bare arms. She forced herself to squeeze between them, feeling the warm, coarse fur brush against her legs and thighs.

She walked unsteadily to the glass door which stood ajar. The air felt strangely thick as she climbed inside. Her skin seemed to tingle as if the very air was effervescing against it. Butterflies pressed against her skin and the air was filled with the whispery beat of a million tiny wings. She could have felt claustrophobic with their wings brushing every bit of her bare skin, even her eyelids. She could see nothing for their fluttering whiteness, and she dared not open her mouth. But she was concentrating on following the feeling of magic to its source, reaching blindly down . . .

Butterflies! Butterflies so thick against her fingers now that she must move slowly lest she bruise them, if they were not killing themselves by straining towards . . .

She had it!

Her fingers closed on the jagged pebble and she backed to the door, fearing the harm she would do if she turned around. The butterflies followed. Unable to see where she was going, she stumbled and stumbled again. Then her leg brushed a more solid warmth. The tigers had come into the cage and were walking either side of her. Guiding her to the door.

Out of the enclosure, the press of butterflies lessened enough that she could see, albeit as if she were in a blizzard. The tigers followed her through the door, and through a fluttering rainbow she saw the Dakini bring his knife to Gerhardt's throat.

'No!' she screamed, and threw the stone.

The Dakini whirled and raised his hands, then his expression changed to one of horror, and he was lost in the thick swirl of butterflies.

Raven ran forward to where Gerhardt lay, pressing his fingers to his stomach. 'Are you . . .'

'I won't die, thanks to you, though I have a few cracked ribs, I think,' he gasped. 'I guess you found it.'

Raven nodded, squeezed his hand gently, then rose and went towards the Dakini. She could not see him, but again she followed the tingle on her skin. And at the eye of this storm of butterflies, she found the Dakini, crooning tunelessly and cradling the Valoria, and understood why Signe's people had used it. The man was utterly harmless now. But when she took the stone from his fingers, the Dakini looked at her with mindless eyes, and she shivered at what it had made of his intelligence. Obviously the Valoria worked immediately if you were in direct contact. She tried to imagine hundreds of men and women like this, and quailed.

The ground lurched suddenly beneath her feet and there was a subterranean rumble that sounded as if it came from the depths of the earth.

'Raven!' Gerhardt cried.

Raven . . .

She stopped, squinting against the butterflies. 'Signe?'

I . . . cannot hold the gate more than a few moments. You must take the Valoria through the rift for me.

Raven gasped and felt the butterflies against her lips. 'But you . . .'

Are too far away. I have barely enough strength to reach you with my mindvoice. I have only a little time left. Too little. Help my people. Help me.

'But you said when the gate failed, there would be no way to reopen it. Will I get back before it collapses?'

A brief telling pause. Then: *I have read you, Raven. The Searchers were trained to quicken to magic so they could locate the Valoria, but your heart quickens to magic naturally. Are you not a Searcher, Raven, and would you turn aside fearing the risks when the thing you seek lies before you?*

A sound rang in Raven's heart like a bell at the centre of her soul. A peel of radiance. A memory of the trembling moment of almost magic that she had felt once as a child. 'What do I do . . .?'

I will open the rift. All you have to do is step through. Prepare yourself.

The ground shook again.

'Wait!' She hurried towards Gerhardt, knelt by him.

'I heard,' he said, struggling to his feet.

'Come,' she said eagerly, startled to realise she did not want to leave him.

He shook his head. 'I can't. I . . . I belong here. I have my brother and my work. I am a physicist.'

'Oh, but Gerhardt. This is magic and . . .' She bit her lip against the other words, for there was no point in saying them now. This is the real world and that is what he wants, she thought sadly.

The ground shook again.

He reached out and took her hand again. That so unexpectedly precious hand. Kissed it. 'Go. You can save Signe's people and help the Dakini.'

There was a cracking sound and the ground jerked impatiently.

Raven. I cannot hold it much longer. Your friend must . . . get clear.

'Goodbye,' Gerhardt said. Then he heard a great ripping sound as if the very fabric of the universe was being rent apart. Raven turned, called to the docile Dakini and, stone raised, stepped forward, flanked by the tigers and a multicoloured veil of butterflies. For a moment, Gerhardt caught sight of a green, verdant land, with a glimmering violet sky, superimposed over the night and the pool.

Raven turned and looked straight into his eyes. He saw her lips shape his name, and a great surge of longing dragged at him.

'Raven!' he cried, and sprinted towards the rift.

Gerhardt wiped the sweat from his brow, turning away from remembering that last moment. There was too much pain in it. How many years had he thought of it, and cursed himself for stumbling, for taking too long to realise that she was the first real magic in his life? If only. The saddest words in the English language. Too late. Of course.

He had barely escaped with his life. He had been in hospital for months recovering from what the authorities had judged as a bomb explosion. By that time, he could not even find out what had happened to Signe. Maybe she just became dust, the way Raven had envisaged it.

He smiled, and though it might have been bitter, it was not. There was pain in it, and loneliness. But there was hope too, because maybe this story of witchlights would be real. Maybe this time the rumour of magic would yield up a longed for truth: a place where the skin between the world where Raven now dwelt, and this one, was torn.

Maybe this time.

He stepped down harder on the accelerator.

Green Monkey Dreams

So, you seek the key to the dream of life, halfling? Look deep, then, and accept the reflections of the dreamwindow, knowing the dreamer and the dream are indivisible. The visions you see in its many facets rise from you and are of your essence, no matter how alien or disconnected they may seem . . .

Random is straight and tall, with the sun in his face and shining from his eyes as he looks away to the horizon.

'I thought you went away,' Jilia says.

Random gives her his slashing smile and winks as if at a joke. Then, with sudden urgency, he says, 'Follow me.' He starts up the hill with his long stride, leaving her behind. It takes her a moment to realise he really means to go up, and then she hurries after him. The hill is much steeper than it appears and by the time she gets to the top, she is panting hard. The walk has taken only minutes, yet it is night already. A dark plain is stretching out, anonymous and bare but for a few boulders, and far off there is another hill rising up. Together, the two hills must look from a distance like giant steps, and who knows if there is not another hill beyond the next, and then another.

Random is nowhere to be seen but Jilia notices a hut a little way from the edge of the steppe. She is puzzled that she did not see it at once, for it is quite close and a light shines in the window.

She makes her way across the stubbled earth towards it, meaning to ask the inhabitants if they saw which way Random walked.

An old woman opens the door before she has the chance to knock, and gives her a surprised look. 'Oh, it's you again. You'd better come in, it's nearly time.'

'I am looking for . . .' Jilia begins.

But the old woman reaches out and pulls her into the hut. 'Of course, but come in quickly.'

Inside, by a fire, there is a child in a night-shirt and a young woman in a stained apron. The woman looks familiar, and Jilia is puzzled by this, and why the old woman appears to recognise her. There is another knock at the door and a big man and three small girls enter the hut, and then a moment later a younger woman comes in with a handsome man who has full red lips. The woman is pregnant and from the way the man holds her arm, he seems to be her husband or perhaps her brother.

People keep arriving and before long the hut is full.

A small child comes to Jilia and holds a hand out to her. A little tarnished key rests in the grubby palm, and Jilia realises the child means her to take it. But a man with a moustache leans between them.

'My daughter would not answer when I called,' he tells Jilia. 'I had to come without her, but I can't be blamed.'

There is a vast muffled whirring as if the air outside is full of birds. Everyone in the hut grows silent and expectant, turning to stare at an enormous window Jilia has not noticed before. She sees a vague movement: a greenish flicker and a hairy little hand that flattens itself gently against the glass for a moment.

'It is nothing, really,' says the man who has spoken of his daughter. 'You need have no fear of them. They are nothing but winged dreams – illusions trying to intrude where they do not belong.'

'Why don't you let them in?' Jilia asks, staring at the face pressed at the window, small and wizened with greenish fur. The creature's eyes are as white and soft as peeled grapes. Behind it, there is a milky blur that might be wings.

'I am sure nothing would happen really. Indeed one does not like to see them striving against the glass like that. It is sickening. But we cannot let ourselves be confused by sentiment. They have to know there are boundaries and limits. There would be chaos if we let them in. No one would know where anything began or ended. Everything would be blurred.'

Suddenly Jilia remembers Random is out there, and, alarmed, she steps towards the door. The old woman strikes a match to light a candle and the flare of the flame is momentarily blinding . . .

Jilia blinks and finds her mother is looking down at her from the door. 'I'm sorry I woke you. I heard you call out and I switched the light on because I thought you were awake.'

'It doesn't matter.' Already the dream is decaying into a few images. The grape eyes at the window, and the little wizened hand fringed at the wrist with greenish fur. Random smiling back at her. The child offering her the tarnished key and that man making excuses about abandoning his daughter.

She realises suddenly that the old woman who opened the door to the hut was her dead grandmother.

'You were having the nightmare again, weren't you?' her mother says in a slight tone of accusation.

Jilia smoothes the doona with one hand. She does not like talking about the dream to her mother. 'It's not a nightmare,' she says at last.

The older woman sighs as if Jilia is being difficult. 'It's not your fault Random died. You didn't leave him. He went ahead of you and took the wrong trail. It might just as well have been you who took the wrong path and was lost, don't you see that? But I wanted to tell you something strange that happened tonight. I was talking about your nightmares and there was a woman there who has a child who was severely intellectually disabled in an accident, and she says he dreams constantly about monkeys at his window. Winged monkeys! What do you think of that?'

Jilia does not know what to think. She can only wonder why her mother is always trying to put things together like a string of beads. Life is random, Random always said in his slouchy voice, leaving the edge of his wit to show in his gaze. Only fools try to make a story out of life.

If you didn't look at him, you might think Random was a fool because of the way he dribbled the words out, hardly moving his lips.

'Sometimes I think you go out of your way to be irritating,' Jilia's mother says. 'Now get up and get dressed because I want you to meet someone.'

'A doctor?' Jilia asks warily, remembering the child psychologist who thought the dreams were because of Random falling off the cliff in the dark. Of course, no one really knows what happened to him because they never found the body. Sometimes Jilia thinks he is not dead at all, but just lost or wandering somewhere. There are times when she thinks she can hear him calling her.

In the sitting room, there are several people. Some are from her mother's reading group and others are colleagues. One of the women has a child on her knee who reminds Jilia of the child from the dream. It has a very red mouth as if it has been eating a red icy-pole, or smearing its mouth with cherry juice. She cannot tell whether the child is a boy or a girl.

'Jilia!' her mother cries in a startled way, as if she is surprised to see her daughter living in the same house. Her mother is sitting beside a long limp noodle of a man with round glasses and white hair tied back into a ponytail. 'This is my daughter, Professor Caleb.'

'Jilia,' the man says in a wet raspy voice that reminds her of a cat licking her fingers. His glasses catch the light so that Jilia cannot see his eyes beyond them. She sees herself diminished and deformed in them.

'As I was saying, Professor,' a woman on the couch says pointedly, 'primitive cultures took their dreams very seriously. They believed they were another level of existence. They would see ours as a poor thin existence by comparison.'

'Miss Allot specialises in primitive cultures,' Jilia's mother says.

The woman gives both of them an irritated look. 'There is some evidence that their minds linked at some level in the fact that we find the same dreams in widely diverse cultures . . .'

Jilia begins to fear her mother has mentioned her dream to these people, and that she will soon be asked to recite it. Being woken so suddenly from the dream has made her feel restless and somehow sad because of Random's presence in it. He had seemed so real, and by comparison, reality seems so pale.

'My research has been focused in a more individual way on the ability to dream, and the reason such an ability exists,' the professor says. 'I have always been fascinated by the fact that anything we can imagine exists at the level of dreams – do we not fly and pass through objects and have great strength in our dreams? The ability to dream affords us enormous power.'

'But it is not a real power,' Miss Allot says sharply. 'It may allow some sort of other level of communication, but that is all.'

'Is it all? I am less certain of that. I think dreaming holds a power which is yet unknown to us. It brings us to a plain of infinite possibility which might be tapped, if we had the key.'

'Plain?' Miss Allot says, looking puzzled.

'I am suggesting that most of the brain is merely a kind of immense storage place for all that we experience. Nothing is ever forgotten. The smell of bread baking in a store reminds us suddenly of a particular day when a friend's grandmother spread jam on her homemade bread for us. Such an insignificant memory, yet out it pops. And if our mind retains this small memory, why not every memory we have ever had – why not every memory that *anyone* has ever had, for are we not born of one another? Who knows that memories are not passed on, just as the ability to breathe is passed on, or the instinct to bear children, and perhaps all memories exist simultaneously in all minds? Or in some vast dark plain to which we all have access only through our unconscious mind . . .'

An elbow digs her deep in the ribs.

'Wake up,' Random hisses into her ear, half laughing. 'You were making noises like a guinea-pig on heat and the lecturer just looked up at you.'

Jilia straightens up, mortified. 'I was dreaming.' She feels groggy and her mouth tastes bad.

'Obviously,' Random says.

'No, really,' Jilia says with soft urgency, waking up properly now. 'I was having this weird dream that I was a kid again and I was wandering in this strange plain and you were there too.'

'Me! I hope I was misbehaving thoroughly.' Random grins and it is so like the dream grin that Jilia has a sharp feeling of *déjà vu*.

'You left me behind. I was trying to find you and I went into this hut to ask directions and there were people in there hiding because flying monkeys were trying to get inside. And then I woke up.'

'You mean I woke you. And you plagiarised my green monkey dream!'

'I mean I woke up into *another* dream. I was still a kid, and my mother was telling me to get up, only it wasn't my mother. It was your mother . . .'

'First she steals my green monkeys and now my mother.'

'. . . and in the dream, something had happened to you. In both dreams. In the second dream you were dead. You fell off a cliff somehow and I had been there when it happened but that wasn't in the dream. I was remembering it.'

'Jesus, thanks a lot.'

'Idiot,' she giggles. 'But in the first dream I was surprised to see you because I thought something had happened to you. Then you disappeared. In the second dream, I got up and went in the lounge room, only it wasn't my lounge room except for the sofa . . .'

'Don't tell me it was *my* lounge room!'

'No, you fool. It was nobody's. I mean I didn't recognise it. And there were a whole lot of people and one of them was him.'

She nods towards the podium. 'The lecturer, only he had another name ...'

'So you fell asleep in a lecture and then dreamed of the lecture – that's what I call dumb. Why didn't you go to Hawaii?'

'But wait. In the second dream, my mother ...'

'You mean *my* mother!'

'Yeah. She told me she had heard of some other kid dreaming of green monkeys like I'd been doing. Dreaming of dreaming of dreaming. Isn't that weird?'

Behind the podium, the lecturer stares pointedly at Jilia who stops talking and pretends she has been clearing her throat.

'A man thinks of his brother on the other side of the world whom he has not spoken with for months and right then, the brother calls him on the telephone,' he says. 'This might be seen as evidence of some sort of mind link between the brothers. Or is it mere coincidence?'

'My own sister called me the other night when I was thinking about her. I said, "You must be psychic. I was just thinking of you",' says the girl sitting next to Jilia to her friend.

'This mental connection can be even more pronounced in twins who grew in the same womb and whose minds might be said to have been irrevocably linked from the beginning,' the lecturer says. 'And in some so-called primitive societies, people saw themselves as possessing one mind, particularly in their dreams. They were not cut off from one another as we are now. They saw the unconscious as a vast country in which all were nomads and there were no boundaries.'

Jilia feels an odd sense of vertigo to hear the lecturer talking about dreams now. It is like looking into mirrors reflecting other mirrors, on and on into infinity. She turns to Random to say this, but he has gone without her noticing.

She looks around but cannot see him anywhere. 'Did you see where Random went?' she whispers to the girl next to her, who gives her a strange look. Jilia realises she was one of the people in the dream hut, and is shaken.

Jilia tries to remember coming into the lecture hall and seeing the girl, but finds she can only see a small green paw resting on thick glass, and grape eyes peering into the light.

Her heart is beating very fast.

'Are you all right?' the girl asks . . .

'Jilia! Are you all right?'

Jilia blinks. Her older sister is leaning over her, a book open on her lap. It is getting dark and there are clouds in the sky. Jilia sits up and rubs hard at her eyes. She is confused by the dreams in which she seemed to be herself but was someone else.

'You slept so heavily I was starting to think you had gone and died on me,' her sister says. 'Imagine if you had. I would have been sitting and reading a story to a dead body. Disgusting.'

'Why? It's not like I would have had maggots yet.'

'Oh, you really are disgusting!' Her sister slams the book closed. 'We better go back anyway. It's going to pour any minute. We should've gone sooner but you were sleeping and this book is so good. I can't believe you fell asleep. And right where the green monkeys were trying to get into the hut . . .'

'I was dreaming the book,' Jilia says but it is half a question, because it seems to her that she has just experienced a sequence of dreams all containing the green monkeys from the book. The strange thing is, she can remember the hut and the face at the window, but she doesn't remember the story from the book.

Random appears at the edge of the field and trots over to the blanket. Jilia pats his black silky ears, thinking of her queer dreams in which he had been transformed into a handsome young man.

'God, I hate this part of picnicking. All this sticky stuff you have to wash later. Yuk.'

Jilia is wrapping the sharp knife in a tea-towel. 'So what's happening in the book so far?'

'I can't just tell it like that. Oh well, all right. The whole village goes to this hut and the monkeys come, thousands of them, and there is this one girl left outside . . .'

'Her father left her.'

Jilia's sister gives her an impatient look. 'No. It was an accident. She was up in the hills and she hadn't heard the warning bell. When she came down, the streets were empty and then she heard the wings and she realised ...'

It starts to rain and they stop talking to throw everything hurriedly into the picnic basket. Grabbing up the blanket they make a run for the car. Inside the Volkswagen, they toot the horn to summon Random. Rain is making a drum of the car and Jilia's ears are hurting.

'Damn dog! Did you get the key?' her sister asks. 'I put it on the blanket.'

'I didn't see it when I shook the blanket.'

'Oh, no!'

'Don't panic. It must be under the tree,' Jilia says. She opens the door, slams it behind her and runs. It has grown darker and is raining so hard now she can scarcely see, but the tree looms up as an unmistakable shape on the flat horizon. The ground under it is relatively dry because of the thick foliage and Jilia begins to hunt for the key. She is distracted by Random barking somewhere. The rain lashes against her face as she calls him.

'Random!'

Jilia is pushing at the sleeping-bag. 'Get up, lazy bones. We're toasting marshmallows.'

Random unzips himself and sits up groggily, rubbing his eyes. He is wondering at the tumbling dreams he has experienced in which he was a boy and a young man and then a dog. He doesn't think he will tell anyone that. But how weird to be dreaming from someone else's point of view. Especially Jilia's. He hardly knows her. He wonders what it means to dream of being dead and disappearing over and over. Was it some sort of weird search-for-identity dream? Probably it was sparked by all that talk of dreams during their hike that afternoon, and then him getting separated from the others. He is actually having trouble remembering what he dreamed and what Mr Allot really said about dreams.

He realises the tree the two girls were sitting under in the dream was the tree where his group ate lunch, and wonders if all this is the result of eating Jilia's crazy chocolate pie. How could anyone think of making a pie out of nothing but chocolate anyway?

'Then there are urban myths,' Mr Allot is saying as he comes up to the campfire. He looks funny in shorts with those knobbly knees, but the old guy is surprisingly fit and it has made them all see him as less of a useless brain.

Jilia and some of the others are spiking marshmallows onto toasting forks and handing them around, and there is a sweet burning smell in the air that makes his mouth water.

'What do you mean by urban myths?' Jilia asks.

'I'll give you an example,' Mr Allot says. 'How many of you have heard the story of a woman travelling home at night, who stops to get some milk from the shop, and gets back into her car? All of a sudden a man is following her in another car, flashing his lights ...'

'I've heard that one,' Jilia agrees, 'but it was a paper she went to get, and she left the car door open ...'

'Yeah, and a killer got in her back seat,' says someone else.

'And the man in the car behind saw him get into the woman's car with an axe ...'

Random thinks he heard that story at a school camp, but it was a knife the man had, not an axe.

'It was a gun,' Jilia says. 'The axe was in the story about this man and woman crossing the desert and they run out of petrol so he has to walk back ...'

'The woman goes to sleep waiting for him, and when she wakes up there is a thumping noise and the police are standing some distance from the car and they tell her to get out and don't look back ...'

Mr Allot says, 'See – we all know how these stories go. Urban myths. But I would be willing to bet that most of you don't remember where you heard either of those stories. Researchers have tried to trace urban myths like these, which change in minor detail but not in substance, and have never managed to find the first person to tell the story, although sometimes they can locate the incident which might have spawned the story in the first place – often many generations back in time. I really think, as I said earlier, that the mind is a country which we choose to think of as fenced into individual and closed blocks, but it is not that way at all. We create these barriers and borders because we need them for some reason. But when we are in a dreaming state we often trespass. I would suggest that is how those urban myths travel from one mind to another.'

Random is thinking how much of life leaks into dreams, and wonders if it works the other way as well.

He has a sudden memory of a small green hand pressed against glass, and pale eyes in front of a blurred shiver of wings. The odd series of dreams in which he was not himself has made him feel unsettled, as if reality might be just another dream. And how do you ever know? Maybe in a minute he will wake again and find he is someone or something else.

'What about recurring dreams?' Jilia asks.

Mr Allot nods. 'An interesting phenomenon. I believe recurring dreams are far more common than we realise. In my experience, a recurrent dream of danger will be dreamed by many different people, but this can go unnoticed because people are reluctant to relate their dreams to life, for fear of being thought fools. We will never know of the dreams that recur and recur, rebounding through out universal unconscious all unnoticed, loud as a klaxon announcing the fall of a bomb, until dreams are taken seriously.'

'But what about one dream recurring in one person?' Jilia asks, and Random senses she is about to tell them about his dream, and wishes he had not told her anything about it. That was the thing about these camps. You ended up getting much more intimate with people than you would have in a classroom. Which of course was the purpose of them. But still.

'And what if a person were to dream of something that was right out of the ordinary – say flying green monkeys?' Jilia says. 'And they dreamt this dream again and again. But it wouldn't be the same dream. Just the same image coming back and back in different dreams.'

Jilia does not look at Random, but his heart is pounding.

'The recurring image is the key,' Mr Allot says, looking intrigued. 'Green monkeys, eh? It's odd you should choose that image; it brings me back to dreams recurring from mind to mind. I was teaching in America at a school called Indian Valley High and I was having trouble with one of the students in my class. I called his mother in and asked if there was anything wrong at home. You see he had been so good up until then. His mother said he was having nightmares, but that the doctor had given them pills saying it was because he was hyperactive. But the thing was the dream was about flying green monkeys trying to get into his window. I had completely forgotten it until you mentioned flying green monkeys. Such a peculiar thing.'

'What does it mean?' Jilia asks excitedly.

'Did he let the monkeys in?' Random asks, without meaning to. Suddenly he is wondering *why* he never let them in.

'His instinct was to keep them out,' Mr Allot says absently.

A tall skinny school counsellor leans forward. 'What if these winged green monkeys are real creatures seeking refuge from their own dying dimension by entering our dreams? Again and again they try desperately to get in, but again and again our minds are closed to them . . .'

'Do you want a marshmallow?' Jilia says, offering a singed pink blob to Random on the end of a fork. She does not like science-fiction. Before he can take the marshmallow, a boy with very red lips leans across to put another log on the fire.

Sparks fly up into the darkness.

'Wake up. You almost fell into the fire,' the old woman says urgently.

Jilia sits up. Her mind is full of vague strange dreams each tumbling into the other, but already the images are fading before the reality of the crowded hut and the fire.

Old Man Random on the stool beside her frowns, his eyes full of leaping flames.

'My daughter is lost,' a man is saying to him. 'My wife sent her to her grandmother's and she never arrived. She was lost in the forest because she left the path.'

The man's mouth is such a moist red colour, it looks as if he is bleeding.

'I was lost when I was a boy,' Random says, plucking at his beard. 'I wanted to find the green monkeys but they hid themselves from me. I had no fear.'

'Listen,' the grandmother whispers, pressing Jilia's arm.

Outside there is a whirring sound as if the air is full of birds.

'It is them,' the man with the lost daughter whispers, and Old Man Random puts his arm around a child in a stained nightshirt who has wandered over to warm its hands at the fire.

'*Why* do they come?' Jilia asks, wishing she was that child being cuddled in Random's arms. She remembers when he used to hold her like that.

'Does not the dream need the dreamer?' the old woman asks sharply.

'I do not believe they are dreams,' the red-mouthed man says. 'I think they feed on dreams and must sow them in us to harvest them.'

'Let them in,' the child whispers, looking up into Jilia's eyes. She sees that it is fearless, and remembers, too, when she was not afraid. The fearlessness of innocence.

There is a tapping and Jilia looks over to the window. She can only see her face reflected as a pale firelit blur against the night, as insubstantial as if she and the room are the night's dream, or the window's.

Jilia closes her eyes for a moment . . .

She hears a tapping and opens her eyes. She has dreamed the green monkey dreams again, but the memories are already leaking out of her, for they are too slippery for her waking mind to hold.

She looks across at the portion of window showing under the sly half-closed eyelid of the blind. Her bedroom, lit by the illuminated alarm clock, presses itself against the glass separating it from the dark night. Her Greenpeace poster of the Rainbow

Warrior looms as a swirl of darkness against the lighter wall, and the handsome Balinese puppet has become a kind of bird. On the dressing table is a picture of Random, smiling forever.

She thinks how odd it is that she now dreams *his* green monkey dream, as if he left it to her as his most precious possession. In the dreams he is so real, she cannot believe he is dead. Sometimes she wishes she will not wake, but will go on dreaming so he will go on living, but the strange sequence of dreams is always the same.

She gets out of bed and walks softly to the window.

As she approaches the glass, a wizened face with grape eyes peers at her. There is a creamy smudge of movement behind it that might be a reflection of her night-gown, or of the creature's wings in constant motion.

She lifts her hand to the window, and at the same time, a small paw touches the glass tentatively on the other side. Their fingers are separated only by a thin invisible barrier.

With her spare hand, she reaches up for the tarnished key that keeps the window closed fast, and in one smooth gesture, turns it.

ABOUT THE AUTHOR

Isobelle Carmody divides her time between her home on the Great Ocean Road in Australia and her travels abroad, during which she writes most of her short stories. She began her first book, *Obernewtyn*, at fourteen, and it was accepted ten years later by the first publisher she sent it to. She has worked as a journalist and radio interviewer and these days, when she is not writing, she lectures around the world on creative writing. She has had five books published, including the highly acclaimed *Obernewtyn Chronicles*, and has won the Children's Literature Peace Prize and the CBC Book of the Year Award for her novel *The Gathering*, soon to be made into a feature film.